Jailbird
(Not Free Yet)

Rose Marie Goble

ISBN: 10-148392176X
ISBN-13: 978-1483921761

DEDICATION:

In a society where justice is not always truth we still have the best laws and system in the world. This book is not to ridicule law enforcement. Instead I wish to encourage those leaving imprisonment to look to Christ and struggle to reinstate themselves into the world in a life style that will bring them success and peace of mind. My father's code said, "Nothing is worth anything without a cost."

Thus I feel the price has been paid. Now let's get on with life!

CONTENTS

ACKNOWLEDGMENTS:

God is good—all the time!

In my Bible studies with the women at the jail I remind them of God's love for them as individuals. It's the same for all humanity, no matter what sin or crimes we've committed.
He died for all of us.

Our part is to believe Him, confess and repent, give Him first place in our lives, and become totally addicted to Him.

Chapter 1: Release

Bailey Berkley stepped through the heavy prison doors onto the street and breathed deeply: free air in, free air out. It tasted so good and clean that she did it again. Across the street of Lakeside, Indiana, immigrating birds twittered from tree to tree, just as free as she felt. A squirrel zipped down a fence post and galloped across the clipped grass with an acorn to bury in the fallen leaves. Fluffy, puffy clouds moved across the sky with the heavens to wander, and the sun beamed from the vast universe with no constraining bars, walls, locked doors, or jangling keys.

"Don't just stand there. Move it. The shuttle is waiting." A guard pointed to the iron grey bus, and she joined the queue of parolees. Five years paid her debt to society. Now the excitement of freedom made her pulse quicken. She'd see James.

She remembered the touch of his perfect little fingers around hers minutes after his birth. His eyelids squinted under the birthing lights in the hospital, but the battle to keep him raged months before she held him in her arms.

"You can't raise a baby. You're only a child yourself." Her grandmother's angry face scowled across the counter of the family's saloon. "Heaven only knows why you'd get yourself in this condition."

"Bailey be sensible. Get an abortion." Her mother's quivering lips turned away as the bell on the tavern's door tinkled, signaling the entrance of a customer.

"No, that's murder!" Bailey remembered the roundness of her belly and the kick that told her James, too, fought for life.

"You're just stupid." Her grandfather left them to pour a beer for a customer and stumble back into the kitchen to fix a sandwich. Bailey watched him, hoping he would return, but again the business had more value than family and an unwanted great-grandchild.

"Well, you're going to have to support it on your own. We didn't ask for it, and we're not paying for it." Her grandmother wiped the counter and joined her husband in the kitchen.

Her mother rose from the bar stool. "I need a drink."

Bailey prevailed and kept the baby, but two years later needing rent money, she was caught distributing drugs. The sentence wouldn't have been so harsh except for her family's testimony.

Her grandfather glared down from the witness stand. "She stole money from the cash registers every chance she got."

"Bottles always missing when she manned the store." Her grandmother sneered at Bailey from above, turned to stare directly into the judge's face, and lied.

And her mother, sober for the first time in Bailey's memory, cried. "She has always been a difficult child. I don't know what to do with her."

"Five years," said the judge with a thump of the gavel, but she hadn't signed the adoption papers. James was still hers.

Had her grandparents forgiven her? Would her mother allow her a place to live? Could time heal the vicious wounds and hopeless scenes? An aching fear that dominated her childhood returned. Maybe this was just a dream. She closed her eyes and stumbled into the steps of the grey bus collecting prisoners leaving the jail.

"Watch where you're going!" A guard clutched her arm to keep her from falling.

The bump was more painful than a pinch. She wasn't sleeping. It wasn't a dream. "I'm free."

"Free, huh?" A hard-faced woman sat next to the bus window and stared toward the sand colored brick building whose striped windows were not a zebra's decoration. "Nobody's free, honey. Not even on the outside." Her leering lips confronted Bailey. "You may look young and innocent, but they'll squash that small body of yours like a man's fist crunching a soda can." She cackled. "I can't wait to see 'em do it!"

Bailey scooted away on the seat until her narrow bottom was perched on the edge, and her legs sprawled out in the aisle as props to keep her balance. Her limp, mahogany hair fell to her chin. She slumped forward on the seat and held tightly to the round steel frame under the bench.

Pale eyes from the gal in front peered back at her. "Just wait until the outside rams into yah like a semi truck. Life isn't free--to people like us. Nobody accepts a jailbird, not even her mama." She twisted around to stare at the driver's back. The clutch popped, and the creaking bus jumped forward like a startled jack rabbit.

As Bailey struggled to stay seated, Rosenbaum laughed. "And that pretty, white face won't mean a thing when you try to get a job. You're an ex-con, always an ex-con. Nobody is going to let you forget it."

"I'm getting myself a McD this big." Hard Face raised her hands to visualize the hamburger. "I can't exactly remember just how they tasted, but I know I love them."

Stupid, thought Bailey. Freedom meant more than food.

"I'm going to a real beautician." Another parolee raked fingers through chopped hair. "Some decent make-up and designer jeans top my list."

Again Bailey disagreed. She never fussed over her looks, and she didn't think now was the time to become a Barbie doll. Her hopes for the future centered on her family accepting her. Would they? The gnawing question began to burn a hole. She grabbed her stomach.

"Don't get sick in here." The woman at the window scooted away. "I don't like the smell."

"I won't." Bailey sat up straighter and looked out at the street. They passed Brickside Elementary where she had attended. Would James be one of the children on the swings or playing ball? The little bundle of energy had her sea green eyes and russet hair except his kinked. He had been a good baby, but an adventurous toddler. Her family rejected him like they disowned her. Social workers placed him in a foster home when she was incarcerated. Now the seven-year old had to be found.

Her mother hadn't written one letter or answered the phone calls Bailey made from jail. She and the grandparents attended the trial only long enough to convict Bailey with their testimony. Bailey's anxiety grew. What would she do if they didn't accept her?

The bus reached the halfway house a few minutes later. Bailey recognized the old residence as a home of a former teacher. She walked inside and ran a hand over the worn fabric. The floors were scuffed hard wood, and the couches and chairs sagged in the middle like tired individuals. Maybe they like her had seen too much human agony.

"There are two bathrooms." Matron Mona Macintyre, a solid

and muscular policewoman, glanced down the line of released prisoners without a smile. Then she turned. "The one at the end of the hall is for those staying in this room to the left. The one downstairs is only for those in the basement." She flipped pages on a clipboard. "Adams, Berkley, Manley, Rosenbaum, and Smith—drop your stuff in the room to the left and report back immediately."

Manley and Smith pushed past Bailey almost knocking her off her feet. She stepped aside and was the last to enter. Two top bunks remained unclaimed. The walls, freshly painted a dull powder blue, smelled clean but not like the antiseptic that she remembered from the prison. Bailey tossed her bags upon the nearest bunk and turned to leave the room.

"I don't want anyone up there." Rosenbaum, the hard faced woman, sat on the bottom. "Get your stuff off my bed."

Bailey reached for her bags, but Manley barred her from the second top bunk. "You chose the other. This one is mine."

There was no time to fuss. Bailey dropped her bags on the floor. She was always the smallest and youngest. Matron Macintyre called them back into the living area. Couches and chairs formed a circle around a small table with half a dozen dog-eared magazines.

"Everyone sit down." Matron Macintyre stood in front of the best looking chair. "These are the rules." Bailey listened half heartedly. Except for bars on the windows the place was run like a cell block. She sighed--so much for being free. Then Matron Macintyre ushered them back into their room and assigned beds. This time Rosenbaum and Manley shared the same bunk. Bailey's was the top of another. When they were by themselves, she looked down at the red head stretched out below her.

“You’re Tink Adams, right?”

“Yea, what of it?”

“I’m Bailey. I just wanted to be sure of your name.” She looked around the room, but no one else tried to get acquainted. Resigned to the unsocial attitude, she curled up with her Bible on the top bunk. As she reread the account of Sarah and baby Isaac, memories of James flooded her mind.

His chubby cheeks always puckered in a grin as he scooted across the floor of the tavern kitchen. She allowed him to play with some kettles that always made her grandmother angry.

“We got to keep this place clean or lose our license.”

Bailey had learned not to reply. Money, the business, and customers always came before her needs and James. When he began to walk, tensions grew tighter. James got under the feet or in the way of everyone, and never could she allow him to roam the dining area. Once he yanked a tablecloth from a paying customer. She could still feel Grandmother’s slap burning her cheek.

“Get out. I can’t stand this trash in my kitchen any longer.”

“I’ll take him upstairs.”

“Oh, no. You’ll take him out that back door. Now!”

Trudging down the street, she’d wandered into the welfare office and stated her story. The woman at the desk had tapped freshly groomed nails on the hard surface. “You’re eligible for food stamps but no rent. You have a job.” The social worker wouldn’t budge from her judgment.

“Who will watch James?”

“Ask your mother or your grandparents.”

"They won't pay me, and they won't watch him either."

"They won't?" The social worker's eyebrows shot up like rockets. "Then look for another position. There's plenty out there if you just look."

Bailey really didn't know how, but Clark arrived with dollar bills dangling between his thumb and forefinger. "Take these to the address on the box."

"It's drugs. I don't want to get caught up in that traffic."

He laughed in her face. "Honey, it's a package I need delivered. Take it, and I'll find more for you."

So Bailey delivered his packages pushing James' stroller down the street. The instant money went to her head. She found an apartment, bought clothes for James, and thought life couldn't be better. Then an undercover cop intercepted a package. When she went to jail, James disappeared in the foster care program. She wanted him back.

"Adams, Berkley, Manley, Rosenbaum, and Smith." Matron Macintyre stood at the door. "Prepare the evening meal, and those in the basement will cleanup." After they ate, they filed one-by-one into the office.

"Berkley, what work experience have you had?" The policewoman looked at her file and groaned. "You didn't have any."

"I worked in my grandfather's bar."

The woman leaned over the desk. "What did you do?"

"I peeled carrots and chopped celery for the relish trays. I drew beer for the customers at the bar. I swept the floors, cleaned, and washed dishes." Bailey looked up. "I don't want to work in a bar again. Please don't make me."

"You will be crying for the opportunity before the month is out. Six weeks is the most you can get for a chance to find your place in society. That's not very long. If you could get a bar job, it would keep you out of prison."

Or send me back, Bailey thought. "Please, don't put me in a bar."

More papers fluttered as Matron Macintyre studied them. "You have a GED and a certificate for secretarial work. That won't help you much in this neighborhood. None of the employers will hire you."

The bubble of hope like a leaky balloon oozed without the squeak. Bailey sagged in her chair. "I got good grades."

"I see, but you have a prison record. Employers are looking for clean girls." Her dark, sympathetic face stared across the desk. Bailey noticed the diamond studs in the small ear lobes, but the woman's smile was like a red boat across her face. "Don't give up hope. We'll find something for you, and we'll find it soon. What about your mother?"

"She's an alcoholic."

Again the sympathetic face frowned. "And your grandparents?"

"They own the bar. I don't want to work there. I'm a Christian." Her voice had become shrill and unnatural. Bailey clamped her lips shut.

The rustle of papers continued. Then the kindly face pursed her lips. "Do you think your mother would allow you to live with her?"

"I don't know." Bailey's hands shook. "I haven't talked to her for five years." When the session ended, she didn't want to leave. She trusted Matron Macintyre, but she had a question. "Do you know where my son is?"

"Your son?" Matron Macintyre looked through the paperwork again. "This doesn't mention a child. How old would he be?"

"Seven. He was two years old the day I was arrested."

"Would he be with your mother or grandparents?"

"No, the social worker put him in foster care. I don't know where he is." Suddenly, Bailey felt naked, more exposed than when she had been stripped of her civilian clothing. She stood and escaped through the door. In the room she kept her eyes down on the green carpet that had seen more feet than vacuums. Then she leapt to her top bunk and the privacy it allowed her. The tears she wept were for James.

Three days later she began to read the Psalms through for the second time since she had entered the halfway house. With nothing else to do except share the few chores with the others, she lounged on her bed and watched TV sitcoms in the living room. The atmosphere hung with depression, and Bailey struggled to keep an attitude of praise. God had safely gotten her out of prison. He would not forget her now.

"Bailey Berkley." Matron Macintyre stood at the door. "Come into my office." This time there was no folder in the woman's hands. "We've located your family, but not your son. He was put into the state's foster care and transported out of the county."

“James.” She slumped into the chair. All her expectations involved providing a home for him. She closed her eyes. What was there to live for?

“Bailey, your mother and grandparents have moved. The business they owned burned down a year ago.”

“We always lived above the bar.”

Matron Macintyre nodded. “But the property is in the process of being sold.” She cleared her throat and looked away. “I don’t know how to tell you this, but they do not want you. Do you have any other relatives? I mean, an aunt, uncle, or maybe a brother or sister?”

“My sister, but we were never on good terms.”

“I see.”

The silence became painful. Bailey twisted in her chair, rubbed the worn suede arms that felt more like the back of a porcupine than a short haired cat. If only she could get out of this place, find her own apartment, and get a job. In prison it had seemed so easy with each lesson returned and marked excellent. She wasn’t a dummy, but how could she prove it? “Ma’am, is there a computer that I could use?”

Matron Macintyre’s head jerked upward. “No, in the past inmates misused them, and the authorities removed them—what was left of them, that is. I have never seen such nice equipment turned into junk so viciously. They even removed the one in here. I have to go down to the office to print out everything I need.” Her voice began with an edge of anger and finished dismally. Bailey let her tongue roll around her lips. “I took a course in the prison and found a site where I could make a little money. If I could just get on line, I think I might be able to support myself.”

Matron Macintyre reshuffled the paperwork, fitted it inside the file folder, and laid it on her desk. "Bailey, that's the best news I've heard all week. I'll see what I can do." She returned that afternoon. "The rules forbid you using any equipment in the office or the jail. They think you might start a revolution or something over there like opening all the cells. But there's the possibility that you could use one at the library. I'd have to put an ankle bracelet on you, but you could walk the three and a half blocks. You'd have to be back exactly on time."

"If I'm late?" Bailey thought of how long it took to get on line and settle down to really type.

"I'd have to put you on lock down for twenty-four hours to a week."

She looked down at her hands and feet. "I promise to be back in an hour."

"Well, here's the bracelet. If you take it off, you'll go to jail for breaking probation."

The mid afternoon air flowed through her veins like a cleansing potion. She had forgotten how cheerful Robins could be and tried to whistle back their calls. The freshly fallen leaves crunched under her feet as the branches waved gaily above her head. Bailey walked rapidly until she reached the library panting like it had been a race. Six minutes wasted, but she entered with gusto and walked to the desk.

A friendly young man behind the desk greeted her. "Good afternoon, may I help you?"

She liked his smile that showed even white teeth and the slightly flaring nose that rose above well formed lips. She could smell the hint of aftershave. “I’d like to use a computer, sir.”

His eyes crinkled at the corners. “I’ve never been called ‘sir’ before. My name is Dave. Do you have a library card?”

Her spirits fell. Would this, too, require a revelation of her past? “No.”

He bent beneath the counter and pulled out a clip board holding a form and handed her a pencil as well. “You can fill this out at that table. I’ll need proof of residency in this community. An envelope with your name and address sent to you from the gas company or your renter or your bank is sufficient.” His encouraging smile beamed across the desk.

She could only stare. Then she handed the clip board and pencil back to him. “I didn’t bring my purse. I don’t have anything like that with me.”

“You could still fill out the form. I’d hold it until you returned.”

Bailey glanced away. It was so tempting to pretend, but she wasn’t even sure of the proper address of the halfway house. “No, I’ll come back.” She took time to scan the shelves of books, the room of glass where multiple computers and hackers collected, and the dangling decorations of fall leaves and flowers. She had almost forgotten that this was the last of September, and summer wasted away like her years in jail. Her feet kicked through the few leaves on the sidewalk, and she wished the crunching sound wasn’t her life crumbling beneath the soles of her feet.

Chapter 2: Conflict

"So where you been?" Rosenbaum, the hard faced woman, scowled across the living room space. "How you get favors to leave this dump?"

"I went to the library."

Rosenbaum mimicked her. "Just a stroll, eh? That's a lie." The woman pulled herself out of the sunken sofa to face Bailey. "Did you get any sugar?"

"I don't do drugs."

The woman's hand rose to slap Bailey across the face, but Matron Macintyre entered the room. Slowly the woman's arm fell limp to her side. "Next time you'd better bring me some." Her whisper grated on Bailey's ears.

"There probably won't be a next time."

"Bailey, come into my office." Matron Macintyre turned, and she followed. The hard faced woman stood with her mouth agape.

Bailey closed the door and slumped down into the chair. The springs relaxed, and she thought she'd hit the floor with her bottom.

"Well, congratulations! You are back on time. What did you discover?" Matron Macintyre's friendly face looked expectantly.

"I can't get a card."

"A library card? Why not?"

"I have to have proof of residency in this community. He said it could be an envelope from a bill or the bank or anything, but it had to have my name and address on it." She focused her eyes on the wretched carpet under her shoes.

"That's not hard." Matron Macintyre made a note. "I'll write you a letter and post it. You should get it tomorrow."

Bailey lifted eyes to hers in disbelief. "You'd do that for me?"

"Yes, it's no problem at all."

"Thank you." Bailey paused. "Have you heard anything about my son James?"

"We're working on it, but you won't get custody until you can prove ability to support him. No welfare or food stamps this time."

"I understand. I'm a felon," but Bailey smiled. "I know I can make money with the computer." She left the office walking on air.

Later Rosenbaum confronted her, yanking her down from the top bunk and letting her fall to the floor. "You got connections. I can tell. Next time you go out, remember my sugar."

Bailey rolled to her back on the floor to face the woman looming over the top of her. She had been right. This was nothing more than cell block rule. She nodded and reached for her Bible that had tumbled with her. The ruffled pages bent when it landed face down like she had. Petting the leaves back into place, she ignored the woman. When Rosenbaum turned, Bailey scrambled to her feet and leaped back on her bunk. The room was quiet until the woman let out a peal of delirious laughter.

"When you get that sugar, I'm gonna light up like a torch."

I wish she'd light up now without the sugar. Bailey rolled over on her bunk and faced the wall. Her Bible hadn't suffered too much from the fall, but she had lost her place. Genesis, Exodus,

Leviticus. The sacrifices and burnt offerings didn't mean much to her, but it seemed God's remedy for sin didn't require five years cooped up with maniacs.

That night when it was too dark to read, Bailey lay on the bunk and allowed her trip to the library to roll through her mind like a motion picture with a happy ending. It was the perfect place to begin working, and Dave seemed so nice, so innocent, and so gentle. She thought he could be a good friend, but who would want to befriend a jail bird? Even the other inmates didn't like her.

Matron Macintyre's letter came addressed to Bailey two days later. When it was handed to her, the girl just stared. Mail was such a rarity, novelty, to one totally rejected by her family.

"Well, open it." Rosenbaum stood at her elbow. Her words brought the curiosity of Smith, Manley, and Tink Adams.

"Who did it come from?"

"Read it. What does it say?"

Bailey shook her head. Could Matron Macintyre have discovered James' whereabouts? She slipped the envelope in her pocket. A letter was a sought after treasure to be opened carefully and reverently while alone. As she stepped into the bathroom, she caught the resentment on Rosenbaum's face through the crack in the door. She shut it soundly and locked it to make a temporary sanctuary. The mirror caught her pale face with scared eyes like green pools. She lifted her hand to lift the limp, mahogany hair from the fraying civilian shirt collar that was her best. Nervous fingers pulled the envelope from her pocket as she ignored her dismal image.

The cheap white paper didn't diminish her reverence for the

only letter that she ever remembered receiving as hers and hers alone. She stroked the face of the envelope as she had stroked the cover of her Bible when a fellow inmate laid it on her lap.

"It's mine?" Bailey slowly opened the new book and smoothed each page open so carefully that the words Holy Bible stared up at her on a flat leaf.

"Baby, it's yours. Haven't you ever seen the Word of God before?"

"No."

"Now I don't believe that!" Her cell mate sat down beside her. "There's Bibles all over creation. Didn't you ever go to church?"

"I don't think so." Once Bailey remembered asking her mother if she could go to Sunday school with a friend and received a slap across the face.

"Church is stupid. Don't ever ask me again." Her mother had grabbed the neck of a whiskey bottle and taken a swig. Bailey remembered the sting on her face and the gurgling liquid. She shivered.

"God's Word isn't anything to be scared of. It's His love letter to us." The woman reached over and began to turn the pages. "Read this, 'For God so loved the world,' that's you and me, honey."

Bailey treasured that Bible. The luxury of Christmas presents or birthdays were non existent because her grandparents called themselves Jehovah Witnesses. She remembered the fateful day when she read the back cover. The plan of salvation was printed in language she could understand and follow. After her simple prayer, a peace flowed through her that she couldn't describe--a miracle. She wanted to hum, sing, and shout, but a glance through the bars stifled her praise.

Now she hooked a fingernail under the flap to ease the adhesive from the paper and pulled out an application for a library card. A small yellow sticky note read, “You will need three references. I took the liberty of asking my friends to vouch for you.” At the bottom were three strange names and addresses. Again God’s comforting peace settled over Bailey as she carefully refolded the paper.

Thumping on the bathroom door bade her hurry. “Did yah die in there? I need that spot.”

Bailey slid the letter back in her pocket before she pushed the dead bolt and scrambled out the door.

That afternoon she sat down in front of a computer hardly believing her good fortune. On line she opened the website used in prison to a blocked page. She backed out of the site and retyped the address. Again the page was blocked. After the fourth or fifth time, she backed her chair away from the screen and hung her head. “What am I going to do?” Her words were mere whispers.

“Can I help you?” Dave, the male librarian, stepped behind her.

“I don’t think so.” Bailey glanced away. “I was trying to open a work site that I’ve used before but for some reason it is blocked.” Looking up, she noticed how intensely blue his eyes were in a round face.

“We block some sites for security, but maybe I can find another for you.” Dave was hovering over her and peering into the screen. His arm snaked around her shoulders to move the mouse. The clicks were rapid and sure. “Here’s a list of on line jobs.”

She ducked her head out from under his arm and rolled her chair to one side. His after shave was pleasant, over-powering. Her heart pounded like she was swimming under boiling water.

"I'm sorry." He stepped away, but she had noticed there was no wedding band on his finger. Few men wore rings, but a heavy, class ring with a ruby center shown on his left hand. His eyes smiled at her, and she ducked her head, sucking in her breath.

He has such beautiful teeth, she thought. "Your teeth are like a flock of sheep just shorn, coming up from the washing. Each has its twin; not one of them is alone."

"What?" His eye lids raised his brows.

"I'm sorry." She looked away. "I was just quoting something I read in the Song of Solomon." Her tongue grew thick, and she feared she babbled. "I didn't mean anything. It was just something that came into my mind."

"Song of Solomon? Did you mean a book of the Bible?"

She nodded.

"Talking is not allowed in here." A tall, angular woman wearing the librarian badge arrived behind Dave. Her blond page boy had every hair in place. Bailey remembered her limp mop and focused on the computer while he turned and left the room. The woman stood guard at the door.

Bailey let out her breath, aware that she had been holding it while Dave was beside her. She glanced at the computer screen and began scrolling down. Yes, the site was what she wanted, but the clock told her time was quickly slipping away. She slipped the envelope out of her pocket and scribbled down the web site's address. Then she closed the computer page.

As she left the room, the woman still remained at the door watching the computer room. Her lips wore a compressed line.

Bailey slipped past and walked to the main desk to sign out.

"Did you find what you wanted?" Dave's voice was quiet, but his face showed kind concern.

"Yes, thanks for helping me."

"That's my job." He lingered, watching her document the time in the column on the page, and she paused.

"Thanks again. I'll be seeing you." She looked up to catch a frown on the other librarian's face. She walked quickly to the door, turned to look at him once more, and caught him staring at her. Outside she broke into a run. If she were a minute late, it would not be pretty back at the halfway house.

Bailey knew she needed more time at the library as well as her own post office box. If the other women knew that she was getting paid for that article she sent in by email, her snail mail might be intercepted. "Please, I just need more hours to work at the library."

Matron Macintyre tapped a pencil on the desk. "I understand, but I've already showed you favoritism above the others. You know how that causes problems."

Bailey nodded. "But I'm not going to get out of here unless I can get a checking account and post office box. I don't trust them, the others." She glanced toward the door, and her voice dropped to a whisper.

"I understand." Matron Macintyre laid the pencil to one

side and leaned forward. "I must talk to my superior. I believe I can trust you, but I have to go through the red tape, too. What are your plans?"

"I'd like to get my own apartment, but I'm trying to get the money for a down payment. If I could just spend a few more hours at the computer every day, I think I can do it." Her eyes locked on Matron Macintyre's. "I know I could support myself, but I need more time."

"I understand." Again Matron Macintyre picked up the pencil. She frowned and stared at the door. "Bailey, do you know who the father of your child is?"

"Uh, I was raped."

The matron sat up. Her eyes resembled those of a frightened deer. "I didn't know. I'm sorry." She swallowed hard and flipped some more pages. "Who was your father?"

"My father?" Bailey pointed to herself. She had asked her mother that question so many times. She remembered her sister sneering. "Your father was a bum. My father is a politician." Her superior air had always haunted Bailey. "I don't really know." She bent her head. "I was born out of wedlock. My mother had many lovers."

"Oh." The matron's face was buried in her papers. "I'll see what I can do, but I can't promise you. You've only been here a little over a week. Your probation is for a year."

"I know, but wherever I go, I would still report in every day."

"Let's cross that bridge when it comes. Right now you need to be patient."

Bailey left to do kitchen duty.

"Did you bring the sugar?" Rosenbaum hovered. Her menacing stance warned of possible violence.

"Where was I supposed to pick it up?" Bailey concentrated on stirring, scraping the bottom to keep it from sticking. The wooden spoon created little eddies in the red tomato soup.

"You know."

"No, I don't. I don't do drugs." Bailey brought her eyes up to challenge the other woman.

"Why you, slut!" Rosenbaum shoved the pan toward Bailey's front, but it hit another pan and bounced to the floor. The soup spread like blood into a lake with no banks. "Now look what you've done!"

Bailey backed off and bumped into Matron Macintyre who entered the kitchen.

"What happened?"

Rosenbaum shrugged. "She said she didn't like tomato soup and threw it on the floor."

"Is that true?"

Bailey saw the smirk on the other inmate's face. Rosenbaum wouldn't take it kindly if she told the truth. Living with the brute of a woman was difficult enough, but Bailey knew it could get worse with just a few of the wrong or right words. "No, ma'am, it was an accident."

"Clean it up. Don't let it happen again." The frown on Matron Macintyre's face included both Bailey and Rosenbaum.

"I didn't do it." Rosenbaum stepped over to the other side of the table where she set out bowls, spoons, and crackers. "What are we going to eat now?" Her voice dripped like the honey comb.

"Crackers," said Matron Macintyre, leaving the room.

That evening with lights out, Bailey's bedding was yanked off the top of her. "I'm serious about that sugar." Bailey waited until Rosenbaum crossed the room and slid in her own bunk before she dropped to the floor to retrieve her covers.

Matron Macintyre summoned her into the office the next morning. "I have to write up the kitchen incident. What happened?" Her face wore no smile. Her eyes showed no warmth or friendliness. A hard, knowing shell had dropped over the warm heart of the official. "You understand this could deny your desire for more time at the library."

The girl nodded. "It was an accident."

"An accident?" Matron Macintyre tapped her pencil on the desk. "Bailey, one of the other women reported that someone ripped the covers off your bunk in the night. Is that true?"

She bent her head and looked at her hands. If she told Matron Macintyre about Rosenbaum, her life could get more difficult. If she didn't, it still had that possibility. She shrugged. "Maybe. I thought they fell."

"Bailey, I need to know what is going on in there. How am I going to be able to keep control if I don't know the truth?" The tapping on the desk counted the seconds of silence. "Okay, I'm going to have to report that you threw the soup on the floor. My superior is going to judge that as violent behavior and prohibit you from the library."

Her head jerked upward. "I didn't throw it on the floor. It was an accident."

"Tell me exactly what happened." She laid the pencil aside and clasped both hands in front of her on the desk.

"Well, I was stirring the soup with this spoon."

"And?"

Bailey wet her lips. If she told Matron Macintyre what Rosenbaum had said and done, the woman might not believe her. Again she studied her hands.

"Did you say you hated tomato soup and threw the pan on the floor?"

"No." Again her eyes tried to communicate to Matron Macintyre what her speech couldn't.

"Bailey, for the last time--tell me exactly what happened."

"It was an accident."

"Okay, it was an accident. Don't let it happen again."

A few days later Bailey was expecting her first pay check. Rosenbaum handed out the incoming envelopes but didn't pass any her way. About mid morning Matron Macintyre summoned her into the office. "How did you acquire drugs to sell?"

"Drugs?" Bailey's head shot up like a baby bird. Her mouth fell open. "I don't do drugs."

"Someone gave me this check that you received in the mail from a pharmaceutical firm. Is this a front for some drug outfit?" Matron Macintyre's eyes seemed to drill into Bailey's.

"May I see the check?"

"Sure."

Bailey studied the piece of paper. "I was expecting this. I wrote an article and put it in a blog sponsored by this company. I'm paid by the hits made on line to read my blog. They asked me for a snail mail address or on line bank account. I used this address." Immediately she thought of Rosenbaum passing out the mail that morning. "I was afraid this would get into the wrong hands. That's why I asked you if I could have a post office box last week." She looked up. "I didn't sell any drugs. I wrote an article about how different drugs affected inmates in the jail."

"I'll have to investigate this. What other articles have you written?"

"Well, you can find them on my blog spot." Bailey wrote the address down. "Please, I just want to support myself and get out of this place."

"I understand, but there are rules that I have to follow. I'll see what I can do. For right now you are banned from the library and have lost your outside privileges."

"But I don't have any other way to make money."

"I know that. However, I have to follow orders." She turned and picked up a file folder. "Bailey, what did really happen with that soup? I have this feeling that you know more than you're telling."

Bailey rose from the chair. "It was an accident. It won't

happen again."

That afternoon she curled up in her bunk and read the Bible. "Behold, I have set before thee an open door which no man can shut." It had been her promise from almost the beginning in her walk with God. The parole board had given her a year's parole. When nothing else opened, she thought the work with the library would be her out, but now that door had slammed in her face.

Matron Macintyre moved Rosenbaum to the basement. Duties and life proved more bearable, but the delay made Bailey antsy. According to the parole papers, she had only a few more weeks to provide herself a home and a steady job. Otherwise the consequences like the Monopoly card read, "Go directly to jail." She knew she could generate the money for an apartment if she had a computer.

"Please, allow me to go back to the library."

Matron Macintyre moved papers on the desk into a file before looking up. She tapped the pencil. "I wish I could, but the soup incident has tied my hands. I'm no longer free to grant your wish. Sorry."

"What do I have to prove? Who do I need to talk to?" Bailey laid her palms flat on the desk and sat on the edge of the chair.

"Bailey, if you would tell me exactly what was going on in the kitchen; things might go smoother for you." Matron Macintyre's voice held a threatening edge. Her eyes narrowed. "I don't believe you threw that pot on the floor."

"I didn't. It was an accident."

The woman's lips compressed. "I see, but I don't think you understand, Bailey. You are not cooperating. You are not telling the whole truth. How did the accident take place?"

Bailey bowed her head. She didn't want to snitch on Rosenbaum. Informers in the prison had accidental deaths. Here would be no different, because the same people were involved. Even if Rosenbaum were sent back to prison, someone would take over her authority, and the playing field would be the same. Bailey had no desire to send anyone back into that den of iniquity and doom. She didn't want to go back herself, and yet, if Matron Macintyre would not allow her to work in the library, she knew it likely she would have no choice.

"I didn't throw the soup on the floor. I like tomato soup. It's one of my favorites. I was stirring. Someone bumped me from behind."

"Pushed?"

"Well, maybe. I lost my balance and before I could get control, the soup was on the floor." This was the closest she could get without lying.

"Who pushed you?"

Bailey shook her head and shrugged her shoulders. "It happens all the time. It was an accident."

"I see." Matron Macintyre set her pencil down on the desk. "Bailey, you have the chance of a lifetime to make a go of it on the outside. Why don't you just tell me the truth so I can give you that chance?" The officer shifted. "Look, I get very few girls in here that will go straight like you if given the chance, but when you don't cooperate my hands are tied."

"Ma'am, I understand, but I had a cell mate who committed

suicide after she talked. I don't want that."

"Suicide?"

Bailey bit her lips. "I've already said too much."

"You mean it looked like suicide, but it was murder."

Bailey bowed her head and stared at the ugly carpet. Rosenbaum knew she was the only witness. By staying within a crowd Bailey preserved her own life.

Matron Macintyre stood up. "I'm getting you out of here, now!" She rounded the desk. "Put your hands behind your back." Without warning the hard, cold, metal cuffs snapped around Bailey's wrists. "You're going back to jail."

"My Bible?"

"Who is your bunk mate?"

"Tink Adams."

Ushered out of the building and into the back seat of the squad car, Bailey feared her probation was over. She felt the tears slide down her cheeks as the door locked behind her. *God, where are you? I thought I was free.* The tears blurred the outlines of the buildings around them. The red, brown, and yellow leaves on the bush beside the drive smeared into a child's rough painting. A cloud passed between the earth and the sun. She closed her eyes and began to sob. It was all so unfair.

Chapter 3: The House

"be thou my strong rock, for an house of defense to save me," (Psalm 31:2).

In minutes Matron Macintyre opened the back door, shoved Bailey's Bible and personal items on the seat, and whipped the door shut. She stood outside talking on a cell phone, her body sometimes turned away from Bailey, and then she'd pivot on the heel of her boot and stare into her face. When she snapped the phone shut, she climbed in behind the squad car's steering wheel and pulled out of the driveway.

They passed the school yard, and again Bailey wondered about James. But he was in another county. She would probably never see him again. They drove down a residential street towards the poorer side of town. The houses lacked paint. Broken windows and sagging doors blended in with the unkempt yards, trash along the gutter, and graffiti rampant on the walls. They stopped before a building with dangling shutters hanging between broken windows stuffed with rags. *That house looks as sad as I feel,* Bailey thought. *Doesn't anybody care?*

"Your mother lives here."

"My mother? She doesn't want me."

"Look, Bailey, your family doesn't want you, but I have a court order." Matron Macintyre got out of the car and opened the car's back door. "Let me take off those cuffs. It was a show to save my face and get you out of the house."

Bailey stood rubbing her wrists. Did a court order have the ability to change them? She remembered the condemnation and rejection. Her heart sank. She might be out of prison, but there were bars of another mode. What happened to her freedom? It had lasted only the moment she'd stepped outside the prison's doors. Now she was bound by society's jurisdictions.

"Here's your Bible and jacket. It's all Tink brought out."

"That's all I had." She looked into the matron's kind face. "You're leaving me?"

"It's the only place I know. The court order is tucked in your Bible. Take good care of it."

"I will." She hung her head. Freedom had sung anthems of hope and cheer. Reality hit with the force of a head-on car collision. Her family lived in squalor. Gone was the façade that faced the public on the front of the beer joint. When the wind blew down the sign, grandfather always called a handy man and demanded it hung immediately. Her grandmother kept pots of blooming geraniums in the windows for the public eye should never know the discord raging in the apartment above the parlor, but now their dirty wash was literally strewn across the postcard sized yard for the world to see.

"Bailey, you are under house arrest, but I will come every afternoon to pick you up and take you to the library. I'm sorry. It's all I can do." Matron Macintyre backed off, turned, and ducked into the squad car. "Good luck."

I'll need more than luck. Bailey turned to walk up the broken sidewalk. She was home, but this didn't look like home or feel like home. Where was the joy? She glanced behind her and saw a curtain move across the street. How many more were watching? She studied the row of houses that looked little better than the one before her and the weathered steps leading to the locked front door. Locks had been her life for years. Would anyone open to her? Matron Macintyre mentioned the court order, and Bailey saw it hanging out of her Bible, but again, what power did it hold? Could a mere piece of paper change her past? Maybe it held the key to the present. She straightened her back, took a deep breath, and forced a smile.

She rapped the hollow sounding door with her knuckles. A dog yapped. She waited until she heard someone growl, "Shut up, mutt."

"Hello." Her friendly call through the wood, glass, and heavy curtain made the dog start in again. Something thumped inside, and the dog yelped. "Let me in. It's Bailey." Again the dog barked, but this time a single thump, thump, thump traveled toward the door.

"Don't matter what you selling. We don't want it."

"I'm not selling anything. It's me, Bailey. Please, let me in."

"Bailey?" The muffled voice coughed. "I don't know any Bailey."

But she had recognized her mother's voice. "Mom, it's me."

"Bailey?" This time the tone went up an octave. "Is that really you?" A dead bolt slid, and the knob turned. The door jerked open, and Bailey saw a haggard creature in a ripped bathrobe, leaning on a cane. As the door opened wider, the sordid contents of the room and rank odor of unwashed bodies, dirty clothing, and spoiled food gushed out like water from a broken dam. "What you doing here? Escaped from jail?"

"No, Mom, I'm free on parole." She stood there waiting to be asked inside, but she didn't want to step across the threshold of the garbage heap. The minutes ticked inside her head, but her mother also waited.

"What do want from me? I ain't got nothing." The door began to close.

Bailey gripped the knob to hold it open. "I have to stay here. The judge has given you a court order allowing me to stay." She flipped the paper in the Bible. "He says I have to stay here."

"He didn't ask me."

The pressure to shut the door increased, but Bailey was stronger. "I have to stay here. Court orders." She stepped inside and closed the door. The dog sniffed at her heels and wagged its tail so hard the hind quarters also wagged.

"I guess I ain't got no say." Her mother turned to creep back to the chair, using her cane. "There ain't no room for you. Not even a couch." She fell into the pillows and sat gasping. The trip to and from the door had taken her strength. Minutes ticked past on the alarm clock at her elbow. Bailey stood as if before the firing squad.

. Around the chair littered Styrofoam containers and other trash of empty liquor bottles and soft drink cans mounded into a pile that leaked into the rest of the room. The couch or what had been one was covered with soiled clothing. The mountain flowed over the back and on both sides. Nothing in the jail or halfway house had prepared Bailey for this. She had desperately wanted out of the prison and the building that held the junkies, the prostitutes, and the thieves—but horror wasn't a word to describe this mess.

Her mind turned to God. *Why am I in this mess? Aren't my desires of a nice home for James pure and holy—like Yours?* Her anger turned on her hopeless mother. How could she live in such a pig pen? Didn't her mother have any dreams or ambitions for something better?

She watched her mother stab the buttons on a remote, and a small color TV buzzed. The screen flipped one line up in fast succession after another. “It’s broke, just like everything else.” Her mother continued to punch the buttons.

Bailey felt her stomach lurch. The matron had left. She had no other alternative.

She stepped into the next room that might have been a bed room, but only a ripped mattress lay on the floor amid the trash. The dog jumped on it, circled twice, and lay down. It rested its head on front paws, watching her.

“You’re stuck in this sty, too.” Bailey’s arms dropped uselessly to her sides, and she kicked at the filthy clothing including a soaked, dried menstrual pad. The dog growled but didn’t move. She backed away, bumping into a door jam. Turning, she saw the bathroom contained a sink and bathtub loaded with more discarded clothing smelling worse than the front room.

She returned to her mother. “Where’s the grandparents?”

“What do you want to know? They left me.” The woman sniffed. “Too good for me, they was. Went south to where it’s warm. They wouldn’t take me.” Then her eyes narrowed. “I ain’t got no money so don’t ask.”

Again Bailey stood aghast.

Her mother tipped a bottle to her lips. After the gurgling gulp she set the bottle upright between her legs and wiped her mouth across the sleeve of the chenille robe. The bloodshot eyes stared without blinking at the television screen that continued to scroll black lines. Only the actor’s talk on the soap opera came through.

“Mom, how can you live like this?”

The woman picked up the bottle for another swig. When it was empty, she swung it across the room. The glass shattered against the wall.

"Is that your answer? Drink yourself to death?"

"Get out of here." Her mother swore.

Bailey's stomach lurched again, and she fled into what should have been the kitchen. Open squares on the dirty and broken linoleum showed where the refrigerator and stove once sat. Open shelves held only a motley assortment of dishes and pans. No edible food existed that Bailey could see—just dirty dishes and more trash.

She covered her mouth and pinched her nose. *Why am I here?* Slowly she turned. *God, I can't stay here. I can't live here. This is impossible!*

God hadn't heard. No savior or prince charming rushed to the door for her. She gingerly stepped around the trash and ventured into another empty bedroom that held only a chest with broken drawers. A tattered blanket blowing in the autumn breeze covered the broken window. Then she saw the mouse scurrying along the wall. Her scream brought the dog who looked at her with a narrow black nose with a broad white stripe pointing at her. It whined.

"You don't like this any better than I do?" She studied the short-haired animal. "I thought rat terriers were mousers, but who am I to judge you?"

The confusion and filth overwhelmed her. Bailey couldn't think. She had to get out and found the back door from the kitchen. The flimsy structure opened easily and hung precariously, above missing steps. Cans, bottles, dirty wet clothing, and garbage lay in heaps an arm's throw away. She searched for a safe place to land and jumped. A torn and weathered love seat lay flipped over. Its six legs or pegs stuck upward like darts thrown at a target. How could anyone live here? She had thought nothing could be as bad as prison, but maybe she was wrong. *Oh, God, what am I going to do?*

"Hi." A teenage boy gawked through the broken fence palings. Then he sauntered through the opening. His baseball cap sat sidewise so the bill stuck out over his left ear. A skull with fiery eyes on the black T-shirt competed with his friendly face. His tan shorts with square pockets on the sides hung from narrow hips. Buttoned down flaps on additional front pockets almost met his knees. Black and white sneakers worn without socks looked too big for the skinny ankles. His shoulders jerked in rhythm to his perky stride.

"I saw you come. You going to live here?" His thumb jerked to the left. "The old people left her here last fall. She doesn't do nothing." He bent down to scratch the dog's back. "They left Bennie, too. Poor dog."

"You live here?"

"Over there." He continued to rub the dog. Bennie wagged furiously in appreciation. "You in trouble with the law?"

"Not any more."

"You gonna live here?"

"I don't have much choice."

"Oh."

He followed as Bailey moved toward the single car garage attached to the house. More junk, broken furniture, and discarded trash cluttered the inside, but a cleared section could have once held a car. Her mother must have sold it with the kitchen appliances, but Bailey could see possibilities of making this area her pad.

"Is there trash pickup?"

"You got to call them. They cost you know." He swung his long skinny arms in a circle. "It will take the whole truck to get rid of all this stuff." His thumb jerked to the left. "My mom says she doesn't throw nothing away."

Bailey nodded and took a deep breath. "Where's the nearest store?"

"Tanker's Pub, down two blocks on the corner."

"I see. I won't be going there."

"Uh, well, they's deliver liquor here almost ever day." He cocked his head to one side. "Don't you drink?"

"No, I never had."

"That's good. She drinks all the time." Again his thumb jerked to the left. "Well, I got to be going."

"Hey, what's your name?" She watched him saunter off with the swing of the nonchalant and wished she could go with him.

He turned one last time. "Teddy Sommers. What's yours?"

"Bailey."

"That's different. See you."

Bailey studied the junk in the garage. The table with the broken leg could have been herself--almost useable, but useless. The chairs with missing parts surely symbolized her missing son, his dysfunctional father, and her unknown father. She closed her eyes. “Oh, Heavenly Father, You said You would be all I need. Help me to know how to clean up this place.”

A broom with only half a handle lay half buried beneath the rubble. It wasn’t much, but like a ray of hope she knew it was an answer to prayer. “Thank You, Father.” A chorus she’d learned in prison chapel came to mind, and she began to hum, hearing the words in her mind.

“He knows my need.

He cares for me.

I’ll trust Him with

A heart set free.”

She began in the corner with the least trash and pushed it to the far front corner. How she wished she could just throw away her past, but the rubble would remain until she had the funds to hire a dumpster. Within an hour she pulled the table into position. Although upright, it wobbled on three legs. She laid her Bible on the top like a deed to her property. This garage would be hers. She would make it work.

“Thank you, God, for freedom and a place of my own.”

She brought the chairs out in the sunlight. The craftsmanship classes in the jail taught her that she could take a leg from one to make the other whole, but she didn’t have any tools. She rested, sitting on an abandoned concrete block. Like the missing parts of her life, she wanted to put the pieces back together, but would that reveal the secrets?

Did it matter who her father was or what had happened to Clark? What if she just concentrated on James and forgot about the sleeping past? Her energy at the moment lagged.

A chilling breeze swept around the corner and through the thin shirt. Shivering, she wished one of those ripped and half-rotten coats were wearable. A tattered blanket would do, but the yard held only garbage, too wet to burn. When she had the money, she could do more, but house arrest meant she couldn't leave the property. Her hopes lie in the library, but that wouldn't happen for another twenty-four hours--tomorrow afternoon.

Laughter and voices caught her attention. The four saw her before she could duck into the garage.

"Yo!" A tall white male faced her from the sidewalk. The black turban around his head didn't hide the long hair held with a rubber band at the nap of his neck or the silver chains cascading down his front. The sleeves of his orange T-shirt were ripped out leaving gaping holes below his arm pits, and the multiple pocketed pants sagged around his hips. "Who is you?"

Bailey tried to ignore them, but the fellow leaped over the pitiful picket fence, and the three rough necks sprinted around the trash in the yard like buzzards flapping around a carcass. The leader cocked his head, and she could see his nicotine-stained teeth when he smiled.

"Looks what we got here."

She didn't like the way his eyes traveled up and down her person, or the ogling of the others.

He reached into one of his pockets and pulled out a plastic bag. "Want some?"

"I don't do drugs."

His eyebrows rose. “I don’t believe you.” He nodded toward the police band around her ankle. “You been in. Now you out. You be hungry, man, mighty hungry.” He laughed and his group laughed along with him. “Now, be honest with Crib. You really want some, but you don’t have money. We can fix that up, yea, boys?”

“Yea.” As they chorused, they stepped closer, but Bailey’s back was already against the wall.

“I don’t do drugs.” She watched him bend closer to her. “Go away!” Her voice rose to a high pitch in her panic. Suddenly, the little dog Bennie was snapping at their ankles. His yapping and attack broke up the group. The four ran through the garbage, leaping over pieces of destroyed furniture, and jumped the fence. The terrier ran back and forth making more noise than Bailey thought possible.

The leader paused and turned to her. “Crib will be back.” That night his leering face penetrated her dreams every time she heard a noise. The night air proved chilly in the garage, but she had blocked the table up with two wooden crates and slept on the surface. She’d thought herself safe from the crawly creatures roaming the floor, but whiskers touching her face awakened her as the sky turned the multiple colors of dawn.

Mid afternoon Matron Macintyre returned. As the police car pulled up next to the sidewalk, Bailey ran out to meet her. She slid into the back seat. “I’m so glad to see you.”

The officer pulled the car out of the neighborhood, drove through the residential streets, and parked in the city park. “Sit up here so I can talk to you. How are things?””

"Not good, but I know I can make it with your help."

"We're going to cash your check and get a post office box for you." Then she just stared at Bailey. "Isn't there any running water in that house?"

"Not much, I mean there is, but the sinks were plugged with garbage and such." Bailey looked down at her broken nails, the dirty jeans, and top. She had ventured into the house that morning and begun the process of straightening in the bathroom. The sewage in the commode required water, and she had found a bucket of sorts to transfer water from the kitchen sink. "Mom's house has few sanitary provisions." There hadn't been any soap, shampoo, or clean towels.

Matron Macintyre grimaced. "The place is that bad, eh? Okay, the first stop is the jail where you can use the showers and get some clean clothes."

Bailey nodded. "Thanks." But she had mixed feelings walking into the cell block. As she passed the women's area, Rosenbaum recognized her through the heavy plate window.

"I told yah, you'd be back."

The raucous laughter followed Bailey down the hall. After her shower she again walked the gauntlet of the cell block.

Rosenbaum screamed through the glass. "You still owe me some sugar."

Bailey shook off the catcalls that followed her and hastened through the last heavy door, stepping out like a liberated colt. Again she knew the feeling of freedom and whirled in delicious joy. She didn't care who saw her. "Thank You, God. Oh, thank You!"

Matron Macintyre waited in her car. "Next stop is something for you to eat, my treat." She drove to a fast food, went through the pickup lane, and ordered.

"Why are you doing this for me?" Bailey held the hamburger in front of her nose. The aroma of warm meat, onions, and a tangy tomato sauce made her stomach rumble.

Matron Macintyre looked out the window. "I guess I just would like you to make it. You seem to be a decent kid." She picked at her own French fries and dabbed one in catsup. "If you went back into prison, you would be dead in less than a month's time."

That was no surprise to Bailey.

They finished their meal, and Macintyre drove to the mall.

"These stores weren't here before."

"A lot changed in Lakeside while you were gone."

Bailey thought of the burned tavern and her mother's house. "More than you know."

The new stores held merchandise and brands that Bailey wanted to study and touch, but she had to be content just to scan the store front windows as she followed Matron Macintyre's fast pace.

The matron stopped at an inside bank. "Bailey, you can cash your check here."

"I don't remember the bank being here."

The matron nodded. "Well, it has been here for almost three years."

"Oh." Bailey felt small and stupid, but so much had changed. Her shopping included a towel, soap, comb, rat poison, and a blanket. Other necessities would have to wait. "I need to go to the library."

"First I want you to get a post office box. Otherwise, kiss your checks goodbye."

"I know." Bailey thought of the four hoodlums. Their visit had made her value locked doors and windows. She couldn't afford any now, but as she transformed the garage, the hardware would take priority.

Chapter 4: Clean Up

She stepped into the library and twirled slowly with her eyes closed, just savoring the atmosphere of books, open space, and orderliness. The smell of a man's aftershave lotion startled her. "Oh, I'm sorry!"

Dave grinned. "I wondered if we had frightened you away." He followed her to the desk where she signed in. "Since you were here, I've found a couple more sites for you to visit."

"Thank you, sir."

"My name is Dave." The big, open smile welcomed her. He opened the web site as she stood and watched. Then he pulled out the chair. "It's all yours."

Her heart glowed. He was so nice. "Thank you very much, Dave."

"No problem. No problem at all."

He stood there, and she studied his clean, orderly appearance, so different from the four that visited her yesterday.

His brown slacks and striped tan sweater reminded her of the pictures of male models in a Sears catalog. His clean and shaped fingernails made her hide her own in tight fists.

Then Dave looked up. “Oops, I have to be going, but if you need me, I’ll be at the desk.”

The frowning librarian guarded the door.

Bailey logged in and began to type. She’d just sent in the third article when she saw the time on the corner of the computer’s screen. She pushed her chair back and stretched. Matron Macintyre would be waiting if she didn’t hurry. She looked for Dave as she signed out, but only the thin lipped librarian manned the desk.

“Excuse me.”

Bailey turned.

The woman stood close. “I know who you are and what you did.” She stepped back, but her low voice continued. “I can’t keep you out of here, but don’t flirt with Dave. He’s a nice young man deserving better than the likes of you.” The triangular chin and smooth skin held memories.

As Bailey stared, she saw the name tag. “Petunia, we went to school together. You were one of the cheerleaders.”

“And you were a bar maid.” She spit the words out like they were poisonous. “I knew you’d end up a jailbird.”

Bailey backed away. The in crowd had always swarmed around Petunia. Bailey wanted to be one of them, but prison taught her to be wary. The price of trusting held hidden costs, and just any friendship couldn’t be considered.

Matron Macintyre didn't stop for groceries on the way back, although Bailey's hunger returned, and her stomach growled. She glanced in embarrassment, but her friend had not seemed to notice. They pulled up to the house.

"How is it going?" The Matron shut off the engine.

Bailey shrugged. "As expected, I guess."

The woman started the motor. "Well, I'll be back, but don't try anything foolish."

"I won't. I promise." She waved goodby and bent to rub Bennie's back.

Inside the garage the table lay on the floor. Smashed chairs and the trash that she had so carefully swept to the corner were strewn over the floor. Her Bible lay in the midst with ruffled pages. She hung the plastic bag holding her purchases on a cupboard knob and picked up the Bible.

"Welcome, home." Crib stood in her doorway. "We had a party, and some things got a little messy." His glance surveyed the room. "You know this could be a nice place if it were really fixed up." He stepped closer. "You and I might just get friendly some."

"Get out."

He peered at the dog at her heels, and his face hardened. "Yea, right, but Crib will be back."

It wasn't safe in the garage. Bailey waited until she knew he no longer lingered outside and made a run for the back door of the house. It had been locked. "Mom! Let me in!" She pounded the rattling window, afraid that it might break. She shook the door knob. Suddenly, the old latch gave way, and she nearly fell when the door opened on its loose hinges. Inside, she turned and relocked the door.

"It won't do no good." Her mother stood, leaning on her cane. The same torn bathrobe drooped around her figure as she waited at the living room doorway. Her hair stood in uncombed spikes. Bailey thought she would have looked like the lady liberty if she would have carried a torch, but the thought wasn't valid.

"Your friends leave?"

"They are not my friends. Mom, I must stay here tonight."

Her mother shrugged. "The chair is mine." She turned and went back into the living room.

Bailey studied the door. She had to fortify it. A drawer gaped beside the sink full of silverware. She found some case knives and slid them under the trim around the door. Just maybe it would hold. Then she kicked at the empty cans, soiled dishes, and discarded cardboard. Cockroaches scurried for cover. Was she really safe? She fled to the living room where her mother still watched the mal functioning TV. A news commentator could be heard recounting some robbery in town.

"Mom, we've got to do something about this place. It's unlivable."

Her mother lifted a bottle to her mouth. "Looks fine to me." She chugged the last sip of whiskey and threw the bottle in Bailey's direction. It bounced against the wall and landed with a clank among others. Then the woman closed her eyes. "Got to get some sleep. I'm so tired." In seconds she was snoring.

The little dog sniffed at some recent Styrofoam containers. He chose one and carried it back into the room with the mattress.

Bailey followed him, wondering how her mother managed to have liquor and food deliveries. The dark room stank, but when she flipped the switch, light revealed nothing had changed.

"Bennie, mind if I sleep with you?" She pushed the mound of clothing off the mattress and to the corner of the room. Taking her new blanket out of the sack, she folded it lengthwise and laid it on the mattress. She shut out the light and then crawled into the blanket. Sleep came. When she awoke, light streamed across the filthy rug from the living room, and Bennie lay at her feet.

Bailey tackled the yard as if she were cleaning up her past. Every discarded item represented a part of her life that she didn't want to remember. She threw it onto the pile that she'd eventually dispose of in a dumpster. Finding the grass underneath gave her hope. In the flower garden around the base of the house, she pulled out the weeds and left what she thought as legitimate plants. An old garden hose screwed to the faucet at the side of the foundation had been cut or broken off, but the water flowed out like blessings of freedom. She soaked the flower patch until the ground was saturated, and small streams flowed over the top of the stones like small water falls. She was determined to find the good inside her, and let it bloom.

She showed the Matron her progress.

"Plants can bend toward the sun, Bailey, but how we use our moisture and the blessings that come, determines our end."

"What do you mean?"

"You've been served a raw deal in life, but you're going to make it." Matron Macintyre kneeled down to touch a small daisy. "See how bent the stem is? All those weeds tried to choke it out, but it still grew toward the sun. Grow toward the Son of God, Bailey. Don't loose sight of Him."

"I won't. I mean I'm trying."

"I know you are." Macintyre stood up and surveyed the yard. "You've made a lot of progress." Then she looked into Bailey's eyes. "We all have scars. Some cover them so others will never see them. They're always looking for a place to hide their memories. We are our memories and experiences. We must use them to make us better people."

Bailey nodded. "I don't think my wounds will ever heal. They are gaping holes."

"Listen to me. You can continue to expose them so others will feel sorry for you, but that will make you dependant on what they think and what they can do for you. Bailey, you've got to be strong."

"How?"

"Child, you are doing fine. Just keep up the good work. Don't get side tracked, and remember this is your healing." Matron Macintyre walked back to her car. "I'll be back tomorrow."

"Thanks." Bailey watched her friend drive away. She would never be able to repay her, but it was like Jesus. She would never be able to repay Him either.

When her next check came, Bailey bought food, garbage bags, and a shovel. Matron Macintyre continued to pick her up on a daily basis. "How is it going?"

"I cleaned up the bathroom. The commode works if I fill

the tank first. The shower trickles, but I got one anyway." She smiled triumphantly.

"I noticed the dumpster in the yard." Matron Macintyre turned the patrol car next to the curb at the library.

"I have to get the garbage out so I can get rid of the pests." Bailey glanced out the window. "Then I'd like to paint and fix it up." She paused. "I've been thinking. Paint will give me a fresh, fragrant start."

"I like what we were talking about the other day. Did you know planting flowers gives the promise of a colorful, beautiful future? Your past is only seed. How we cultivate and weed our gardens gives the character to our soul."

"Well, I didn't think of it that way. I do plan to put more flowers out, but they do cost money, you know."

As the matron chuckled, her eyes lit up.

Bailey knew she was loved. "Do you think I could get a bicycle? It would save you the trips to pick me up and such."

"Bailey, you are still under house arrest. I must know where you are at all times."

"Oh. I could call you on the telephone."

"We'll have to see." Matron Macintyre smiled. "I must admit that I thought you'd be begging to come back to the half way house by now. But you seem to be making the best of a bad deal." She paused. "Did you ask your mother about your father?"

"She won't tell me anything." Her eyes lifted. "You know, I have to make it by myself. You are the only one who will help me." Suddenly she thought of Dave working with the computer.

"Well, just about the only one." Bailey looked down at her hands. "I want my son, but I can't even begin to work that out until things look better here. But I couldn't have made it without your help. You've been good to me." They passed a church. "When can I start attending church?"

"Church?"

"Yea, I always went to chapel in the prison and Bible studies, too, but since I've been paroled, I haven't had a chance."

"I'll have to find out about that, too." Matron Macintyre smiled. "When I report your good attitude and the work you've been doing, I don't think it will be a problem."

"Thanks."

She was coming out of the library that evening when she saw him. Clark hadn't changed. The bags under his eyes were as blue black as ever, and his rounding middle puckered his shirt front around the buttons at the bottom. She didn't want him to notice her, but he did.

"Bailey, I didn't know you were out of the slammer." The smile didn't reach his eyes. "Didn't you get ten years?"

She turned away.

"Come on. You don't treat an old friend that way."

"You're not an old friend." Her temper blazed. "I remember how you fed me drugs and raped me. Then you testified against me."

He laughed. "Don't be so angry. That's life. It happens to everybody. I can set you up. Just give me the word."

"Get lost." She saw Matron Macintyre's car slow and park at the curb.

Clark put out a hand to detain her. "I'll see you later, Bailey."

"Not if I can help it." She shook off his heavy hold and ran. Bailey slid into the car and heaved a big breath of relief. "Thanks for coming."

"I was a few minutes late." Matron Macintyre appeared flustered.

"You came just in time."

"Who was he?"

"Clark, I don't know his other name, but he's the one who set me up, and I landed in jail."

"Don't have anything to do with him."

"I won't. I don't do drugs."

"Did he sell them?"

"Maybe. Once he gave me ecstasy. I was raped and became pregnant. To support my baby, I delivered some packages for him. When I got caught, he vanished. Nobody believed me. Even my own mother and grandparents witnessed against me." Bailey could feel the old anger suffocating her. "They took James away. I don't know where he is."

That evening Bailey pondered how she could avoid Clark. If he ever discovered where she lived, he would hound her just like he had before. She wondered why he had never been arrested for pimping or rape. Maybe nobody had ever turned him in. The thought lingered. If he started bothering her, she would inform Matron Macintyre.

Her mother never voiced any comments about Bailey's cleanup, but neither did she raise a hand to help. When the living room was actually livable, Bailey set a plastic trash can beside her mother's chair. "Put your garbage in there."

"Are you ordering me around in my own house?"

"Look it should be easier to just drop it in the bucket than throw it across the room."

"What if I need the exercise?" Her mother's refusal to cooperate included no baths or showers.

"Mom, it isn't healthy."

"I've lived this long without being healthy." But she did start combing her hair when Bailey put up a mirror in the bathroom and set out a plastic glass of combs on the sink counter.

As Bailey's checks from the work at the library on the internet continued, she purchased a small stove top and an apartment sized refrigerator for the kitchen. Her mother said, "You could have bought some real appliances."

Bailey didn't answer. She reformed the bedroom in the back to be hers by ripping out the old carpet and cleaning the floors, the windows, and adding fresh paint. The change was wonderful. She didn't have the money for fancy curtains, but the old blanket was gone. She divided a clean sheet lengthwise, tied it back on both sides with ribbon, and hung it over the window. Civilization suited her just fine.

A week or so later, she typed rapidly in the library computer. A shadow passed, and Bailey looked up into David's eyes. "I've missed you. I thought you didn't work here anymore."

"My schedule changed. I've been promoted to the children's department, or so I've been told. My job is to read them stories on the weekends and after school. I show them where books are and such."

"Oh." Bailey saw the misery in his eyes. "Don't you like kids?"

"Yes, I do, but I prefer working with computers." He looked away. "I'm having trouble with the decorations, too. I never was much good in art. My fingers are all thumbs when it comes to cutting paper." He glanced around. "Well, I've got to be going." He nodded toward the stairs. "Come up and visit sometime."

"I will, but I have to work."

Petunia came into the room, and Dave spoke to her. "I need a banner made for upstairs."

"Come back when no one is working the computers." Petunia's eyes traveled from Bailey to David and back again. "Then you can make all the banners you want." She smiled triumphantly. Bailey glanced in his direction. Dave paused at the door to wink at her before he ran up the steps to the children's department. His shoes thudded on the carpet.

Later Clark slid into the chair beside her. "I figured I'd find you in here. How are you doing?"

"Get lost. I don't want anything to do with you."

When Bailey realized that he wasn't going to move, she closed the computer screen and collected her purse.

"I've got to go."

She didn't expect Matron Macintyre to return for another hour, so she slipped into the ladies' restroom and hid in a stall. She would have stayed there except she didn't have a watch, and there was no clock on the wall. After a few minutes she avoided the computer room and came to the stairs. It seemed natural to climb the steps into the children's department. David sat at a desk littered with scissors, paste, and construction paper.

"Hi, Bailey." A smile erased the frustration on his face. "I'm trying to cut out some leaves to go around that bulletin board."

"Would you like some help?"

"Sure." He passed the scissors across the desk. "I'll punch out the lettering. That's so much easier." The minutes flew. She laid the red, yellow, and brown maple leaves like fans on his desk. "Hey, I like that arrangement. Hand them up, and I'll staple them." Soon he stepped back. "It's beautiful." His eyes met hers. "Thanks, I couldn't do it by myself."

"I enjoyed it." Bailey glanced at the clock. "Dave, I must go. See you."

"Thanks for helping."

"It was fun."

He waved when she reached the top of the stairs, and she waved in return. Then she glanced down to see Clark slowly turn.

A smile that didn't reach his eyes alerted her.

"Hello, Bailey."

She had to get out to the car.

Clark waited for her. "Stop."

But she brushed past and ran to the curb. Inside the car she regained her breath. "Thanks for coming on time. He was there again."

"Who?"

"Clark. He came into the computer lab. I left so I didn't get my work done." She heaved a sigh of relief. "Thanks. I always feel safe with you."

Matron Macintyre nodded. "Tomorrow, if Clark shows, call this number." She handed Bailey a card.

"I don't think I would be allowed to use the phone."

Matron Macintyre frowned. "Here." She handed Bailey a cell phone. "It's mine. Don't get any ideas, okay?"

Bailey nodded and tucked it into her purse. "I promise. I hope you arrest him."

"We can't without proper motive or evidence." Matron Macintyre touched her arm as Bailey was sliding out the door. "I'd like to prevent his bothering you, but I need more identification than the name Clark. Should he show up again, I could possibly have him apprehended for fingerprinting. He probably has a record on file."

That evening Bailey finished her dishes from an evening meal in the "purged" kitchen. Now she wasn't afraid to cook and keep food in it. A knock on the front door sent her running.

"Coming!"

Through the peephole, Bailey saw her sister Narla in an attractive pantsuit with pearls at her neck. A large diamond flashed on her left hand, and the shiny heels were the latest. "She hasn't changed. Nothing but the best and most expensive," Bailey muttered as she opened the door. Bennie barked a welcome.

"Hello, jailbird." The mocking smile on Narla's face took in the whole living room. "I see you've become Mom's maid. Well, she needed someone, and I couldn't do it with a husband and three children. My time is completely busy all the time. I just stopped in because Mom told me you were living with her. I don't trust you, jailbird. You can't live off Mom's money. She doesn't get enough to support herself properly." Her eyes roved around the room at the decrepit furniture and sagging drapery. "You'd best find another hotel."

Bailey froze.

Her sister pushed past. "Hi, Mom, you're looking good." Her eyes turned to Bailey. "I don't see how you can stand having a jailbird living in your house. I'd be afraid she might slit my throat in the night or make off with the television to the pawn shop. You can't trust any of them that come out of prison, you know. They pick up habits from all the others they associate with and come out worse than they went in."

Before Bailey could stop her, Narla wandered into the front bedroom. "Well, this is an improvement. What did you do?" She turned to Bailey. "I know. You have to be selling drugs to afford this bed and bedding." Her eyes seemed to miss nothing. "Even the drapes are new." Her fingers rubbed the fabric. "Cheap cotton." Her eyes narrowed. "Sheets! I bet you found them at the dollar store." She smirked. "This *your* room?" Before Bailey could say anything, Narla crossed the room to the closet.

She yanked at the old sliding door which fell to the floor and gave it a healthy kick. "Cheap, cheap, cheap." Her glare at Bailey said more, but she stared at the neatly hung clothes and folded items on the top shelf. Her contempt and scorn soured the face that could have been beautiful.

Bailey reached down to lift the door. Narla's kick had dented it until she didn't know if it would slide back in the channel. It took hours the first time to hang it and get it to slide somewhat in the groove on the floor. Now it probably wouldn't work again. She propped it up against the wall to follow Narla. Her sister made the rounds through the kitchen and bathroom, but Bailey didn't want her crossing the threshold of her room.

As Narla stood staring at the dish water whose suds had disappeared, Bailey gained the doorway of the other bedroom. If it had a door, she would have shut it. The next time Narla appeared, there would be doors and locks on both bedrooms.

"Afraid I'll find you've been using drugs?" Her mocking face challenged Bailey. "Move. I have as much right to all parts of this house as you do."

"This is my room. You've seen everything else, but this is private." Little Bennie who had been following them around suddenly chose Bailey's side. He barked. Narla kicked at him. He began to snarl. "You'd better leave before you get bit."

"He's just a noise box." Narla kicked again, and the dog's teeth latched on the fold of her pants. As she swung her leg around, the dog let go, and her foot hit the door jam. She screamed. "You broke my foot, you dumb dog."

Bennie's teeth latched on the other pant leg. He let go when Bailey reached down and picked him up in her arms. "Narla, get out of here before I turn him loose." Bennie growled.

"You'll pay for this, you beast." Narla limped to the front door. "Mom, that dog is vicious. Get rid of him before he bites someone, and you get sued for it."

When the front door closed, Bailey locked it and leaned against it. Narla had never been friendly. Her mother pushed the buttons to turn on the TV. Again the lines rotated rapidly. "Everything's broken around here."

Especially relationships, Bailey thought as she and Bennie went back to the kitchen.

Chapter 5: The Search

Early the next morning Matron Macintyre knocked at the front door. "Last night a woman filed a report that there was a vicious dog here, and you were sponging off her mother." She looked around the room. Bailey's mother was still wearing the torn bath robe and sleeping in her chair. Her snores punctuated the officer's sentence.

Bailey led her into the kitchen where a small card table and a plastic lawn chair resided in the former corner of the refrigerator. "That was my sister Narla."

Matron Macintyre sat down and watched Bennie who was sniffing at her feet. "Is this the vicious dog? What happened?"

Bailey explained how she had prevented Narla from invading her bedroom. "She accused me of hiding drugs in there. It's not true, but when she tore down the closet door in my mother's room, I didn't want her destroying my room."

"I see. I do need to search it, because she filed a report regarding that, too, and you are on probation." She stepped into the room with the single cot and the sheet at the window.

"I haven't replaced the light fixture yet. It was like that when I came." Bailey pointed to the bare wires hanging from the ceiling. "Light fixtures are so expensive, and I can read in the kitchen."

Matron Macintyre nodded. She opened the closet doors and carefully shut them. "I don't see any evidence of drugs, but we'll have to bring in a dog. You'll have to take this one outside while the search is made."

Bailey nodded. "I understand." Then the tears came. "I've cleaned this place up, washed all of Mom's clothes, and used my money for the furnishings, and yet, my sister could only destroy me."

Matron Macintyre's arms came around her. "Bailey, listen. You won't have to live like this much longer. I've seen the money you're making. Soon you'll have an apartment of your own where your sister can't touch you."

"Why are you doing this for me? My own family hates me."

"I think I've located your father. His name was on your birth certificate. There are better days ahead. I promise."

"Who is he?"

"I'll tell you later."

A few minutes later the canine control arrived. Bennie and

Bailey sat in the back seat of Matron Macintyre's car. A large German shepherd trotted up the broken sidewalk and concrete steps into the house. Bailey waited for her mother's scream as she held the barking Bennie, but she didn't hear one. Minutes later the handler and dog sniffed around the house where Bailey had planted a few flowers after her purge of the yard. They disappeared into the garage to come out and give the all clear signal. The van disappeared around the corner before Matron Macintyre came out of the house.

"How did Mom react to the dog sniffing around her chair?" Bailey dropped Bennie on the ground. The little dog began sniffing around the house and garage like the other dog had, but every so often he hiked his leg and scratched the ground with his claws.

"She slept like she was in a drunken stupor." Matron Macintyre frowned. "She needs to get into a rehab center."

Bailey shook her head. "It'll never happen."

"Are you paying for the whiskey?"

"No, she must have a stipend from the grandparents. I think the house is still in their name. They pay for the utilities, the phone, and the taxes."

"I see. Are you ready? I can take you to the library." For some reason Matron Macintyre didn't mention her father again, and Bailey forgot to ask.

Crib and his gang returned the evening after the police search. "I saw the whole thing. They know you do drugs, or they wouldn't have come. You're pretty smart, but where you hiding them?"

"I don't do drugs." Bailey had a hose and was watering the few asters along the side of the house. "If you don't leave, I'll soak you good." She flipped some water at them, and they left.

But the next morning she awakened to the graffiti spray painted on the garage in black paint, toilet paper hanging from the singular maple in the yard, and plastic forks jabbed in the lawn. It looked like a kid's prank, but Crib wasn't going to take her denial seriously.

Bailey was busy at the computer when the library began to fill with kids. She heard the many thumps on the steps and the excited chatter. Earlier Dave showed her *Horton Hatches an Egg* and allowed her to read it. Then he showed her the bean bag he'd placed on a library table with a large papier-mâché egg.

"I'll sit up here like Horton to read the story." His eyes danced. "The kids will be on the floor, so I'll be above the crowd."

"That's neat!" She gestured at all the Dr. Seuss' books he'd displayed around the room. "I bet there will be a run on them when you're done."

"I hope so. Readership is down since Petunia placed me up here. Most kids gravitate to a female."

"It's just because they don't know you."

"I guess so."

As she thought about it in the evening, Bailey realized even Dave had his troubles. She wished she could help him, because he had been so nice to her and smiled every time she saw him. If he knew of her background, he wouldn't be so friendly. Like the other librarian, he'd try to get her to leave the library, but she couldn't yet. She was saving for a computer, but the one she wanted was so expensive. Not only that, she didn't think it would be safe in her Mom's house. As long as everything was cheap, nothing would happen, but if Crib thought there was anything of value inside, she knew the doors would never keep him out although she had replaced both outside doors with new locks and dead bolts.

She was painting the garage to cover up the graffiti when Teddy Sommers sauntered into the yard. "Hi, I haven't seen you since you welcomed me into the neighborhood."

"Mom, wouldn't let me come over because she thought you'd get me in trouble, but since you've cleaned up the place and are painting over the graffiti, she doesn't think you're a bad person at all." He bent down to pet Bennie. "Miss me, fella?"

"Yes, he has. He likes you."

"He likes you, too. I saw how he chased Crib off that time. Crib isn't anybody to fool around with. I saw him slice a guy once who was fooling around with his girl."

"So he has a girl?"

"Not any more. Her family moved away."

Bailey finished painting. She dropped her brush into the thinner. "I'm making pudding for supper. Want to watch?"

"No, I've got to go home." Teddy turned, and Bennie started to follow.

She whistled. When the little dog came, she picked him up. "I like Teddy, too. He's a decent kid." The words hung in the air, and she thought of when Matron Macintyre had said them about her. Would there ever be the chance that she would be deemed a decent mom and get James back? Maybe the answer came with knowledge of her father. The matron hadn't talked about it lately, but she had to know.

The session of *Horton Hatches An Egg* was so successful that one little boy asked Dave to tell it again. "My mother ran off from me, too." His eyes looked into Dave's confidentially. "I have a foster mom, but she didn't hatch me, 'cause I asked her. She thinks that some day my mom will get out of prison and come back for me. My mom didn't sign the papers that would let me be adopted."

Dave glanced over to connect with Bailey. His face wore a sad expression. "What's your name?"

"Gary, but I don't like it. I told my foster mom that it wasn't my name. She laughed and showed me how it was on the papers. It was Gary all right, but I still don't like it."

"What do you want to be called?"

"I don't know, but I sure don't like Gary. Gary stinks."

"What makes it stink?"

"'cause it's not my name!" Gary wandered over to the book case. "Can I check out a book?"

"Do you have a card?"

"I brought my foster mom's card. She said I could get one book with it."

"Okay, you can get one book." Dave went over to help the boy find the right book. Bailey slowly walked down the stairs. Her son James was in foster care but outside the county. She hadn't signed any papers releasing him for adoption. Did that mean she might be able to get him back? Would he want to come back and live with her? She thought of her mother's old house--not the safe environment to raise a child. If she were going to get James, she needed to start looking for the right apartment.

She began her search on line. One-by-one she scratched off possibilities until she thought she had found the perfect place right across from the school. She called the number.

"Do you have children?" The woman's voice sounded warm over the telephone.

"I'm single, but I need two bedrooms. There's the possibility I may get custody of my son if I can find him."

"Well, that apartment has been rented." Without further comment, the receiver clicked. Bailey continued to search the internet and the newspapers.

Bailey hated to have to rely on Matron Macintyre for every major need, but she didn't know what else to do unless she could find another place. When the apartment across from the school was still advertised two days later, she mentioned it to the police woman. "I don't understand why I couldn't rent it."

"I'll check into it."

"Well, I'm going to look again."

"I'll still look into the situation. It's possible that it could be rented, and the ad was never removed from the internet."

"Thanks." The next day Bailey searched for the apartment

ad, but it was gone. However, another ad with only a phone number had been listed. This time she didn't mention the possibility of James. The address hadn't changed.

She told Matron Macintyre who nodded. "We'll check on this together right now."

The renter's eyes smiled until her eyes saw the bracelet on Bailey's ankle. "The apartment has just been rented out this afternoon, but you can fill out an application."

The police officer motioned Bailey aside. "I'd like to see your renter's agreement."

"It's confidential, ma'am."

"The judge will give me a search warrant." Matron Macintyre wore her "don't mess with me" attitude.

The woman backed away. "I don't want to get in trouble with the law."

"If you've really rented it out, you won't be in any trouble."

"Well, I promised it to a young fellow this afternoon, and he's coming in tomorrow to check it out. I'm sorry for the inconvenience."

When the door closed, Bailey shook her head. "I know it would be ideal because it's so close to the school and the library, but she'll never be happy with me. She'd find a way to evict me as soon as she could. Let's look for another place."

"That's another issue. She's publicly advertising the place. According to local laws, she has to provide it without stipulations of gender, race, or other stipulations."

"I understand." Bailey studied the band around her ankle. Would she never measure up to society's standards? Then she remembered. "Could you tell me who my father is?"

The matron's face looked blank. "I've left that paper at the office. I'm sorry. I meant to give it to you the other day." She turned a corner. "Right now, let's concentrate on finding you an apartment, okay?" She took Bailey to three different real estate offices. Only one listed apartment was close to the library and school.

"It's strange. That's the same place where we were told it was already rented."

The real estate woman looked surprised. "If it's rented, it happened just hours ago." She picked up her telephone. When no one answered, she nodded to Bailey. "I'll check into it for you."

Finally, Bailey conceded defeat. "I already know I can't have that apartment."

"We've just started to look." Matron Macintyre gave her a smile as she dropped Bailey off at her mother's house. "We'll find something."

"Why are you helping me?"

The officer glanced across the street before answering. "I believe you deserve a chance. Bailey, I believe in you. Don't destroy my trust."

Narla had been there. Her mother didn't say anything, but the locks on both bedroom doors were broken. Marks of a pry bar marred the new wood. The dumped contents of the shelves and dresser drawer as well as the stripped beds made Bailey cry. Why would her sister hate her so? She called Matron Macintyre.

"Let's take fingerprints. Don't touch anything." In a few minutes a couple of squad cars came roaring up the street with blinking lights.

Bailey allowed them inside. She held the furious Bennie as the search dog moved from room-to-room. Her mother ignored the whole process. The German shepherd left the house. Bennie whined and relaxed on her lap.

Soon the other officers left. Only the chatter on her mother's TV disturbed the silence. Bailey went into the front bedroom and began to pick up the clothing, refold it, and put it back on the shelves. With a flip of her wrists, she straightened the bed covers, but this time the closet door would not fit into the groove no matter how hard she tried to force it. She left it against the wall, closed the damaged door, and went to her own bedroom.

The carnage was so senseless. The intruder had used her few pieces of underwear to wipe muddy shoes. One of the emptied bureau drawers was pulled apart. Bailey found her hammer and tapped it back together. Again the tears came. Why did her sister behave like this? She didn't want to hurt Narla or her family. Why did Narla seek her out to destroy her?

Again she smoothed the pages of her Bible which had been thrown across the room. The most rumpled page spoke to her. "Lo, I am with you always." Bailey bowed her head. "Thank you, Lord, for your protection and Matron Macintyre. I don't know what I'd do without either of you."

The next afternoon Matron Macintyre motioned for Bailey to go to her car. "Your sister didn't break in your house. Prints from several people were taken. The sergeant found them on file. Do you know a fellow who calls himself Crib?"

"Yes, he's threatened me a couple of times. Once his gang destroyed some furniture and painted graffiti on the garage." Bailey turned away. "Why would my mother allow them in the house?"

"They could have threatened her."

"But the door was locked. She was safe."

"People are only as safe as they feel. She opened up because she was scared."

"Well, that explains some things." Bailey looked down at her hands.

"What?"

"The refrigerator and stove were gone. Mother didn't have the energy to think about selling them, but they had disappeared." She looked out at the garage. "I wonder if the grandparents left her a car. None was here when I arrived."

"I'll make note of that." Matron Macintyre dropped her off at the library. "Remember to call if you happen to see Clark."

Bailey's hand touched the cell phone in her pocket. "I've been thinking about getting my own phone. Can we do that before you take me back?"

"Yes, we can find you a reasonable phone." The matron grinned. "That's what I like most about you. You don't sponge." She paused at the stop sign and turned left. "I wish I knew more people like you—hard working and determined to do the right thing." They reached the library.

"Thanks you so much!" Bailey stepped into the serene scene and took a deep breath. The relaxing environment of books and magazines was so invigorating. She found herself smiling at her thoughts.

"You look happy." Dave touched her arm. His v-necked, red cardigan revealed the white shirt collar and a shiny tie. Every hair on his head was slicked into place. She couldn't believe that he ever had any problems. "I could use some help upstairs. Do you have time?"

Her eyes traveled to the computer room, but she nodded. "Only a few minutes." She followed his quick steps up the stairs and into the children's room. He had moved the book shelves into a "U" shape, and Horton's bean bag and egg sat in the middle of the carpeted floor.

"Look!" Dave pointed to a small desk in the corner by the window overlooking the front entrance of the library. The monitor and keyboard of a new computer waited. "I bought it myself so you could sit up here and talk to me every afternoon."

Bailey glanced at him in surprise. "Won't the other librarian be unhappy?"

"I don't see why. You have just been named my voluntary assistant." His beaming face spoke volumes. "I told the directors how you helped me the other day and recommended you for employment. They said the budget couldn't allow another employee, but if you cared to volunteer, you could work up here." The broad smile almost reached his ears. "It's best that you're a volunteer. Otherwise Petunia would have you putting books on the shelves down stairs."

"I don't know what to say."

"Say, yes, and we'll get to work. First of all I want to show you a new website that I've discovered." He led the way to the computer and seated her. “It promises to be more lucrative than the others.”

“Thank you. I don’t understand your kindness, but thank you so much.”

He laughed. “I’m going to work your fingers to the bone.”

“Well, let’s get started.”

The time flew so quickly that Bailey just happened to glance down at the street and see the squad car come to the curb. “Dave, I must go, but I’ll be back tomorrow at the same time.”

“Okay.”

That evening before she slept, she allowed her mind to replay his touch as he laid his hand on her shoulder, the gladness in his eyes as he spoke to her, and the gentle way he had seated her at the computer. She had never had a friend like Dave.

“I’ve discovered that your son James has been brought back into this community.” Matron Macintyre started her car engine. “He’s in the second grade at Brickside, but I’m not allowed to tell you more.”

“How many classes of second graders are there?”

“Three, but I wouldn’t go there until you have been cleared. The social worker is preparing his paper work so you can get him when you have a proper home.” She smiled. “I don’t think it will be long now.”

Bailey felt her frustration rise. “I haven’t found a place, but couldn’t I have visitation rights?”

"You are right. I'll look into that, too. Did you know there's a low income apartment complex across town? You could afford to rent one in another week or so. We'll see if there's an opening."

Bailey knew the building. Actually two or three of the brick structures stood in a row with a park between them with children's swings, jungle gym, and slides in the center. "Low income?" Her eyes met the matron's. "That's where I lived when I was on welfare before prison. The place reeked of drug addicts."

"Bailey, I don't know what else to recommend unless you would purchase a house, but I don't think you are ready to do that yet. Are you?"

She licked her lips. If buying a house meant living in a neighborhood like her mother's, she didn't want it for James. She could live in the apartment complex, but she didn't want to raise her son there either. "Let's see what opens, okay?"

"Okay."

Dave caught her house hunting that afternoon. "I wondered where you lived. The library sent you a new card in the mail, but it returned this morning stamped, 'Return to sender. Unable to forward.' We need your new address."

Bailey stared at the envelope. "I have a post office box." Quickly she tore it open and removed the permanent card. Then she wrote her new address on the envelope and gave it back to him.

He frowned. "That doesn't tell me where you live."

"Do you need another proof of residency?"

"Not really, but…" He looked away. "I was hoping to find out where you live."

She didn't supply any other information but turned back to the computer. Above all else she didn't want Dave to discover her Mom's house. As she tucked the card into her pocket, she looked up. "Thanks for the card."

He stood there for a few minutes. "Ah, yes, when you get time, I'd like you to cut out these Halloween figures. We'll tape them to the window and hang them from the ceiling."

"Okay." She had them ready for him before she left. "Thanks, Dave. I really enjoy working for you, but there are some things you don't know about me."

"Like your address?" His eyes showed hurt.

She lifted her pant leg to reveal the bracelet. "I'm under house arrest at present." She tried to smile, but her lips felt like wooden fixtures. "Do you need me tomorrow?"

"Sure." Confusion covered his face as he stared at her feet and glanced up into her eyes.

She waved at the top of the stairs and nearly collided into some kids. At the front door someone grabbed her arm and whirled her around. "Clark!"

"You squealed on me, didn't you?" His pinched face wore fury like a red devil's mask. "The cops have been circling me like buzzards."

"Let me go." She shrugged him off and slipped through the door. As he followed her, she fled to the squad car. "Matron Macintyre! That's him! Clark!"

"Clark?"

Bailey looked back. Clark was gone. "He must have

doubled back into the library when he saw your car."

Matron Macintyre pulled down her CB radio mike. "Backup needed at the rear entrance of the library immediately." The answering car swerved around the corner in seconds, but Clark had disappeared.

"Next time I pick you up I'll have a car waiting in the back. We'll get him. We always do." Her confidence didn't assure Bailey. If Clark could give them the slip as easily as he had in the last five minutes, it would be impossible to catch the weasel.

Chapter 6: Her Mother

"Bailey, I have great news." Matron Macintyre's face glowed as the girl slid into the car. "You are allowed visitation rights. We need to set up a time and place. The foster parents prefer the first one to be in a non-threatening atmosphere."

"Where would that be?"

"How about a restaurant?" She pulled out into the street. "There's Cindy's Cup over on Ninth Street."

"When?"

"It could not be during school time. How about a Sunday afternoon?" The matron stopped at the corner and looked both directions. "I would pick you up, drop you off, and then return for you."

"Could we do it Saturday or another evening? I'm not able to go to church, but I'd like to keep God's day as holy as possible." When the matron frowned, Bailey added, "I'd have to buy something at the restaurant, and the Bible says not to do that on Sunday."

"Well, I think the ox is in the ditch this time. Remember Jesus' disciples plucked grain on the Sabbath which displeased the Pharisees." The matron turned a corner "I didn't realize how important church attendance was to you. What if we both went to church and then visited James afterward?"

"You're kidding!"

"No, just pick a church. I can't take you to mine. It is several miles away, but I'll go with you this once."

Bailey looked out the window. They passed several churches each time they went to the library. She had prayed God would help her find the right one to attend, but she didn't want to enter with the bracelet on her leg. "How much longer will I be under house arrest?"

"I don't know, but here's the copy of your birth certificate." Bailey studied the name given in the paternal blank: John Doe. Matron Macintyre pulled beside the curb of the library.

"She didn't give his real name." Bailey stared at the paper. "Was she hiding him, or didn't she know?" Scenes of her childhood replayed in her mind of men and her mother. There were so many traipsing in and out of the bar. Her mother flirted with every one. She looked up at the Matron. "What do I do now?"

"You will have to ask your mother."

"She'll never tell me."

"Bailey, do you talk to your mother?"

"I try, but she ignores me."

"She needs to go into a detox center."

"She won't." Bailey couldn't handle the situation at the

moment and slid out the door. “Thank you for bringing me every day.”

“It’s my job.”

Bailey turned to watch the squad car drive away. Just as she thought her life might be gaining normalcy, another important door slammed into her face. She entered the library and walked right into Clark. When she sidestepped to head for the stairs, he grabbed her arm.

“We have business that won’t wait.”

She tried to shrug off his hold, but the pinching fingers continued to tighten. “Leave me alone.”

“Scream if you wish, but you’ll only make a fool of yourself.” He turned her toward the back door. “Walk out.”

“No!” She kicked him in the shin. When he yelped in pain, she dodged into the woman’s restroom to sit in a stall and tremble. Quickly she yanked the cell phone out of her pocket and punched the buttons. “Matron Macintyre, Clark tried to pick me up as I entered the library. He’s there right now.”

“Where are you?”

“In the bathroom.”

“Walk out and keep an eye on him. Don’t let him disappear.”

She wandered about the library, but he had disappeared. As she raised the phone to her ear, Petunia faced her. “Inside all cell phones are to be turned off.” She pointed to the sign on the door. As Bailey stepped outside, Clark grabbed her, knocking the cell phone into the grass. His hand cupped over her mouth. She tried to bite his fingers, but Clark was too clever. However, she could still kick.

"Bailey, stop it. All I want to do is talk to you." When he dropped his hands, Bailey dropped to the grass to get the phone. "Don't." His warning came as a squad car rounded the corner. He started to run, but Bailey pursued.

"Stop!"

He skidded to a stop as the squad car pulled up beside them. "Officer, arrest this woman for assault. She attacked me."

"This is Clark!"

The Matron handcuffed Clark. Another police car pulled in behind her vehicle. The male officer nodded his head as he opened the back door. "Get in the back seat."

"This is a false arrest." Clark scowled angrily. "I'm innocent."

Matron Macintyre turned to Bailey. "I need you to come with us." As they rode along, she asked, "What happened?"

"He grabbed me inside the library and was going to force me outside. I kicked him and telephoned you in the lavatory. The librarian told me not to use the phone inside, so I stepped out to call you, and Clark grabbed me again. When he saw you, he ran."

Bailey repeated it for the recorder. Then the matron took her back to the library. "I don't think he'll touch you again, but keep your phone handy. I don't know what he'd do to you."

"Please, take me home. I don't think I can work in there today."

So the squad car passed the library and headed down the

residential street to her mother's house. "Bailey, you are under house arrest until Clark no longer bothers you." Matron Macintyre's eyes showed compassion. "We're doing this to protect you."

Bailey nodded and walked up the crumbling sidewalk. Her heart beat too quickly to be normal. She inserted her key in the lock. When the door opened, she found her mother on the floor. Immediately she pulled the phone out and dialed 911.

The ambulance's siren and flashing strobe lights woke up the neighborhood. People who had not ventured from their front door to meet her leaned over their fences to peer at the stretcher being carried from the house to the vehicle. Bailey saw them lined up along the street in whispers and knew what they were saying and thinking.

"She killed her mother."

"It would have happened sooner or later."

"Nobody can trust a jailbird."

"No matter what they go in for, they come out murderers, addicts, and rapists."

But it wasn't true. Her mother was still alive. Bailey wanted to crawl into the back of the ambulance and ride to the hospital, but the bracelet on her ankle constrained her. She didn't know her sister's number, but maybe Matron Macintyre could help. Soon the two were speeding down the streets with the sirens blaring over head.

"How bad is she?" Matron Macintyre never took her eyes off the traffic sliding off the street in front of her.

"I found her breathing but unconscious. I think she must

have had a heart attack and fell."

"So she wasn't in her chair?"

"No, she was right in front of the door."

They drew up in the hospital parking lot and jumped out. Inside, Matron Macintyre led her down the confusing halls at a fast pace. Their shoe soles slapped on the glistening tile. At the emergency counter they turned to see Bailey's mother being unloaded and carried in on the stretcher.

"Do you know if she has insurance?"

"No, I don't even know the name of her doctor if she has one."

"Was she on any medication?"

"Not that I know of."

The woman passed a sheaf of papers into Bailey's hands. "You can fill these out over there." She pointed to a row of padded chairs with a small table on the end loaded with outdated and well thumbed magazines.

Bailey sat down in a stupor. "I don't know how to do this."

Matron Macintyre dropped into the seat beside her. "Do the best you can. The medic said she was so drunk the fall didn't leave a mark." She sighed. "That keeps you out of trouble."

Bailey looked at the blurring words and lines. From her earliest memories she had always been guilty. Nobody ever thought her innocent. She looked down the sterile hallway where her mother had disappeared through a door. This would cost money, the money she had been saving for an apartment and a computer. She closed her eyes. "Oh, God, help me."

"Bailey, don't sign your name at the bottom. This isn't your responsibility." Matron Macintyre pulled the clipboard away and handed it back to the woman. "The daughter doesn't know anything about her mother's medical condition or records. Surely you have something already on file."

The woman nodded and turned away.

"Come, Bailey. They won't know anything for awhile. I think both of us could use a cup of coffee." She led the way down the hall and to the left to a large cafeteria. Tables and chairs sprawled through the middle while the edges were vending machines or ledges holding the supply of napkins, cups, and plastic ware. Matron Macintyre strode purposefully across the space to the cappuccino machine. "What would you like?"

"Regular, but I can pay for my own."

"Not now. It's my gift. You can have any flavor you want." She stood aside so Bailey could see and choose. Then they made their way to a table in a more secluded area against a window that looked out over the back lawn of the hospital. "The asters and mums are really colorful this year."

"I found a couple next to the house when I cleaned the yard."

"Bailey, you've done a great job against terrible odds. I want you to succeed." The police officer stirred her coffee.

"What happens to you if your mother dies? Will you be able to stay?"

"I don't know. It belongs to my grandparents. They might give it to my sister. They always preferred her to me."

"Why?"

Bailey shrugged her shoulders. “I guess she was prettier or smarter than me.” The tears dripped, and she wiped them away with the side of her wrist. “I wasn’t wanted, ever.”

The matron nodded. “I know that feeling. I was the youngest of seven. Mama was struggling to feed the other six, and here I came. Bailey, that’s past. We need to think of the future. If you can’t stay in that house, we need to find you another. Are you still against the projects?”

“Is that my only choice?” Bailey lifted the hot cup to her lips and blew across it.

“I think so, unless…”

“Unless what?”

“We can find your father.”

“After all these years do you think he’d do anything for me?” Bailey’s anger flared. He's never shown any interest in the past.”

“Maybe he wasn’t allowed.”

Bailey set down her cup. “You really think that’s it?”

“It’s highly possible.”

They entered the intensive care unit where her mother was stretched out on a gurney. “Is she conscious?”

“Yes, and her heart beat and breathing are normal.” The nurse’s voice and demeanor showed disgust. She made a note on a chart and slid it into the file case on the wall. In deliberate slowness she faced Bailey and the police officer. “The doctor will see you in a few moments.” If the snobby nose could have risen any higher, Bailey figured it would have flipped the white cap from her curls.

Her mother turned her body and face to the wall.

"Mom, are you okay?" Bailey bent over her.

"Leave me alone. Let me die." The woman pulled the sheet over her head.

Bailey looked around. Matron Macintyre had slipped away. She was just about to pull the document out, when a heavy set, white haired, and pudgy fingered doctor on call walked into the room. He smiled. "She'll pull out of this, but she must quit drinking if she's going to live. Her liver is almost destroyed." He looked at his chart. "Are you her daughter, Narla?"

"No, that's my sister. I'm Bailey."

"Your name isn't on this list as next of kin." He scribbled on the page. His multiple chins quivering as he signed his name with a flourish. "Have you contacted Narla or your grandparents?"

"No, I don't have their numbers."

"I see." He waddled over to her mother and pulled the sheet off her mother's face.

"Don't touch me!"

He recoiled. "I was just going to take your pulse."

"It's normal."

The doctor shrugged, wrote another entry on the paperwork, and shoved it into the slot. "I have just released her. She can get dressed, and you can take her home."

Her mother sat up in bed. "I am not going home. I'm a sick

woman."

"Not sick enough to stay in the hospital." He left the room without a smile.

Bailey stepped out into the foyer to look for Matron Macintyre. The police woman was not in the waiting room. She returned to the clerk who had given her papers to fill out. "Did Matron Macintyre leave me a message?"

"No."

Bailey took out the phone and punched the buttons. "This is Bailey. My mother has been released from the hospital. How will I get her home?"

"You'll have to call a cab. I can't come right now."

"Okay." She asked for a phone book and dialed the number. Her mother was pushed out in a wheel chair, and they went home. As Bailey paid for the ride, her mother stumbled up the broken steps and into the house. Before Bailey could get inside, the door was closed, locked, and the dead bolt set in place.

Bailey stood there, feeling the cold wind of October needling her bones as it blew through the porch. Some leaves flew like kites in a down draft, but she felt only resentment. She'd done everything she could to help her mother, even paying for the cab, and she was locked out. She had a key in her hand that would open the deadbolt and the lock, but the unfairness burned inside her. Why did her mother hate her so?

Chapter 7: James

A car's brakes screeched to a stop in front of the house. Narla jumped out and stomped up the walk.

Bailey studied the fur jacket and tam on flowing curled hair shoulder length, heels, pearls around her neck, rings on her fingers, bright lipstick and impeccable make up. The shiny, green dress sparkled in the bright sunlight.

“Why didn’t they keep mother in the hospital? Why did you sign her out? Do you want her to die?” A crafty look came over the woman’s eyes. “Oh, if she dies, you think this place is yours.” Her eyes glanced around the yard. Bailey had mended and painted the picket fence. The dumpster was gone with all the trash. The revived grass, new paint on the garage, and blooming asters gave the place respectability. “I must say this is the best it has ever looked.”

“Thank you.”

“But I warn you. It’s not yours. The grandparents have life long rights, and it’s mine.”

“So you’re paying the taxes and utility bills?”

“Oh, no.” Her eyes shifted. “Why do you want to know? It’s none of your business. You’re not getting a dime of that money either.” She selected a key and tried to open the door. When the key wouldn’t fit, she turned on Bailey. “So you’ve changed the door and the locks. Are you trying to keep me out?”

Bailey shrugged. “Well, it worked.” She gestured to the door bell. “Try that. It works, too.”

In seconds their mother opened the door and allowed them inside. Narla fussed over the woman who was demanding a bottle of whiskey.

“The doctor said she couldn’t have any. Her liver is almost gone.”

“But mother can’t live without her liquor.”

“She won’t live with it, either.” Bailey stood before her sister. “Look. You accused me of wanting her to die. Well, if she keeps drinking, she will. She’s got to quit.”

Narla snapped her fingers. “Oh, just like that?”

“Just like that.”

“But she can’t.”

“Who says?” Bailey left her standing there waving an empty bottle. She closed the door to her room and locked it. She didn’t know what would happen next, but she needed some quiet time.

“I’ve got to get out of that house.” Bailey could feel the frustration taking over her body. “It belongs to Narla.”

“I thought it belonged to your grandparents.” Matron Macintyre stopped the car in front of the projects. “There are a couple of openings here for a single bedroom and kitchenette.” Her head nodded. “I think you should look both of them over and choose.” She opened the car door, and Bailey jumped out the other side. “It’s not that you have a better option.”

“Okay, I’ll move, but am I still under house arrest?”

“I think that can be lifted as you are paying your own rent, but you’re still on parole. You have to report in every week.”

“I can handle that if I can have a car.”

“Can you afford one?”

Bailey nodded. “I’ve saved enough for a down payment, and I can do payments. That is, if the rent isn’t too high.”

“Would it be cheaper to get your own computer?” The matron lifted an eye brow. “Fuel is high priced right now. The winter is coming and utilities will be sky high.”

“I’ll consider it.” She sighed. “Let’s see these apartments and their price.”

The first was on the ground floor next to the office. The other was on the fifth floor and overlooked the complex. Bailey pulled the blinds to the top of the picture window. “I want this one.” She leaned on the window sill and looked out over the park. “It almost makes me feel like a free person to be up here among the trees.”

“Like a bird?”

“You might say that.” Bailey chuckled.

Matron Macintyre pivoted. “It’s not bad, although it does have a lingering smell of tobacco.”

Bailey glanced at the floor. “I can get rid of that even if I have to shampoo the carpets.”

“You’re not afraid of work, are you?”

“No, why do you ask?”

The police woman shrugged. “I think that’s what I noticed first about you. Remember that first day? I told the group to mop the floor, and you were the only one who did.”

“Oh, yea.” Bailey had opened a closet door. The empty shelves needed minimal cleaning, but she was slowly calculating her possessions. “I’m going to have to buy everything: a bed, a sofa, a desk, a computer." She stopped. "I don't even have any cooking utensils."

"What about those at the house?"

"I'm not taking anything out of there." She faced Matron Macintyre squarely. "Narla and my mother would accuse me of stealing although I purchased it."

"That's another quality I like about you." The matron walked to the window and looked down at the parking lot below. "If you had a deck, this would be a nice spot to spend your evenings in the nice weather."

Bailey shook her head. "I wouldn't want a deck. I'd feel unsafe."

"I never thought of that. You're right. Intruders might take advantage, but do you think you could bring James here?"

"We'll see. I haven't even met him yet."

"I think you will be more accepted and be able to slide easier into a large congregation." Matron Macintyre brought her personal Chevy into the parking lot. In a tan pant suit with a Hawaiian print blouse she didn't look like a police officer. Her makeup gave her face a soft, feminine glow. "I asked my husband if he wanted to come with us, but he had promised to teach Sunday school in our church this week." Her eyes glanced in Bailey's direction. "I like that mint green dress you are wearing. It looks very nice."

"Thank you." Bailey felt her palms sweat. Three lanes of cars as well as those parked on the west side told her the church was well attended. The inoffensive building with the smiling double glass doors welcomed every person who entered, but to Bailey the sand-colored stone walls spoke deeply of other institutions.

"Bailey, lift your chin. You are free."

She raised her eyes to the Matron's concerned face.

"If you don't like this one, we can go to another. There's plenty of time."

"I'll be okay. It's just my first time." Bailey stiffened her spine and picked up her feet. She had worn ankle boots to hide the ankle bracelet. The tap-tap of the little heels cheerfully accompanied them down the sidewalk, but her fingers nervously rubbed the soft cotton of her skirt. She was glad she hadn't chosen to wear a hat. None of the other women or girls had one.

An usher gave her a folded brochure with many printed paper slips inserted on the inside. Bailey shoved the bulletin into her shoulder strap purse that also contained her Bible. Her gaze swung to the groups of people talking and laughing, ignoring her and the matron. She gave a sigh of relief.

"There's a Sunday school class just down this hallway to your left."

"Thank you." Matron Macintyre took the lead and strode down the carpeted hall. Bailey followed. Again she compared the light, cheerful walls with the halls of the prison. She began to breathe easier. The matron chose chairs half way into the room behind a full row of couples. Someone greeted them and handed each a booklet.

"We're glad you're all here, and we have some new ones." The man in the navy blue suit pointed to Bailey. "Would tell us your name and where you're from?"

Bailey's mouth went dry, but Matron Macintyre answered for her. "I'm Mrs. Mona Macintyre, and this is my friend Bailey Berkley."

"We're glad you are here and welcome you back." His genuine smile entered into the Bible lesson, but every eye in the class studied her. Bailey saw the Matron listen to the story and the values being exposed, but she felt her bones grow cold. In the prison the other inmates positioned themselves around a table with their eyes on their open Bibles.

Later in the dim sanctuary with all the lights focused on the platform, Bailey relaxed. She listened to the lively songs and choruses. Power point posted the words on the huge screen reaching from the ceiling to the floor of the platform. Standing with the rest of the congregation, she watched six men and women with microphones on the stage like rock stars on television. When everyone sat in their pews, Bailey felt at home. She didn't know why, but a peace settled over her soul.

As they left the church, Matron Macintyre patted her on the knee. "Did you have a good time?"

"Yes, God was there."

Bailey entered the café ahead of the matron. Her eyes searched for a seven-year-old. "He isn't here."

"We're early. Let's choose a table close to the back."

The waitress was serving them coffee when Bailey saw the child. "Gary?" She had to be mistaken, but the boy that enjoyed David's stories in the library stood there in the middle of the room.

"Where is she? Where's my mother?" His strident tones

focused every eye.

Bailey froze, but the Matron motioned for him and the woman in the tan, calf length coat to the table. The woman's gaze brought memories of high school English. Serine had been the teacher's favorite. Bailey remembered the young girl always smiling except the time Serine's term paper landed on Bailey's desk.

"Don't open it!"

But Bailey had already flipped the cover. A fat red "B" stared at her. She closed it and handed it to the girl whose face resembled that of an angry bull dog. The square chin and fierce eyes held her at bay while thick fingers snatched the folder from her hands so violently that the heavy chain bracelet on her right wrist jangled in protest.

"I'm sorry."

"Don't touch my stuff." Serine added in a whisper so the teacher couldn't hear, "Bar maid."

Now Serine pulled the boy close to her legs, but Gary struggled and stopped three feet away. "You're not my mother. You work in the library with that nice man." His eyes traveled to the Matron. "Are you my mother? I have a policeman mother?" He reached out to touch the Matron's sleeve. "Wow, I can't believe it. My mother is a policeman." His body stopped. "But my mother is in jail." Again he turned to Bailey. "Are you really my mom?"

"Yes, but your name is James." Her eyes confronted Serine.

"Gary, this is not your mother." Serine turned him to march to another table.

"Mrs. Barnes, this is Gary's mother." Matron Macintyre

rose from her seat. "The paper work showed that the foster mother before you changed his name because she had another boy named James in the household and couldn't handle the same name for both boys."

Serine's arms held James closely to her legs. The sleeves of the coat covered him like the wings of an eagle protecting its young. "Oh." Her eyes traveled to Bailey. "I can't believe that such a nice boy could belong to….her."

"You know each other?" The matron smiled. "That should make this meeting easier for both of you. I need to go, but I'll be back in an hour to take you home, Bailey." She turned, and Bailey watched the uniformed back move out the door, across the parking lot, and into the squad car. Serine stood staring. "Come, Gary, let's go home."

Staring drilled holes into Bailey's composure. She licked her lips and motioned with her head. "Wait. Why don't you sit down?"

"Are you really my mother?" James pulled himself free. His little face had screwed itself into a mixture of hope, confusion, and fear. His shoulders squared like a soldier's, but his head swiveled back to Serine. "She is in the library. She's really nice. I like her. I like her a lot, but why didn't she tell me she was my mother?"

"I didn't know." Bailey rose. "James, I haven't seen you since you were two years old. That's five years ago."

Serine's face showed no leniency. "What is his birth date?"

"September 22. He'll be eight in less than five months."

James chose the seat beside Bailey. "I told you that my name wasn't Gary. I like James so much better." His eyes traveled back to Serine. "Will you call me James from now on?"

"We'll talk about this later." The woman dropped her gaze and slid into the chair across the table. A waitress appeared, and she ordered for herself and the child. Then she stared at Bailey. "How did you do this?" She looked around. "I mean, is Gary really yours?"

Bailey slid her arm around the boy. His kinky, dark hair was soft. The green eyes studied hers. "Yes, I think so. I didn't realize it before when I saw him in the library, but I can see what I remember. It has been so long, and he has changed so much." She reached for his hands and studied the pudgy fingers with blunt ends. When the fingers circled her thumb, a sigh of contentment escaped.

"I see his eyes are the same as yours."

Bailey nodded. "I know."

"And yet you didn't recognize him in the library?"

"I wasn't looking for him there." Bailey removed her arm. "I had been told he was in another county."

"Are you going to take him home with you?"

"I don't have a proper place right now, but yes, soon."

The boy reached for his French fries when the waitress returned.

Bailey watched Serine eat. "Thank you for taking care of him."

Serine ignored the remark. "I don't think this is going to work. Gary might have the same color of eyes as you, but look, so do I."

As Bailey's mother sobered, she became more talkative. "Your father had those same eyes that followed me everywhere. Don't mention him again."

"How am I going to find out who he is?"

Her mother shrugged. "You were a mistake—no, a punishment. I should have had an abortion. I could never get married with a child. Men want to marry a virgin."

Bailey went to her room. Her mother's words echoed in her mind. "You were a punishment. Men want to marry a virgin." The evidence grew. She had never been wanted. She reached for her Bible and hugged the volume to her chest. Only God loved her. Only God wanted her. But something made her desire to continue the hunt to know who had sired her. All the Bible characters had fathers. She wanted to know hers.

"Why do you want to know his name?"

"I want to know who I really am."

"Ha!" Her mother picked at the food set in front of her. "You're spawn of a bar maid who never married."

"But Narla."

"Leave Narla out of this. She doesn't have those green eyes that tell the world exactly where she came from. Narla is normal. You never were."

Again the words cut deep into her soul, but Bailey had to know. "How can Narla be normal, and I'm not?"

"If you can't find your father with those green eyes, you're hopeless!" Her mother pushed the button on her TV. "When are you going to get this fixed or buy me another?"

Bailey pivoted to stare at the appliance which was more important that she. A pain of laser magnitude chewed up her insides, and she bent as if she were going to vomit. Her mother's TV flipped lines, but music floated into the room.

"I never did love yah. I never did care.

Go jump in the river and see how you fare."

She ran to her bedroom.

"Mother won't tell me anything except to look for a man with these green eyes."

Matron Macintyre nodded. "You said Serine had those same eyes."

"Yes."

"Don't you think you could be related?"

"Related! But I don't look anything like her." Bailey pulled the visor down to peer into the mirror.

"It was just a thought."

"Yea, I guess I should look into it." Being related to Serine tied her stomach into knots, but the feeling had almost become a constant lately. "How do I start?"

"Do you remember what Serine's last name was when you were in school?"

"No."

"Well, I'd suggest you look in the library at some school annuals."

Bailey didn't want Dave mixed into her problems, especially the one of discovering her father, so she asked Petunia for help.

"School annuals?" Petunia pointed out a bottom shelf in a corner of the room. "You'll have to use them here. We don't allow them to leave the library."

Bailey could feel the woman hovering, watching her every move. Nevertheless, she found the copy that would have been her junior year. Serine wasn't in her class. She looked through the senior pictures. Below Serine's picture the name smeared into a black blot. Bailey had to know. She showed it to Petunia.

"Oh, you wanted to know her real name?" The librarian sneered and pivoted away. "Good luck. Serine was a foster child, adopted by the Dodge family, but she hated it."

Bailey sifted through more annuals, but Serine's picture did not appear. She reported to Matron Macintyre. "It wasn't there."

"I guess we'll have to look elsewhere. My husband in the detective department can help us."

"But I don't have any money."

"This is police business. We need to know your background before we can end your parole."

"Really?"

The Matron nodded. "Bailey, I want to do this for you. My husband and I have discussed you before, and he said he would do this if all other angles failed." She laid a hand on the girl's thigh.

"Bailey, my husband and I don't have a family. I can't understand why you have come to mean so much to me, but he understands. Okay?"

"I could talk to Serine."

"You might cause a problem there. If she thought your identity questionable, she might be able to wrest James away from you. Your mother is being so secretive. I suspect something deeper is going on."

"Like what?"

"I don't know." Matron Macintyre's head turned to check the traffic and stared out the window at the porch. Bailey's asters were fading in the cool autumn air and drying into little seedy knots. The dark skies threatened rain, but the cold wind blowing from the north boded snow or ice. "This is the perfect atmosphere for something sinister—like a mafia figure or somebody political trying to preserve his image."

Bailey shuddered. "I can't believe my mother being involved in anything like that."

"You don't really know your mother, do you?"

"Nor my father."

Chapter 8: Green Eyes

The next week Matron Macintyre couldn't take Bailey to church, but she gave Bailey the freedom to walk to the closest church for worship. "It'll be good for you to canvas the churches before you choose the one you decide to join. You've been confined. You need to get out more, and I can allow this."

"If I can't buy a car, can I get a bicycle?"

"That will come in time. Let's get you in an apartment first since I can take you to the library. I know you are saving for that computer, too." She drove around the neighborhood to help Bailey locate the churches.

Bailey entered the Catholic Church on tiptoe. The dim-dark interior was as foreboding as an earthen cave. The chandeliers dripped like stalagmites, but the beauty of the stained glass drew her like a child to candy. Jesus was easy to recognize on the cross or with the children or on the hillside with the sheep, but the other figures required the placards: Peter, John, James, and Thomas. Their similar faces needed more than different colored garments for distinction.

Mary fawning over the child brought Bailey's compassion to the front. This young woman, too, had a fatherless infant, but Mary had Joseph. Bailey bit her lip—she had no one to share the stigma. The brief thought of Dave flew through her mind, how tenderly he tended James as he searched for the right book. But her integrity rejected it. Dave was too nice for the likes of her, so her son would just have to go without a father. Clark would never touch her child.

The cathedral beams structured like the ribs of a whale surrounded her like Jonah imprisoned in the great fish. She turned to see the priest genuflect before the altar. Bailey slid into the nearest seat. When the service began, she couldn't understand the chanting or the orderly liturgy exchanged between the priest and those around her, but she listened and let her eyes wander to the closest icon set in a niche along the wall. A ledge held a flickering candle; the motion of the dancing flame hypnotized her.

"Hello."

Bailey looked up into the green eyes of the priest. She

looked around her. Sensing that she had fallen asleep, and everyone was gone, her wonder turned to fright as in a nightmare. The narrow face could have been hers except for the shadow of a shaven beard. She gasped.

"Oh, don't be afraid. You're new, aren't you? I thought you were waiting on me for confession." His fingers touched her shoulder, but Bailey ducked and slid away. She reached the middle aisle and looked back. He waved. "Wait! I don't know your name."

She forced her feet to walk down the long, long path to the door. Outside, she paused to gulp in fresh air as if she had been Jonah escaping the fish.

"Wait!" The priest waved from the vestibule as he hurried toward her. The tassels hanging from the golden cords around his neck flopped against his chest. Again she fled. At the bottom of the front steps she glanced back.

"I just want to know why you are afraid of me. What is your name?" His breath came in gasps, and one hand against the ornate door supported his figure. The face in full sunlight convinced Bailey. The priest had to be her father.

She turned away and jogged back to her mother's house. "Mom, I know who my father is." Now her breath came in spurts while a pain surged through her side. "I saw him. . . at the church."

The empty whiskey bottle hit the wall. "I told you not to go to church. Don't you ever follow directions?" Her mother rose, her legs wobbled, and she fell backwards in her chair. "I don't want to have anything to do with him." Her breath wheezed out like an emptying balloon. "Don't go back there again, hear me?"

Bailey fell on her knees in front of her mother. "Why didn't you tell me? Why all this secrecy?"

The woman's gaze avoided her daughter, but old memories were bubbling from her lips. "He said it was an act of worship, and that he loved me. Then I got pregnant, and he called me a filthy child, a whore. I had caused him to sin. I was headed for hell. He told me to go home and not tell anybody. He said I would go to hell if I did."

"Do the grandparents know?"

Her mother looked almost sober. "They knew. Why do you think they joined the Jehovah Witnesses? They no longer wanted anything to do with the church."

"Is that why they hate me? Is that why *you* hate me?"

"You had no right to look like him. You even have his eyes." She motioned for Bailey to go away. "I don't want to look at you ever again."

Bailey went to her room and pulled out her Bible. "The truth shall make you free." She had underlined it and written another reference in the margin. "Jesus said, 'I am the way, the truth, and the life. No man cometh unto the Father except by Me.'"

"Oh, God, what does this mean? Mother knew the truth, but she wouldn't or couldn't acknowledge it on the birth certificate or even to me. Now that I know the truth, why don't I feel free or happy? Why do I feel worse than when I didn't know?"

The face of the priest haunted her dreams through a restless night. Bailey slept late the next morning, but when she awoke, she reached for the only comfort she had—her Bible. She laid the open pages on the table and read as she ate her oat cereal with the miniature pastel marshmallows. "Let not your heart be troubled. You believe in God, believe also in Me."

Her mother entered the room swinging a whiskey bottle. "I

ought to kill you and that priest, too. Both of you have made my life a hell on earth."

"Mom, let me have that bottle. I'll throw it in the trash."

"I ought to throw you in the trash." She lurched forward, but Bailey caught her and removed the bottle from her hands with little resistance.

"Let me get you a cup of coffee. It will help you get sober."

"I don't want a cup of coffee. I don't want to be sober." Her body swayed, and then she began to cry. Bailey walked her back into the living room and seated her in the chair.

"Mom, you don't have to suffer like this."

"I'm so afraid."

"You don't have to be afraid. There is forgiveness that brings freedom and peace." Again Bailey knelt before her mother. "God sent Jesus to die for our sins."

"That's what that Catholic priest told me. It's all a lie, a terrible lie."

"No, Mom, it's the truth. Forget about that priest. Think about Jesus and what He did for us. He shed His blood to pay the debt for our sins. Then He rose to life with the keys of death that we might have eternal life." Bailey bowed her head so her mother couldn't see her green eyes. "Believe me, oh, believe me."

Her mother sobbed and thrust Bailey away.

Bailey walked into the kitchen no longer hungry. Bennie ate the rest of the cereal, and she washed the dishes, dried them, and put them away.

When Matron Macintyre heard Bailey's tale, her body trembled with anger. "Do you think Serine's mother was raped by this priest, too?"

"I don't know."

"It's worse than I thought. All these years a pedophile lurked in that building." The car nearly ran onto the sidewalk as she drove beside the building. "There's not a child or young person safe in this community!"

Bailey shivered at her venom. "A case of whiskey arrived this morning for my mother. I emptied every bottle down the sink before she wakened. Then I called the company on the packing list and deleted her order."

"Do you think that will keep her from getting more?"

"I don't know, but I found out who ordered it."

"Who?"

"My sister." Bailey let her hands drop lastly to her lap. "She knows that Mom's liver can't stand any more whiskey. Why does she want her to die?"

Matron Macintyre's hand shook as it rested on Bailey's shoulder. "I don't think she really wants your mother to die. It's the way she's always lived. She doesn't know what else to do."

"Matron, I have to go back to that church and that priest. I have to know the truth."

"I thought you already did."

"What if the priest is my half brother?" Bailey could feel

the anguish flowing out of her soul. "What if he is a victim, too?"

"Bailey, that's highly unlikely, but allow my husband to investigate this, please." Matron Macintyre had gained control of herself. "It's a matter for the law authorities to investigate."

"It's my problem."

"Don't think of it that way."

Bailey clamped her lips tight and glared at the arched windows beneath the majestic steeple. She would find a church, but this one was scratched off the list.

That afternoon the neighbor boy, Teddy Sommers, showed up in the yard to scratch Bennie's ears. "My Mom told me to come over here." He looked away. "Our church is having a contest. Would you come? I'll get ten points. That's all I need to get me a new ball. I need a new ball bad. My old one leaks and won't bounce no more."

"Where do you go to church?" Bailey couldn't resist his plea. The boy's anguished face and yet derisive tone sparked memories when she wanted something. Rarely had she gotten what she wanted. Right now she'd like to have a real home with her son.

His body perked. "You mean you would come?" A bright smile replaced the sullen, duty-driven attitude that had marched him across the block.

She nodded. "First tell me where you go." She didn't want to get caught in the Catholic Church again.

"It's across town."

"I don't have a car." Something died inside her. Teddy's

sincerity had given her an identity or ego stretch she had not felt for years. He wanted her. A nice person had actually invited her to go with him. "I'm sorry."

"Oh, Mom would take you with us." His smile widened. "Please, would you come?"

"I'll have to ask my probation officer, but I don't think it would be a problem." Bailey laughed at Teddy's dance routine across the street. She was wanted, needed. So what if it were just a one time happening to help the neighbor boy? It made her feel wonderful.

Matron Macintyre smiled. "That's the best way to find a church. Go with someone you know and respect." Her gaze roamed over the yard. "I was going to move you today, but we'll wait until next Monday."

That evening Bailey decided to inform her mother. "Mom, I'm going to move into an apartment on Monday."

Her mother was too drunk to reply.

"Where'd you get this?" Bailey grabbed the bottle, but the label didn't give her any clues. "Did Narla bring this?"

"No, Tanker's Pub." Her mother smiled. "You can't keep me from drinking."

"You couldn't walk that far."

"Didn't have to."

"They delivered it." Bailey spat the words out in disgust. "Who ordered it? Who paid for it?"

Her mother looked away.

"Did Narla?"

"Why do you want to know? Narla loves me." Her mother shut her eyes.

Bailey stomped away. Narla needed to be spanked. No, she reconsidered, Narla needed worse than that, but Bailey couldn't think what would stop her sister from killing her mother.

Teddy rang the door bell on Sunday morning as Bailey hung up the wet towel from drying her dishes. She grabbed her coat and Bible and rushed to the front room, thankful that her mother no longer slept in the chair.

His mother waited in an older Ford model at the curb. "Thank you, Bailey, for coming. Teddy has talked about you ever since that first time he met you." Her smile reached across the back of the front seat as her handshake. "My name is Tonia Sue Sommers." She turned and drove slowly down the street. "Teddy has invited everyone on the street. We're going to pick up Ma'am Kuhn and her two children. Then we'll head for church."

Ma'am Kuhn carried an infant in one arm and drug a two-year-old. Bailey helped buckle little Amy in a child seat while Teddy moved so the woman could sit in the front seat beside his mother. The little girl played peek-boo with them until they arrived at the church.

Inside the church Tonia Sue introduced her to everyone. "This is our pastor Brown and his wife. Bailey is our new neighbor. She's the one who cleaned up that lot on Sixth Street." Bailey shook their hands and returned their smiles. They seemed so delighted in having her. It made her heart sing. She turned and gasped. Dave had just entered the foyer. She stared as he removed his sunglasses and stepped beside her.

"Bailey, I'm so glad to see you. I'd invite you to my class, but it's the younger set." He motioned to the pastor's wife. "Stella teaches the adults in the sanctuary. She's a great teacher." He paused, and his eyes searched her face. "Don't go away. I'll see you later." He turned. "I teach downstairs." His head nodded at Teddy who waited.

She couldn't keep her thoughts on the lesson although the quarterly lay open on her lap. Stella had each of the eight adults on the left side of the sanctuary read one after the other, similar to the Bible study Bailey had in prison. Dave was downstairs. He had welcomed her although he knew she wore an ankle bracelet. A song in her heart obliterated what Stella and the others said. At closing exercises Bailey discovered herself between Tonia Sue and Ma'am Kuhn. She was counted in with the others as points for Teddy who was grinning from ear-to-ear on the platform where Rev. Brown presented him with a ball as the winner in the Sunday school contest. When the women scooted together to make room for Teddy at the end of the pew, Bailey felt like an orange being squeezed for juice. She looked up in time to see Dave's beaming smile directed right at her.

Rev. Brown preached a long, long sermon.

Bailey counted bricks to avoid Dave's eyes. The altar was seven high. She couldn't see past Tonia Sue, but she judged the middle brick to be forty-eight, so the altar probably doubled that in length. To make sure, she counted them again. Then she studied the paneling lines behind the pastor. Some were wide and some narrow, but there was a pattern beginning at the right side: fat, skinny, two skinnier yet, a moderate width, and then the fat one again. The pattern repeated six times. At the doxology Bailey rose in relief. She followed Tonia Sue down the aisle toward the double door until Dave nudged her. He clamped his hand around the upper part of her arm and drew her aside.

"Bailey, do you live on the same street as the Sommers?"

She nodded.

"I'll see you." He picked up his teaching materials. "What about this afternoon?"

"Dave, I'm moving tomorrow."

He stopped. "Where? Out of town?"

"No, into the government projects. I've signed a lease for an apartment." She saw Teddy and his mother exit. "Talk to you later. I've got to go."

Later that afternoon while she packed her clothes in boxes, she wondered why she always tried to discourage him. He was so nice—too nice for her. Then the door bell rang. Could it be Dave? She didn't want him to see her in this squalor. She deemed her ankle bracelet embarrassing enough. She waited. If no one answered, he would have to go away, but she heard her mother's shuffling steps to the door, and she couldn't stop her.

"You didn't bring my whiskey?"

Chapter 9: Dave

Her mother's screech would have scared an owl. "Bailey! Some tramp wants to see you. Don't you let no guys start any foolishness 'round here. I won't have it in my house."

Bailey's embarrassment cemented her feet to the floor. If she could have only said, "No," to Teddy, Dave wouldn't have tracked her down, but her common sense and reasoning knew he was bound to meet her mother sooner or later. Well, it had happened, but she didn't know what to do.

"Bailey!" The high pitched scream pierced the air. "Get out here right this minute 'for I come after you."

She knew her mother held no power over her, and yet the command wielded an ax over her head and threatened untold punishment. Bailey padded barefoot through the kitchen and into the living room. She stopped at the edge of the kitchen. His pinched face relaxed as she crossed the room, and a wobbly smile surfaced.

"Hi, I didn't know you were coming." Slowly she crossed the room.

"Bailey, I thought I had come to the wrong house." Dave's hair was slicked back and glistening wet. The aftershave lotion created a potent aurora most likely found at a cosmetic counter or the library. "Did I come at a bad time?"

She forced a smile and lied. "I'd like you to meet my mother." When the introduction ended, her mother settled down in the chair and watched like a cat licking its chops. The uneasy silence between the three of them settled down like an unwanted wake before a storm. Bailey wished she could use the remote to start the television.

"Do you have time to go for a ride?" Dave gestured through the still open door.

"Yes." Bailey sprang into action. "Let me get my jacket."

"Okay, it is a little nippy, but this is October."

"Bailey, you didn't ask permission."

She turned to her mother. "Don't you think I'm a little too old?"

"Don't talk back to me. I'll slap you silly." Her mother glowered at both of them. "Anything you got to say to each other can be said right here in front of me."

Bailey chose to ignore her. "I'll only be a minute. I'll get my jacket." She ran to her room and used a comb to straighten her hair, but the mirror told her nothing could be done for her blanched face. She grabbed her purse and slipped on shoes. With the jacket clenched in her hand, she raced back to the living room.

"I'll not have my daughter out at all hours of the night. You get her home, understand?"

"Mom, I'll see you later." Bailey headed out the open door without a backward glance. She could hear Dave behind her and sighed relief. Inside the car she turned as he started to snap on his seatbelt. "I can't go anywhere. I'm under house arrest."

"Okay." He let the belt slide and twisted to face her. "I just wanted to talk to you."

She slid one arm into the sleeve of her jacket, and he reached to help her. His arm circled her shoulders temporarily. Then he with drew.

"Thanks, Dave." She looked down at her hands and down at her feet where the bracelet was only half hidden under the denim cuff. "I'm sorry things are like this. I didn't want you to know, but it's not as bad as you think. I'm moving out tomorrow into my own apartment."

"Is there anything I can do?"

"Not really. Matron Macintyre is going to help me. I don't

have much to move—just some clothing." Her eyes slowly came up to meet the blue of his. "Please, understand."

He settled back into the seat and stared out the window. The wind blew an oak leaf across the windshield and into the street. Then he turned back to her. "I was so glad to see you in church this morning. I had been trying to find you, but now I know why you wouldn't tell me. I'm sorry, Bailey. I didn't mean to hurt you." His mouth opened as if to say more, but he closed it. "I like you very much." Then his head tipped downward. "Bailey, you're the nicest girl I've ever known."

"No!" She startled herself at the vehemence of the word. Closing her eyes momentarily, she tried to compose herself. "Dave, I'm not for you. You deserve a really nice girl, a virgin. I've had a son out of wedlock. I've been in prison for selling drugs."

He laughed. "Yes, Gary, uh James as he now demands to be called, ran into the library the other evening and told me."

"Told you?"

"Yes, that you are his mother. He is so excited."

She bowed her head.

He caught her hands. "Don't you like me a little?"

"Yes."

"Then that's all that counts." He pulled her close. His arms encircled her. "Bailey, I want to help you. I want to protect you."

The warmth of the embrace satisfied something inside of her. His hands touched her back and prickled her skin even through the layers of material. She could sense the strength of his fingers bringing her closer and closer. His head bent down, and his breath like a warm breeze moved her bangs. She wanted the moment to last forever. Then he lowered his face so his nose met hers.

"May I kiss you?"

His words broke the spell. She pushed back, shaking her head. Like a cracked shell, his hands dropped from the cupping hold on her, and she was free.

"Oh, Dave, you deserve somebody better."

"Like who? I like you." A grim set of the lips squared his jaw. "Don't I get to choose whom I like and whom I don't?"

She grabbed the door handle and forced her way out. "You deserve a nice girl like Petunia--not a jail bird like me!"

"Bye, Mom, I'm moving." Bailey held the dog and stood by the chair. Matron Macintyre waited in the squad car just outside the door. "I thought I'd give you a bunch of keys. This one fits the front and back doors and the dead bolts. This works on your bedroom door, and this one is for the back bedroom."

Her mother accepted the keys. "You're really leaving?"

"Yes, I'm going. The matron is waiting for me." She glanced through the door's window. "I'm taking my clothes and Bennie, okay?"

"Bennie?" Her mother rose from the chair. "You can't leave me alone."

"You want the dog?"

"I can't live alone."

"You were alone when I came. You didn't want me." Bailey turned. "I've got to go."

"You are going to leave me?"

"Mom, the place is cleaner than when I came. You'll be okay. You didn't want the dog, so I'm taking Bennie."

Suddenly the woman stood and hissed like a mad cat. "You're just like the rest of them. You got religion, and now you're too good for me. You won't get me whiskey, and you won't let me drink it when it comes. Get out of here. And don't come back." Her body fell back in the chair. Then she straightened. "Oh, now I get it. It's that tramp. You're just like all the other modern girls. You're moving in with him."

"No, I'm getting my own apartment." She wondered if her mother would understand her desire to have a nice place to live so James could be with her. "I want my son."

"I see. The tramp is moving in with you." Her mother laughed. "He's crazy!"

Bailey felt the tears coming to her eyes. Why did her mother have to make it so hard?

"Go on. Live with whoever you wish, but don't come crawling back." She turned on the television. The picture came on in perfect color and conversation. "I hate you. I always have."

Bailey received no thanks for her cleaning or paying the repair bill on the TV, but she felt a tug of remorse. "Do you want Bennie?"

Then her mother started to cry. "Don't take Bennie. He's the only friend I ever had. I can't bear to be alone and without him."

Bailey walked through the door with one backward glance. Maybe she would never see her mother again, but those were her thoughts when she had been sent to jail. Cotton candy had filled the hole in her soul but now it melted and evaporated before she could strive for another bite. The bitter taste was the worst medicine she had ever swallowed.

"Life will be easier for you," the Matron said quietly.

Easier? Bailey tried to contain her tears, but they dripped on jeans leaving little wet dots.

"I thought you'd be glad to leave."

"She didn't take it well."

"I can understand that." Matron Macintyre turned the corner and pulled into the parking lot by the apartments. "Your mother has to make her own decisions. You cleaned her up and set her in the position to change, but you can't change her. She will have to change herself."

Bailey could only nod.

"Well, let's go sign the lease for your apartment. It's going to take a day to find the furniture and items you need to make it a home."

She went back to the library to say good-bye. Petunia guarded the lower level, but Dave wasn't in the children's department. An older woman whose white hair reminded Bailey of a grandmother puttered behind the desk. "Can I help you?"

"Do you know where Dave is?"

"Dave? Oh, the fellow who used to work up here." Her

merry face nodded several times. “He was transferred to the computer department in one of our branch libraries.”

Bailey glanced around the room, noting the computer by the window had disappeared. The small desk stood empty looking out over the driveway. Matron Macintyre sat in the squad car waiting. “If I wrote a note, do you think he would get it?”

“Why, sure! We have an inner mail route in the library. Just give it to me.”

“I don’t have any paper or pencil.”

“Well, I can supply that, too.” The congenial woman produced a simple envelope, slip of paper, and pen. As soon as Bailey had finished, she took the note. “Have a good day.”

“You, too.” Bailey left the library with a backward look. Matron Macintyre waited to take her to purchase a new computer, but the joy that she had anticipated had disappeared like the warmth of summer. The wind whirled around the building sending dried leaves flitting across the dead grass. She slid into the warm car and shivered. “It’s cold out there.”

The matron laughed. “It’s Halloween. Tomorrow is November.” She brought the car into the mall parking lot. “Let’s go shopping.”

Soon Bailey’s mood matched the excitement of her friend. They bought the computer first, and then the Matron took her to a used furniture store.

“Do you like this settee?”

Bailey would have accepted anything, but she knew the Matron hoped for the best. “It’s nice, but how will we get it to the apartment?”

"For a small fee they will deliver."

Together they chose a desk, a bed frame, and the settee.

"You'll want a new mattress which we can get across town."

In a discount center Bailey purchased bed sheets, towels, and some pots. She added cleaning aids and came out of the building laughing. "I feel free!" Her face sobered at the sight of the squad car.

The furniture arrived that evening, but Bailey couldn't go on line with her computer although she set it up on the desk.

"You'll need to visit the telephone company tomorrow, but I must call it a day." The matron turned slowly inside Bailey's apartment. "I am so happy for you. See you tomorrow."

Bailey had finished making her bed when her door bell rang. She peeked through the hole in the door to see Dave wearing a mask and standing before her door.

"Trick or treat." He handed her a basket loaded with fruit. Then he pulled off the clown mask. "Actually, this is a house warming gift." His smile broadened as he viewed the room. "Bailey, this is nice." Then his eyes focused on the ankle bracelet. "Let's call out for pizza." Without waiting for her reply, he pulled his cell phone from his pocket and punched in the numbers.

"How did you find me?"

"You told me you would be in the apartments. With a little research I found you. Lakeside just isn't that big."

"I went by the library this morning."

"And you left a note. That's what encouraged me to stop

by. Okay?"

She nodded. "Come in and have a seat." She motioned to the settee. "You have no choice, but it doesn't sink to the floor."

He laughed. His eyes focused on her computer. "You won't be coming to the library."

"I can't." She gestured to the ankle bracelet. "I'm still on house arrest until Matron Macintyre can persuade her superior that I won't run off to Timbuktu." Then she studied his face. "You are no longer at the library."

"I transferred to the computer lab in a branch library. It doesn't pay as much, but it's what I like to do." He gestured to her computer. "Can I look it over?"

She nodded.

"You chose a good brand. It'll do fine. When you get your e-mail address, we will be able to keep in contact all the time." He pulled a card out of his pocket. "Here's mine." Then he turned on the machine and brought up the Outlook Express so he could type the e-mail into her address file. "I wanted to be first." Then his eyes met hers. "Okay?"

"Yes."

He stood to his feet and pulled her close to him. "Bailey, I always want to be first with you." His face was coming down to kiss her, when the door bell rang. She pulled away to receive the pizza. Dave paid the bill. Then he smirked. "Well, let's eat." He chose to pull the settee up close to the window so they could look out as they ate.

She knew as soon as he set the empty cardboard on the floor that he would reach for her. Bailey jumped to her feet knocking over the pizza boxes. She watched as he picked them up.

"I should have disposed of these in the trash can." His concerned face centered on hers. "What's wrong, Bailey? You look scared."

"Oh, nothing." She took the cartons from his hands and marched to the kitchenette. Her shoulders shook as she dropped the remains into the can. Memories of Clark and the back seat of a car rose vividly in her mind. His arms, too, had circled her body. She turned, brushing against the front of Dave's shirt. Startled, she yelped.

"Bailey!" His hand stretched out to her face.

She backed away.

"What's wrong?"

"I'm not the girl for you. I'm a jailbird, remember?" She looked down at the condemning anklet. Fears erupted from the inside of her soul. "I've had a child out of wedlock. I'm not good—good enough for you."

Tears trickled down her cheeks and dripped from her chin. She brushed them off with her arm and then picked a fairly clean napkin out of the trash to wipe her face. When she managed to raise her sight to look in his face, she was surprised at the shock. She attempted a smile. "Surprised that a bag lady would use a napkin out of the can?"

"No, you're not a bag lady." His voice held the husky rasp of disbelief. "I like you. You're different from anybody I've ever known. You fascinate me." Again his hand came toward her face. She backed off. His arm dropped to his side as though useless. "I don't understand." He turned away and walked to the door. Then he stepped forward once more. "Bailey, you're hurting inside. I want to help you, but I can't unless you give me a chance."

She shook her head. The saturated napkin dripped into her hands, but the tears continued to flow. She had to blow her nose and turned to the can to search for another napkin. As she rummaged through the trash, she felt his hand on her spine. He guided her back to the settee.

"You must talk to me." His fingers touched her chin and turned it toward his face. "There. That's better."

"I'm a jailbird." The sobs came from the pit of her stomach. She bent over, folding her arms over her abdomen. Another napkin was thrust into her hands, and she felt his arms cover her shoulders. They pulled her to his chest. The warmth and rocking of his body calmed her.

"Bailey, speak to me." Again those tender finger tips tilted her chin upward. "That's better." He sighed. "Did you know those glistening tears have blackened your eyelashes? They curl upward ever so slightly and brighten those beautiful green eyes."

"Don't kiss me."

He drew back. "Okay, I promise not to kiss you unless you call yourself a jailbird one more time." A slight smile drew his lips together. "I really, really want to, you know, but I'll make this pact. Say jailbird once, twice, or a hundred times, and I'll kiss you every time!"

She knew he meant it and wiggled away.

"I'm going." He stood up and stretched. "But I will return."

Chapter 10: In Court

Anxiety surged through Bailey's veins as she mounted the courthouse steps. She saw the same crack on the surface of the top piece of granite that she'd seen before prison and paused to trace it with her toe.

"Bailey, straighten your shoulders." Matron Macintyre paused before the double doors. "You look very nice in that olive pantsuit."

The glass doors that allowed them into the hollow building mirrored her small figure with the new bouffant hair cut. She had smiled at her reflection in the beautician's shop, but today her ego plummeted to the bottom of her shoes. Every step and voice echoed in the chamber. She stared up the curving wooden staircase that led to the judiciary department. It had been no ladder to heaven the last time, and she was scared of what the judge would say this time.

Earlier the Matron explained all the reasons at least twice. "We're going to end your house arrest. Otherwise, you won't be allowed even visits from James."

"Why?"

"You have to be able to get to the grocery. You'll probably want to take him to a matinee or out to eat. Under house arrest you can't go anywhere, and I don't think you need me."

"But I do need you."

The Matron's smile lit up her whole face. "You're special to me, too. I'm going to ask to continue to handle your probation, but you need more freedom. Bailey, you need to stretch your wings. You still have a lot to learn about living these days and only experience will teach you."

The Matron's boots thudded on the thin carpet as she led the way to the front. Bailey found herself counting the steps—thirteen, fourteen, fifteen.

"Bailey, you haven't heard a word I've said." The Matron stood before a door with a frosted window. "Stand up straight. Square those shoulders, and walk in like a person." She waited for the girl to comply. Then she smiled. "Now lift your chin. Smile. That's so much better." She turned and opened the door.

The vast room of seats hit Bailey's esteem like a blow to the belly. She followed the Matron's solid back, marching to the front. The woman formed a shield between her and the judge, just like the scripture she had read that morning. "Fear not Abraham. I am your shield and your very great reward." Bailey had read it over and over with her own name in it. "Fear not Bailey. I am your shield and your very great reward." The thought brought peace.

"Bailey Berkley."

She startled at her name being called so loudly and echoing in the room. "Yes?"

"Are you Bailey Berkley?"

"Yes, ma'am."

"Speak up." The petite woman judge leaned forward over the huge desk, an insurmountable mountain of polished surfaces.

Bailey trembled like a dwarf rabbit and looked up into the light brown eyes that glowed like a cat's. She licked her lips. "I am Bailey Berkley."

"That's better." The judge leaned back in the padded, black leather chair whose wooden frame made it a throne. She peered intently at a few sheets of paper as she spoke. "You've been in jail five years?"

"Yes, ma'am."

"Umm, and you've been on good behavior. That's good." She moved the paper to the back of the others. "You are presently under house arrest."

"Yes, ma'am."

The judge turned to Matron Macintyre. "Is there any reason to continue the house arrest?"

"No, your honor. Bailey has proven to be peaceful and industrious."

"What's this about moving into an apartment? How do you pay for it?" The judge leaned forward again. Her intent eyes bored holes into Bailey's confidence.

"I have a computer and work on line."

"Do you make enough to support yourself and pay for it?" The judge's interest in how Bailey earned her money needed the Matron to explain certain aspects until Bailey realized what the judge wanted and could completely answer. "You're not going back to selling drugs?"

"No, ma'am."

"That's good." The judge glanced at the court reporter. "I'll lift the order so you won't be under house arrest, but you will continue to wear the ankle bracelet and report to Matron Macintyre every week. Case dismissed." She looked beyond them. "Next?"

Bailey held her breath until they were back in the hall. "That was it?"

"That was it. You did fine." The Matron glanced down the hall. "The juvenile department is down here on the end. Let's stop in and fill out the paper work needed to start visitation rights for James."

The clerk handed over a sheaf of papers. "They will need to be notarized before you return them. Then a social worker will have to evaluate you and your apartment. It should take two to four weeks. If you have any questions, feel free to call this number." She reached through the small window to circle a telephone number and smiled.

"Thank you." Bailey turned away. Her euphoria had slithered out the door and disappeared. She looked up at the frowning face of Matron Macintyre.

"What's wrong?"

"I don't know if I can do this."

"You can. Trust me, Bailey. I know you. If anybody can do it, you can." She led out the door and down to the squad car. "We have a few more errands today, but first I want to take you out to eat. Then we can look over these forms."

The first snag was paternal rights.

"I don't want Clark touching James." Bailey pounded her fist, and the silverware jingled.

"By law he has rights, too."

"But he raped me. He hasn't shown any interest in James. He lied about the drugs and sent me to prison." Bailey's tears turned to anger. "He can't touch James. I'd rather James stayed in foster care than that."

The Matron looked at her watch. “Put the papers away. We’ll talk about it again, but you need to get a bicycle. I suggest we visit the discount store for a bargain.”

Bailey couldn’t resist purchasing two chairs and a small table.

Then the Matron took her to the mall. “You’ll need a cable to secure your bike.”

“I’m taking it up to my apartment all the time. I can’t leave it down there for someone to steal.”

“But you can’t take it into the stores with you or wherever you go. You’ll have to lock it up.”

“Okay.”

Bailey thought they were on the way home, but the Matron turned into the opposite direction. They stopped in front of the Bureau of Motor Vehicles. Inside, Matron Macintyre picked up a small booklet. “I suggest you take one of these and study for a driving test.” Her smile held a glint of humor. “You’ll want to be ready when you buy that car.”

Dave arrived just a few minutes after he finished work. “Now that you’re not under house arrest, I can take you out to eat. Where do you want to go?”

The only place Bailey knew was the little café. Dave chose a corner booth. “Tell me about your day.” His hands reached across the table top to hold hers.

“Well, the Matron told me that I can buy a car as soon as I pass the driving test.”

His extended smile showed every perfect tooth. “I can help you. I have a friend out in the country that will let you practice on his harvested bean field.” Right after the meal he drove them out to see his friend. It was quite late when he brought her back to the apartment.

“I can find my own way up the stairs.”

Dave shook his head. “Bailey, I don’t want anything happening to you.” He was out of the car and around to open her door before she could protest. His hand seemed to automatically hold her elbow as they walked up the stairs. His breath came in little puffs when they stood before the door, and she searched her purse for her key. She inserted it and opened the door. He had not moved. She twisted around.

“Dave, thanks for the beautiful evening.”

His tongue passed over his lips. “I enjoyed it more than you.” His eyes searched hers.

“Good night, Dave.” She stepped inside.

He waved. “Good night.”

She wondered if it were her imagination, but as she closed the door she thought she heard him whisper, “Jailbird.”

Filling out the visitation rights paperwork brought Bailey more grief. When she took them back to the juvenile department, the clerk was adamant.

“The father has to know.”

“But he didn’t come to the baby’s birth. He paid no support. The child was placed in foster care without his consent.”

Bailey threw her hands up in despair. “I don’t want him to know about James or me. He’s an unfit parent. He’s,” she paused, “He’s dangerous!”

“A judge will have to determine that.” The clerk would not accept the forms.

Matron Macintyre nodded. “I was afraid of this, but I thought maybe we could bypass it since Clark is in jail.”

“He’s in jail?” Bailey’s hopes rose. “Then he can’t possibly have any say in my life or James.”

“Bailey, he’s still the father.”

“How am I going to get rid of Clark? He caused my problems in the beginning. He’ll only be more trouble and more trouble as time goes on. Isn’t there anything I can do?” Bailey could feel her stomach tightening. She wound her arms around her middle to hold it still.

“The clerk was right. We’ll have to take this back to court and see what a judge can do.” Matron Macintyre stared out Bailey’s window. “I suggest we both pray about this. The laws have changed until the father has as much right to a child as the mother, no matter how evil he is.”

Dave rejoiced to hear about Clark being behind bars. “I feel you are safer. I was afraid he would find you. You don’t know how hard I’ve prayed that God would protect you.” She allowed him to look over the forms. “You know, there is an easy solution.”

“What?”

“Marry me. I’ll adopt James, and we’ll live happily ever after like the three bears.”

Her mouth dropped. "But I'm a …." She looked at him.

He laughed. "Go ahead. Say it." His arms circled her shoulders. He looked down into her eyes. "I dare you to say it. Come on, Honey. I've been waiting for this opportunity for all my life." His nose came closer and closer.

She could feel the warmth of his breath over her face. His fingers drew her closer.

His cell phone began to beep. Dave ignored the noisy beast in his pocket, but it wouldn't shut off automatically. He clutched it with one hand and punched the numbers with his thumb. Then his forefinger shut it off. "There. Now where were we? You were saying?"

The spell had broken. Bailey pivoted on her heel and slid out from under his arms. "I'm sorry, Dave. I can't marry you. Don't you understand? I'm not good enough." She turned to see his shoulders sag and knew she had hurt him very deeply. She reached out to touch his arm. "I'll never be good enough." She shook her head. "No matter what I do, you're too good for me."

"I refuse to go out and kill someone or rob a bank." He swallowed. "Bailey, the past doesn't matter. Put it behind you. Let's live for the future. I know you care for me." His arms reached for her, but she ducked and headed for the kitchen.

"I made cookies for the first time. Would you like one?"

"No, I'm going home." His abrupt departure shocked her. He walked to the door and slammed it behind him without looking back.

Matron Macintyre set up another court hearing for

visitation rights. This time Bailey walked in with her head held high. The judge beamed at her. “How are you?”

“I am fine.”

“What can I do for you?”

Bailey handed her the filled out forms. “I want visitation rights and eventually my son.”

“How long has he been in foster care?”

“Five years.”

“And you’ve seen him…”

“Once. Ten days ago.” Bailey explained her relationship with Clark and her feelings. The judge listened, nodding at times, but mostly frowning.

“A father is as important as a mother to a child.”

“I know that.”

“Do you plan to remarry?”

Bailey blushed. “I don’t know.”

“What do you mean, you don’t know? You’re a bright and pretty young girl. What man wouldn’t want to marry you?”

“I have a jail record.”

The judge slammed her gavel down on the desk pad. “Matron, talk some sense in her and bring her back with all the information. I’ll need a case worker history and credentials.” The judge shoved the papers back across the desk and turned to her court recorder. “Who’s next?”

Bailey e-mailed Dave. "I've read the entire test book. Will you teach me to drive?"

When Dave's car pulled up in front of the apartments, the phone rang. "I'm here."

Bailey grabbed her new woolen coat and the matching tam and scarf. She ran down the stairs and out into the howling November wind. The icy cold shocked her body so forcibly that she almost tumbled into the car. Her freezing hands made her remember. "Oh, I forgot my gloves and purse!"

Dave turned off the motor. "Go get them."

She cocked her head.

He shook his. "I guess you'll have to go get them. I'll wait."

"My keys are locked inside."

He groaned. "Okay, let's go find someone with a duplicate." He strode into the building like a drill sergeant. She followed him like a punished puppy. He talked to the girl at the desk. She didn't have access to keys. The girl used an intercom to get security. Security procured a key but would not allow her to have it because she had no identification.

"My purse is upstairs, locked in the apartment."

The girl made more phone calls. The long hand of the clock on the wall moved from the one to the ten. Dave talked to this person and another. Finally he turned to Bailey.

"You are not going to be allowed inside until tomorrow morning at seven when the manager can come in and verify that you are really you."

"What am I going to do?'

"I guess you come home with me. It's too cold to make you sleep on a park bench." He ambled out to the car and opened the door for her.

She was so cold her body shivered and her teeth chattered. "I'm sorry, Dave. I didn't mean to cause you so much trouble." She continued to shiver although he had started the car and turned on the heater. The blast of cold air on her feet made her yelp.

"Bailey, I'm sorry about all this. If I hadn't been so angry, I'd have come up to get you."

"You were angry?"

"Couldn't you tell?"

"Well, no. Other people scream and yell and cuss. I didn't know you were angry." She glanced over at his profile. The car was so cold his breath came out in puffs. "Dave, why are you angry?"

"Because, because you won't marry me. You don't even trust me enough to allow me to kiss you. I want to help you, but you keep running away. Bailey, I don't know what to do!" His voice had gradually crescendo-ed until he was shouting.

"Now I can tell you're angry." She reached down to rub circulation into her foot. "I can feel it getting warmer." She squirmed around in her seat.

"Bailey, put your seat belt on."

"The judge told me to get married."

"What?" He turned to look at her, and the car swerved to the right.

"Watch out!"

He braked, missing the parked car with an inch to spare. Then he looked at Bailey. "I'm glad I'm taking you home. We've got a lot to talk about."

Chapter 11—His House

Snow flurries spun in the headlights. Dave drove, but he turned to look at her frequently.

"So what are you thinking?"

He grinned. "I can't believe I'm taking you home with me. It's like I'm dreaming."

"Well, I'm not a dream. I'm a …" She had almost slipped with the word, "jailbird."

Dave laughed. "Go ahead, Honey. Say it. Say it loud and clear. Repeat it a dozen times or a million. I'll keep count." He slowed the car and reached across her body to point to a shadowy building beside two others. As the car turned, the lights brought out the rough brick walls, the windows trimmed in white and dark shutters. The garage door opened and overhead lights showed her a motorcycle parked in the other space. Shelves held swimming gear, a couple of skate boards, and camping equipment.

She turned to see Dave watching her. Never had he appeared as an outdoorsman, but she had met him in the library.

"Stay inside until I close the garage door." He stepped out of the car to push the button and came around to her side as the rumbling door slid to the floor. "There. My nosy neighbors won't know I have a visitor." He opened the door and bowed deeply. "'Welcome to my parlor, said the spider to the fly.'" He frowned. "I can't exactly remember how the poem goes, but it ends, 'And I'll eat you by-and-by.'"

As she twisted in the seat to come out, her skirt hiked up past her knees. Bailey pulled it down quickly, but Dave's grin told her he hadn't missed a thing. His eyes came up to meet hers, and he reached out to get a gentle grip on her forearm to help her to a gracious standing position.

"Oh, Bailey, I can't believe my good fortune!" His arm circled her shoulder and drew her body next to his. Her hips touched his, and his arm slid down to her waist. He was slowly turning her to face him.

"No, Dave." She didn't duck, but her spine stiffened. "I'll stay in the car if we don't lay some ground rules."

"Bailey, what happened to you that you don't like a man's touch? Am I that barbarous?"

She twisted her hands in front of her. "Dave, I like you. I like you very much, but there are memories."

"Bad memories?"

"Very bad memories." She looked down at the flawless cement floor. She had come out of prison to be imprisoned in her mind and feelings. "I'm sorry."

He pulled away. "I'm sorry. I get carried away around you." Then he heaved a huge sigh. "Just having you here makes me—*love* everybody!" He threw up his hands and did a little jig. Then he motioned with his head. "Come in where it's warm, and I'll make a cup of tea."

She could hear his breathing behind her as she went up the three steps and through the door. His arm came around her to turn on the light. She looked up into his face, a face she could love. His brows rose over honest eyes, and she shook her head.

He sighed and dropped his arm. "I'll hang up your coat." He held it by the collar, his fingers touching her neck and sending little tingles down her spine. Then he brushed past. "The closet is in here next to the front door."

She raised her hand over her thudding heart as she heard the clank of metal clothes hangers. Slowly she turned and surveyed the kitchen. It was basically clean except for a couple of coffee cups on the butcher board counter. The new appliances matched and fit snugly into the maple cabinets lining two walls. Matching chairs surrounded a glass topped table covered with envelopes and papers.

"That's my file system." He shoved the mess into a pile that covered only half of the table. Bailey turned to watch him set two mugs of water in the microwave to heat. He opened a small door and brought out a box of tea. "Is orange pekoe okay?"

"Yes. Do you always have your blinds drawn?" She pointed to the window over the sink.

"It keeps the neighbors from seeing what I eat or don't eat." He laughed. "When I first moved in, the old lady across the street was always telling me to drink more milk and eat more green vegetables. I discovered she had a pair of powerful binoculars that zeroed in on everything I did through that window. That must be why the other couple moved out and sold this place to me."

"It's a very nice home." She wondered what living in this mansion would be like with someone as friendly and loving as Dave. Surely it would be heavenly.

"Sugar?" His eyebrows danced. "Oh, you're sweet enough."

She could read the message. He wasn't giving up. "Dave, don't you understand that there are millions of girls better than I am?"

"I want you." Again his voice had finality, don't try to change my attitude. "I know what I like, and I know what I want." He set the sugar bowl in front of her. "If you just dip your finger in my tea, I wouldn't need any of this white stuff." His grin compelled her to smile.

"Oh, Dave." She shook her head. "But I'm not good enough for you."

He smiled. "Just keep talking, Honey. I'm listening." He stirred sugar into his tea and brought it to his lips. His eyes held hers. "Your eyes are the most fascinating in the world."

She looked away. All her life she had been told how ugly those green eyes were. Now Dave told her they were fascinating. She couldn't believe him. How had she gotten herself into this predicament? She had only wanted a lesson about driving a car. Her fingers drummed the table nervously.

"Am I that boring?" Again his voice teased.

"No."

"Bailey, I'm not good at cat and mouse games. If you keep blinking those lashes, I don't know how I will be able to wait for the code word." Again his eyes stared into hers. "How do I break down your determination?" He glanced down at his cup. "But I don't want to break it. I want it to be mine." He reached out for her hand and began to stroke the palm. "If I were a pagan, I'd read the lines. I bet they'd tell me that you and I were meant for each other, and we'd live happily ever after."

"Dave, why do you even like me?" She was afraid of what he would say, but she had to know in order to judge how truthful he was. Clark had a line, too, but it hadn't led to happiness.

He studied her face. "You're beautiful. You're kind."

"How do you know?"

"Remember I asked you to cut out paper leaves in the library? You didn't have to help me, but you did." He turned her hand over. "You don't give up. That first day you asked for an application and could have quit, but you found a way and came back. Petunia did her best to put you down, but there's something like flexible steel in you. It bends, but it always flips straight up."

She laughed. "You're tickling me."

His face beamed. "That's what I wanted to do. I wanted you to laugh, relax, and enjoy our time together." He rose. "I'll shove a couple of TV dinners in the stove. While they cook, we'll start a movie, okay?"

The entertainment center held a library of tapes. She looked up at him. "In the prison we saw very few movies. I haven't seen any of these."

Dave's eyes gleamed. "Then I'll show you a love story, and we'll live it out on the couch."

Fear gripped her. She stepped back. "I get the chair."

He shrugged. "Then I'll watch you instead of the movie. I've seen it several times, and you are far more interesting."

Half way through their meal, the doorbell rang. Matron Macintyre stood on the doorstep that was covered with an inch of fresh snow. The wind whirled around the building, swirling more flakes. “Is Bailey Berkley here?”

Dave stood back. “Come in. It’s cold out there.”

Bailey stood. “How did you know I was here?”

“Your ankle bracelet. Bailey, I know you’re no longer under house arrest, but when I checked the monitor, I was afraid.”

“Of Clark?”

The matron nodded. “He was released from jail this morning.”

Dave brought her inside and seated Matron Macintyre on the couch.

Bailey began wringing her hands. “I can explain. Dave offered to teach me how to drive a car. I was so excited that I forgot my purse and locked it in my apartment. Security wouldn’t allow me inside because I didn’t have any identification, so Dave brought me here for the night.” Bailey’s hands twisted the tail of her blouse.

The Matron turned to Dave. “Who are you?”

“I’m a librarian. I met you when you came in to get an application for a card.” He placed himself between the two women. “Look, I’m sorry if I got Bailey in trouble. Blame me, not her. If I’d gone up to get her from her apartment, she wouldn’t have forgotten her purse.”

The Matron’s head nodded. “I was sure that I’d met you before.” She turned to Bailey. “Do you think it’s best for you to spend the night here?”

Bailey and Dave exchanged glances.

"Well, under the circumstances I think you should get a motel room, Bailey. Shacking up just after your house arrest lifted doesn't look good. Remember you still have ten months of parole."

Dave helped her into her coat and then swept the snow from the door to the Matron's car before he'd allow the ladies to walk down the sidewalk. Bailey used the time to finish her meal although the fun had disappeared, the meat and potatoes had cooled until they were tasteless, and she really wasn't hungry.

The Matron stopped the car in front of the hotel. "I'm sorry it has to be this way."

"We weren't going to do anything."

"I know, but conventions must be considered. Have a good night. I'll see you in the morning."

"Matron Macintyre." Bailey turned before leaving the car. "Thank you for bringing me over here, but could I borrow some money? Remember, I left my purse in the apartment. I can pay you back tomorrow." She bit her lip. Was life always going to be a humiliation?

The Matron's car rounded the complex, leaving Bailey at the front door of the motel. She squared her shoulders and stepped into the steamy office. A glass wall separated her from the swimming pool. "Room for one, please."

She paid the clerk, picked up the card key, and looked at the number.

"Bailey, we didn't finish the movie." Dave stood waving the black box. "I brought it over." His eyes studied hers. "I knew you didn't have your purse. I thought you might need some money."

"Matron Macintyre gave me some." She turned to leave.

"Wait a minute." He turned to the clerk. "I want a room beside hers."

"What will the Matron say when she finds you here tomorrow morning?" Bailey stood in the hallway sliding the card in the door lock.

"What can she say? We have separate rooms." Dave looked down the hall. "I just wanted to keep an eye on you. Remember Clark is out of jail again."

"He can't do anything here. He doesn't even know I'm here." Bailey looked down at her ankle. "I'm still being monitored."

"Right, but that won't protect you." He pushed her door, and it opened. "There are two beds. We shouldn't have any trouble at all."

"But you have your own room."

He smiled. "That is for convention's sake."

She fell asleep before the movie ended. When she awoke the next morning, the blanket from the other bed had been carefully laid over her. Dave had disappeared.

With the Matron's help Bailey regained her apartment, but the police woman took her down to the local hardware store to have a key made. "I'll keep this one so you won't ever have that problem again. It's on my chain."

Bailey looked at her apartment. She had a computer, a kitchen, a view, her own bed, a bicycle, and a clean bathroom. All of her needs had been met, but unrest like dissatisfaction filled her as she listened to the wind howl over the building. There was an eerie whine that chilled her bones. She put on another sweater and turned on the computer, but the wind still howled, and the whine made her irritable. With all the talk of removing house arrest, she was still a prisoner.

She e-mailed Dave. "Thanks for everything."

His reply came quickly. "Keep safe, and don't forget our code word."

Her body began to relax. She found her site and began to type. The phone rang. She picked it up. "Hello?"

"Bailey, this is Clark. We've got to talk over these visitation rights."

"No!"

"Well, if you don't talk it over with me, neither one of us get any rights." He chuckled. "Uh, where are you?"

She hung up and redialed the matron's number. "Clark called. He wants to talk over the visitation rights."

"Give me his number. Let me talk to him." The Matron took the number. "Bailey, don't give him any idea where you are. That's an order."

A tension had built itself into her day. Bailey couldn't do any more writing. She made herself tea and a light lunch. She stared out the window at the snow. Her body stretched out on the settee, and she watched the flakes swirl from the heavens. Did God keep count of all the snowflakes? She knew He had the hairs of her head counted. He had promised Abraham, children as many as the sands on the sea shore, so God must have counted every granule.

She began to count. A phone was ringing.

She awoke. The sky had turned dark. Evening came quickly this time of year. She sat up. The phone rang again. "Hello?"

"Bailey, this is Dave. Do you want to go out tonight?"

"Yes."

"I'll come up to your apartment in about an hour."

She found herself humming as she quickly showered, dried her hair, and dressed: warm wool slacks, two sweaters, and the boots she'd picked up at the bargain center. The doorbell rang. "Just a minute." She grabbed her coat and purse. "I'm coming." She opened the door with a flourish.

Clark stood grinning. "Baby, I didn't expect that greeting, but let's get out of here."

"No!" She tried to back into the room. "You over-stuffed ferret."

"You're not bad looking yourself." His foot held the door open, and his body strength overpowered hers. In a second he had grabbed her upper arm and yanked her into the hallway. "You never could follow orders right." Before she could scream, he had stuffed her mouth with a man's handkerchief. Bailey kicked, squirmed, and pinched while she tried to spit out the rag.

He dragged her down the hall. She went limp except for pushing the high heel of her boot into the carpet as hard as she could for a brake or drag. The effort kept her from getting the right position to kick him into the privates, but she kept the thought in mind.

When they reached the stairs, he stooped to pick her up in his arms. The gag fell out, but her mouth was dry. “Help!” sounded weak and sick. She closed her mouth to bring more moisture to her tongue. He slapped his hand over her lips. Again he struggled to pick her up, but she rolled and elbowed him. He pulled her upside down and started down the stairs. She bent one knee and pushed her foot against the stair. He lost his balance and fell forward, but his grip on her increased.

“You’ll pay for this.”

Her shrill, whistle-like scream was absorbed by the carpeting up and down the stairs and the stair wall. He thrust his fist into her mouth.

“Shut up!” As he stumbled upright, she bent double, pulling his weight upon her back. Again the two lost balance and rolled down another flight of stairs. He landed on the bottom, his head striking the floor. She stood over him gasping for breath as the building manager and the janitor came puffing up the stairs.

“He tried to kidnap me.” She stepped away as the two men bent over Clark.

“Call the police.”

Bailey ran back up the stairs, grabbed her purse and coat that had fallen in front of her door, and leaped inside the door that was still ajar. She whipped it shut, slid the dead bolt, and sagged to the floor with her back against it. Her phone was ringing.

“Bailey, I’ve been detained. I’ll be another half hour,” Dave said.

She flipped the case shut and bowed her head. As the doorbell rang, she opened the phone and dialed Matron Macintyre.

"Open up, police!"

"You should have checked the peep hole." The Matron sat beside her and held her hand inside the police station. "It would never have happened if you hadn't opened the door."

"I know, but I thought it was Dave." She glanced at Dave's worried face on the other side of her. The Matron dropped her hand and rose to talk to another police officer. They walked a short distance away and Dave laid his arm over her shoulders.

"If you would marry me, I could protect you. Bailey, I'm going to move in with you whether the police like it or not!" His fingers squeezed her arm as he leaned closer to her. The individual bucket seats in the lobby prevented him from scooting closer.

However, she laid her head into the hollow of his body next to his heart. His heart beat thudded beneath her ear, and she began to count. His strength seeped into her body. As his hands slid down her arms, she turned. "I'm not afraid any more." She gazed into his eyes.

"What?" Dave pulled her closer so that her chin nearly touched his. "Bailey, what do you mean?"

"I can't explain it, but I feel it."

"Bailey." The Matron came toward her. "You have to make a report. Clark claims that you were chasing him. That's why he fell." Her lips quivered. "He's charging you with assault and battery."

Dave helped her to her feet.

"Am I under arrest?"

"Not exactly. I talked to the chief of police and explained that you wore an ankle bracelet. He didn't have any cell space open for a female, but you are not to leave your apartment without permission, understood?"

Bailey nodded. "Iron bars do not a prison make."

"The quote is, 'Stone walls do not a prison make nor iron bars a cage'." Dave's arm slid around her waist. "What do we do now?"

"Dave, she has to make the report." The matron nodded to Bailey. "Tell everything from the very beginning. I mean, go back to when you were a teenager, and Clark came into the bar."

"Yes, ma'am." Bailey's eyes turned to Dave. "I told you there was a lot you didn't know about me."

"It's okay. That's the past. We're the future." His lips came together in a line, squaring his jaw. "We'll fight this together, okay?" His hand squeezed the side of her waist. When they walked across the room, his hand slid to the small of her back. Bailey leaned slightly into the open palm. It felt so good, so right, and so secure.

Chapter 12: Bennie

Sunday morning Bailey awoke with unspeakable joy. Dave was picking her up for church. She tried to tell herself that true worship made the day exciting, but being with him meant so much to her. The more she thought about it, the more she wondered. Who was he? She had known him for such a short time, a little over a month, and yet she trusted him more than any man she had ever met.

She hummed as she showered, dressed in the new woolen pantsuit that the Matron declared made her a movie star, and touched up her face with the slightest of makeup. Caring about how she looked began when she knew she cared for Dave. He deserved the best. She might not be the best, but she would do her best to make him proud of her.

“Bailey, your hair is naturally limp and fine,” the beautician said, “but this new product will give it body when I cut it in this new style.” She had given the mahogany hair a few discreet streaks of lightness that gave the girl an urchin look. “You are just naturally beautiful with those green eyes and narrow chin.”

Now Bailey donned the apple cinnamon suit and smiled at herself. “I look better than a Barbie doll. I’m me.” She donned her coat and hoisted the long strapped purse over her shoulder. Bible in hand, she left the apartment.

The November sun drenched the front of the building which blocked the west wind, and Bailey waited for Dave. The full parking lot would someday hold her car, but she knew the Matron’s caution towards the purchase held sense as well as cents.

“Keep that money in the bank drawing interest for awhile. It won’t hurt a thing, and there are multiple cars on the market. When the time comes, you’ll pay less if you can throw down the whole payment right before the seller’s nose.” She laughed. “You are something else, Bailey.”

“And so are you, Matron Macintyre.” Bailey couldn’t believe the love that they had for each other. It patterned more like what a mother and daughter should be than an officer of the law and a prisoner, but Bailey wasn’t about to change it. She knew God had given her this best friend.

Dave’s Saturn rounded the corner and parked in the closest hole. He leaped out and guided her to the passenger side. “Hello, beautiful.”

She smiled. "Hello, yourself." She watched him walk around the car with the gait of a happy man ready for an adventure. His whistle was slightly off key, but his broad chin tilted upward in confidence. He slid under the wheel of the car and started the engine.

His eyes met hers before he backed the car and turned it onto the street. "It's not going to stay nice much longer. The weather is forecasting snow this week." He grinned. "What do you say we elope this afternoon?"

She had to laugh. "I need to know you better."

"Ah, what do you want to know?"

"Where were you born? How did you get here? Who are your parents?" She cocked her head to one side. "Do you have any brothers and sisters?"

"Too many." He faced the street. "I was born in Indianapolis, the second son of six. I had three sisters and two brothers. My oldest brother is in Iraq. My sisters are scattered from Los Angeles, California, to Atlanta, Georgia, and Westchester, Massachusetts. I don't think I pronounced Westchester correctly. Ilene said it is almost like saying "whisper" but that's not the way I heard her say it." He laughed. "My parents have retired from the retail business and own a condominium down in Florida. Tampa Bay is just too hot and muggy for me, but they want the whole family down there for Christmas. You're invited. Do you want to go?"

Suddenly Bailey shrank into the leather seat. "I don't think so." Her mind whirled. "I'm still on probation. I don't think I'd be allowed to leave town."

"Oh."

She could sense his disappointment and looked out the

passenger window. The empty elementary school yard reminded her of her childhood. “I went to school here. Where did you go to college, and why did you decide to become a librarian?”

“Actually I didn’t see myself as a librarian. I studied computers. When I came out of Ivy Tech, the jobs in the offing were few and scattered.” He pulled the car into the church parking lot and unhooked his seat belt. Then he turned to her. “The pastor’s son, Ernest Brown, was my best friend at school. He died from congenial heart failure just before graduation. At the funeral Pastor Brown and his wife encouraged me to come here. Through their help I obtained the position at the library.”

She lifted her eyes to his. “I’m sorry. I mean, I’m sorry you lost your best friend.”

“Bailey, you remind me a lot of him. Ernest had green eyes like yours.” He smiled and turned to open his door, unaware that she was speechless. “Come on. I could use some help in setting up my classroom. Believe it or not, I need to change the bulletin board. Do you want to cut out some figures?”

She stumbled from the car. The pastor’s son had green eyes. When would the curse end? Where would it take her? She glanced at Dave who had opened the trunk of the car and was pulling out folders.

“Bailey, can you carry these?”

Just before church Teddy Sommers entered the small basement room. “Hi, Dave.”

Bailey handed Dave the last letter she had clipped from the gold construction paper and stepped back to study the balance of the bulletin board. The cornucopia dominated the middle of the space with fruits of the Spirit spilling out of its broad mouth. The bright colors made the corner sparkle with the outline of glitter in just the right places.

Teddy's face glowed with the joy of youth. "Hey, Bailey, my mom wants to talk to you. Your mother has been taken to the nursing home. Bennie is at our house, and I've been taking care of him. She wants to know if you want him."

"Bennie?" She remembered the loyalty of the little dog. "Yes, I'd like to have him."

Upstairs, she searched the crowd for Tonia Sue Sommers and bumped into Stella Brown. Immediately she searched the woman's eyes which were a light blue under the blonde eyebrows. "Good morning. Have you seen Tonia Sue? Teddy said she was up here somewhere."

"I think she is in the ladies' restroom checking on the necessities."

Bailey wandered through the foyer in that direction.

Pastor Brown held out a welcoming hand. "Good morning, Bailey. I'm so glad you're here. Did Matron Macintyre come?"

"No, Dave brought me."

The man smiled. "He's a wonderful boy. We love him very much."

"Yes, sir." She shook his hand and stared at his dark brown eyes.

"Is something the matter, Bailey? I mean, did I miss a spot when I shaved this morning?" His hand came up to feel his chin and cheeks.

"No, everything is fine. You didn't miss any spots." Her embarrassment fried her face, and she escaped into the ladies' room. She turned to the sink to splash water on her face, careful not to touch the makeup around her eyes.

Tonia Sue came out of a stall behind her with a roll of toilet paper in each hand. "Hi, Bailey, it's good to see you. I wanted to talk to you about your mother and that little dog. Did you know she was admitted into the nursing home this week?"

"Teddy, just told me. I want Bennie, if you don't mind."

"Oh, I'll be glad for you to have him, but Teddy is quite attached to the little fellow." She opened a cabinet and set the toilet paper on a shelf that contained multiple rolls in military stacks. "Do you know where your mother is?"

"No."

"Hmm, I don't either. The ladies of the church would like to take her a care basket for Thanksgiving like we have in the past." She smiled. "Let me know if you find out where she is."

"I will." The thoughtfulness of the ladies and Tonia Sue for her mother melted Bailey's heart. "Thank you. Thank you so much!" She felt the tears running down her cheeks.

Tonia Sue wrapped her arms about Bailey. "There, now. I'm sure your mother is in good hands." Her warm hug continued to hold the girl for several minutes. "Are you going to be all right?"

Bailey nodded and pulled away. She used a paper towel to dab at her eyes. "I just don't know how to thank you. You have been such a wonderful neighbor." She composed herself and went to class. Another woman whom Bailey had seen before scooted over to give her room in the pew. Stella Brown bowed her head for prayer, and Bailey joined her with a silent mental petition. *"Thank you, Lord, for such loving, wonderful people. Teach me how to care for others like they have cared for me and my mother."*

When Dave and Bailey arrived at the Sommer's house that afternoon, Bennie's barks warned Teddy who turned and dropped the leash. Then the little dog welcomed her with a whining and wiggling body about her legs. She scooped him up, and he rewarded her by licking her chin.

"I think he's glad to see you." Teddy's grin reached across his face.

"He didn't forget me." Bailey held him close to her chest and looked across at her mother's house. The back door hung open. "Does anybody live there?"

"Crib and his gang hang out over there every night or so. I believe they've made it a drug hangout."

"I've got to see." Bailey turned to Dave as she set the dog down. "Please stay here." She walked across the street with Bennie trotting on leash beside her. Inside the furniture lay broken beside strewn clothing. Bennie sniffed at the floor and abandoned food cartons, but he stayed next to her as she toured the living room with littered whiskey bottles. The TV had disappeared, and her mother's room no longer had a bed or dresser. "They must have taken it with her to the nursing home." Of all the rooms, it seemed almost vacant except for the broken closet door.

She walked out the back, shutting the door firmly, but the lock wouldn't hold. The wind blew around the corner as if to shoo her away. She glanced at the barren flower bed and the garage with new graffiti on all four sides. Once again she left, but this time without regret.

Bennie heeled beside her up the stairs of the apartments when she bumped into the janitor. "No pets allowed in the building."

"My lease permits a small dog or cat."

He shook his head. "Rules changed just last week. The manager said the place smelled like a barn lot. Sorry. You're going to have to find the little dog a home." He bent down to Bennie's level. "Nice little terrier, too. What you say? I'll take him home to my kids. They'd love to have him."

Bailey shook her head. "He's my mother's dog. She's in the nursing home. I thought I could keep him."

The man rose. "I'm sorry, but those are the rules. I didn't make them. I just work here."

She turned to Dave. "What should I do?"

"I'll take Bennie outside to the car. Find your lease agreement, and bring it down. We'll look it over."

The fine print over her signature said, "Rules are subject to change without notice."

"Now what do I do?"

Dave shrugged. "Bailey, I honestly don't want the dog in my house unless you are living there, too. I was hoping he would bring you added security. I've always had an allergy to animals." Already his eyes were tearing, and he sneezed. "I'm sorry, Honey."

She held Bennie on her lap and stroked his little body. "I could take him back to Teddy who wouldn't mind keeping him." Then her chin rose. "I have the money. I'll find a house to buy of my own."

"Bailey, don't. Not yet." Dave's face entreated. "If Bennie means that much to you, I'll take him home with me."

She could feel the tears threatening her eyelids. "Bennie needs me. I need him. Maybe I can smuggle the little fellow up to the apartment."

"He's going to need a bathroom break at least twice a day or more. Can you smuggle him in and out that many times?" Dave's tone was cynical. "I don't think so. Besides, you're a Christian. Christians follow the rules." His eyes said more than his words.

Bailey nodded. "Let's take him back to Teddy Sommers. At least Teddy loves him."

She opened up her computer when Dave left her that evening. Again she searched the rental sites, looking for a congenial place. "What kind of town is this that doesn't like pets or children?" As Bailey shut it off, she thought of her mother. Where had Narla placed her?

Chapter 13: The Police Report

The Matron held the door for Bailey and Dave as they entered an office tucked in the back of the police station.

The older fellow taking the report smiled at Matron Macintyre. "You don't have to be here."

"Do you mind if I stay?" Her eyes connected with Bailey's.

He looked directly at Bailey and his nod indicated the Matron. "Will her presence bother you in telling the truth?"

"No, sir, she will help me. I need her." Bailey clutched Dave's hand. "And I'd like him to stay, too."

The officer raised his eyes to Matron Macintyre. "What do

you think?"

She nodded. Then she spoke to Bailey. "Begin with the first time you ever saw Clark. Don't leave out anything, understand?"

"I was fifteen, a junior in high school. Every morning and afternoon I worked in my grandfather's tavern on South Street. My mother, sister, and I lived above the tavern with my grandparents." She looked at Dave. "Living that way isn't like normal people. The kids teased me and called me a barmaid."

His hand found hers and squeezed it.

"Of what did your work consist?" The interviewer had turned on a taping devise. "Remember this recording will be used if there is a trial."

She licked her lips. "In the morning I'd get up to peel carrots and potatoes. Grandmother always told me or left a list of how much needed to be fixed. I'd make salads and set them in the cooler. Sometimes, if my mother wasn't able, I'd serve early breakfast to customers."

"What kept your mother from serving?"

"She is an alcoholic." Her eyes studied the broken toes of her boots. Clark's dragging her down the hall had ruined them. The fancy silver cap had come off the toe. "I never knew her to be sober for very long."

"Did you do any of the cooking, like the grill or stove?"

"No, grandmother and grandfather did that. Besides I didn't have time. I served meals and drinks, cleared tables, and washed dishes. At quitting time it was my job to sweep and mop the floors." She stared at the three. "I didn't know anything else. It was what I did since I was little."

“Did your sister help, too?” The officer adjusted his glasses.

Bailey shook her head. “Mother wouldn’t allow her to do it.”

“Why?” He adjusted some papers on the desk.

“Mother always claimed my sister was different. Narla did other things. I worked.”

The officer swore, and Matron Macintyre’s grimace appeared almost violent. He pushed his glasses back and searched through the paperwork. “How did you meet Clark?”

Bailey’s fingers wound around Dave’s. “Clark was Narla’s boyfriend. She brought him into the bar one evening when I was about fifteen. He got drunk and began verbally abusing her, so that night she dumped him right in front of everybody. He paid the tab and left.” She looked away to study the shadows of their heads moving on the wall. Taking a deep breath, she turned to Dave.

“Clark returned the next evening and the next. I didn’t want to serve him because of what he’d said and how he touched me. Mother laughed about it. ‘That’s the way men are.’ Narla teased me about Clark at home and at school in front of her friends. Grandmother didn’t do anything. Sometimes I thought I saw pity on her face, but grandfather told me I had to serve Clark. He was a good customer.”

“What happened after that, Bailey?”

She looked up in the Matron’s eyes. Bailey’s tears dripped from her chin, and the Matron pulled a couple of tissues from a nearby box and handed them to her.

“Clark kept touching me. One night he was drunk. It was closing time, and I had already cleaned off all the tables except his. I’d swept the floor and was mopping it when he grabbed me by the arm and took me to his car." She stopped. "I didn't want to get in, but he pushed me in the back seat and raped me." Her gulps became sobs. "I hurt so bad that he took me to another bar and put something in my drink. It was a powder. I drank it and passed out. I don't know how I got home."

"That rat!" Dave rose from his chair.

The officer held out his palm to indicate Dave to sit down. Then he adjusted his glasses. "Did you see Clark again?"

"I was sick for almost a month. I didn't work, and I didn't go back to school. Then I discovered I was pregnant. Mother wouldn't let me return to school. The grandparents made me work in the bar. They tried to get me to abort the baby. I couldn't. It just didn't seem right."

"Did Clark come back?"

"No. He wasn't there when the baby was born. Grandmother kicked me out. She told me to go to social services and support myself. They gave me some food stamps and a little money, but it wouldn't pay the entire rent. I asked the woman for more money, but she told me to go get a job. I didn't know how." She looked up into the three faces. "I really didn't know how. I didn't have a high school diploma, and James needed me. I came out of the apartment office crying one day and saw Clark. He told me he would give me some money if I would deliver packages for him."

Bailey blew her nose. "I told him I didn't do drugs. He laughed and told me to starve. He didn't care what happened to James or me. Then he came back with those packages. 'Hide them in the baby carriage.' He told me where to take them and gave me the rent money."

"How long did you deliver packages?"

"Almost two years. Once Clark tried to move in with me, but I wouldn't let him. Then he gave me a package to deliver to an undercover cop. I was arrested. My mother and grandparents put James in foster care. I didn't hear from them for the five years in prison. They wouldn't answer my phone calls or my letters. I didn't know what was going on."

"Bailey, tell him what happened at your trial." The Matron handed her more tissues.

"Clark testified that I was a druggie trying to pull him into jail. My grandparents said I had stolen money from their cash register. Mother said I was guilty of stealing vodka from the cellar because I had a hidden drinking problem. Then she claimed I pawned her jewelry for drug money. It was all lies, but I couldn't prove it. I was sentenced for ten years." She looked up at the Matron. "An inmate gave me the first and only Bible I ever had. I read it and gave my life to Jesus Christ. She introduced me to Bible studies. The parole board let me out on good behavior. For the first time in my life I had hope."

Dave's hand reached over and covered hers. She could see the love shining out of his eyes. He hadn't rejected her although he knew all the evil. Her body relaxed.

"I finished my high school in prison and passed the GED test. Then I took some bookkeeping and computer courses. I learned how to write and earn money on the internet. When I got out, the Matron allowed me to go to the library." She turned. "Dave helped me find web sites. I am earning enough to support myself and my son. I want to get James back."

The officer nodded. "Tell me about your connection with Clark. When and where did that begin?"

"Clark bumped into me at the library. I managed to dodge him because Matron Macintyre was driving me everywhere since I was under house arrest." Her eyes rested on the matron. "I thought he was put in jail, but somehow he must have been released."

"How did he happen to be at your apartment?" This time the officer pushed his glasses back and continued to stare at her while she replied.

"The judge acquitted me from house arrest. Dave called to ask me out for dinner. I was waiting for him when the doorbell rang. I opened it expecting Dave, but it was Clark. He dragged me out into the hall and stuffed my mouth. I fought. When he got to the stairs, he tried to pick me up, and I knocked him off balance. We fell down, but he still held me." Bailey took a deep breath remembering her fright. "I couldn't scream, so I kicked the stair step, and we tumbled down the other stairs. He hit his head. I screamed for help. When the manager and janitor came, I ran back to my apartment."

Dave's hand squeezed hers. "I'm sorry. I was helping someone who came into the library at the last moment. The computer crashed, and it took an hour to get the information the customer wanted. I couldn't come as early as I planned."

"Bailey should have used the peep hole." The Matron's frown could not hide the concern in her voice. "This wouldn't have happened if Bailey hadn't opened the door."

"I'm sorry."

"Well, I guess that wraps this up." The officer stood to his feet and reached for his jacket. "It's late. My wife has been waiting for me for hours."

They filed out. He turned off the light and shut the door.

Dave held her coat as Bailey slid in her arms.

She looked up in his eyes. "I'm not afraid any more."

He gave her arm a little squeeze and turned to put on his own coat. Bailey saw the Matron having final words with the officer. Then Dave helped Matron Macintyre with her coat.

As the woman slipped on her gloves, she said, "He just told me that Clark was set free. Bailey, I'm taking you to your apartment."

"I'll take her home." Dave's offer came with a special squeeze around her shoulders and a guiding pull towards the door.

The Matron tapped him on the shoulder. "That's my job. I must make sure she is securely locked in her apartment and safe."

"How can she be safe alone if Clark is running free?" Dave faced them. His smile lost in a grimace of concern.

"He's not as free as you think. He's under observation."

The police could be satisfied with Clark on the outside, but Bailey froze. She slipped into the squad car. The snowstorm had plastered everything in white including the streets. By counting the tire tracks she could tell how many had passed through the street.

"When you are inside, don't open for anybody, understand?" The Matron's face with the stern set to her jaw could have been etched in stone.

"Yes, but why does Clark continue to harass me? He should know he'll just get in trouble."

"He's scared of what you know and what you'll spill." The Matron concentrated on her driving. "Don't let him in, and call me as soon as he shows up or telephones, okay?"

Bailey nodded. She could see the lights of Dave's car almost on their bumper. The wipers brushed the snow from the windows leaving an arc for her to stare out at the flakes blowing down in the headlights. The tracks of others ended, and theirs were the only vehicles in the blinding storm. The Matron's car slid around the last corner.

"There's ice underneath." No fresh tracks appeared in the parking lot as the Matron brought her car in between two others that were completely covered with the white stuff. Bailey stepped out and turned to see Dave park two or three cars away. She waved, and he jumped out to return the wave. The Matron smiled. "I still have to see you inside." Like an army sergeant she marched up the stairs behind Bailey. At the door she waited while Bailey found her key and unlocked the door.

"Are you coming inside?"

"No, that's not necessary. Bailey, let me know if Clark shows up. Don't let him in even if the hall is on fire. Shut the door and slide the dead bolt." The Matron stood there waiting.

Bailey searched the hall for Dave, but when she didn't see him, she obeyed and leaned against it on the inside. The dull thuds down the hall announced the Matron's retreat. What had happened to Dave? She thought he would come up to the apartment, but maybe he had just turned around and went home. The storm raged around the building, the wind rattling her window. Crystallized frost framed the bottom third of her large window. She crossed the room to stare out at the parking lot. Matron Macintyre's squad car entered the street to follow the tracks they had already made. She looked for Dave's car or retreating tracks, but the storm prevented her detecting his car from the others.

Bailey's phone buzzed.

"Honey, did you mean it? You're not afraid of me?"

"Yes." A warm feeling ran through her. "Dave, you can start counting. Jailbird."

He laughed. "I'm coming up."

"You're here?"

"I'm coming up the stairs."

"Did you see the Matron?"

"We just passed. She looked the other way. I don't think she wanted to see me."

"She told me not to let anyone in."

"You know who she meant."

A thump on the outside as the doorbell rang alerted her. "Let me in immediately. I am coming to collect."

Insistent pounding like a pagan drum beat drove her to the door, and she looked through the peek hole.

"Bailey, let me in before I awaken all your neighbors!"

She pulled back the bolt.

An impatient thump sounded as he pushed the doorbell button again. "I can't wait, Bailey."

She twisted the knob, and he charged into the room with his arms opened wide. She leaped into his embrace and squealed. "Dave!" He swung her around, kicked the door shut, swung her one hundred eighty degrees and locked the door behind her.

"Bailey!" His breath came in puffs. He looked into her eyes. "I can't believe it!" He squeezed her again.

"Jailbird," she said softly as her hands crept around his neck. Her chin came up to his, and she felt his breath on her lips.

But his cell phone in the coat pocket played, "Dixie." He stopped. Then he smiled. "I'm kissing you this time. Let it ring." His lips brushed against hers.

She leaned into the kiss, and a magic thrill zinged down to her toes. He pulled away to turn off the phone and shrug out of his coat. It fell to the floor beside hers. Then he wrapped his arms around her little body. His hands traveled up her spine to pull her closer, but her arms had circled his neck as her feet left the floor.

"Oh, my Bailey!"

"Jailbird."

He kissed her again. He was still keeping count.

Her phone rang. After the third ring she turned to answer it.

"Bailey, send Dave home soon. The roads are awful out here, and we both want him safely home."

"I love you, too," Dave said into the receiver, and they both laughed.

They stared out the window at the storm. The wind blowing gusts picked up tons of snow and whirled it around like an egg beater.

"It's awful out there, Dave. You'd better go before it gets impossible."

He squeezed her waist. "I like it better here." His lips found hers again. "There isn't anything this sweet back at my house."

She gently disengaged his hands while their lips seemed to be glued together. Then she pushed him back into the settee. "You can't stay here."

He pushed the cushions. "Why not?" His smile showed all his teeth and eyes in a glowing face.

"Because."

He pulled her down beside him. Her head lay on his shoulder, and his arm snuggled her close. "Because, why?" He kissed her again. "This is addictive."

"Dave, we're Christians."

"We're not doing anything wrong."

"Not yet." Her eyes met his.

Chapter 14—The Winter Storm

"Bailey, I'm marrying you so you won't send me off in a terrible storm again."

She looked out at the blizzard. "Dave, you are going to get home safely, aren't you?"

"No problem." He rose slowly, bringing her up beside him. "I wish I could take you with me." He studied her face, his fingers touching her chin. "You will come home with me, won't you some day?"

"Some day after we're married."

"Let's do it soon."

She walked with him to the door. "We'll get married, and then I can get James."

"James?" He drew back. "Is that the only reason you are

willing to marry me?"

"Well, that's one of the reasons."

He picked up his coat and turned to the door. "Don't forget to lock it and slide the dead bolt." He stepped out into the hall. After the lock clicked, and the deadbolt scraped into place, she leaned against the door and listened to his shoe soles brush the carpet down the hall. When the door at the bottom of the stairs slammed shut, she danced to the window to follow the red taillights of the car venturing out of the lot and into the street. They faded in the swirl of the ongoing storm.

Her phone rang. "Bailey, you didn't answer my question. Why do you want to marry me?"

She knew he was referring to James and bit her lip.

"Bailey?"

"Because I love you."

She heard a screech of tires and a loud crash. "Dave? Dave, what happened?"

A loud whack almost broke her ear drum. The phone line buzzed momentarily before the busy signal began its steady beat. "Dave? Are you all right?" He didn't answer.

Quickly she punched 911 and impatiently stepped around her phone as it rang several times. Before someone could reply, she blurted, "There's been an accident. I don't know where or what happened, but Dave's car just crashed, and he's unconscious."

"Are you in the car?"

"No, I was talking to him on the phone. He was headed home. I heard a crash. His phone died."

“Ma’am, he probably dropped it. There is no record of an accident.”

“But it just happened seconds ago.”

“Do you have the name of the street or general area?”

“He just left the government apartments.”

“Can you see the accident?”

“No.”

“Who am I talking to? Is this a prank call?” The line went dead.

Bailey began to seethe and dialed 911 again. Dave was in trouble. The house arrest restricted her from leaving the apartment, but she couldn’t let him die. The soft pulse of the busy signal kept her from connecting. She punched in the Matron’s phone number. This time the phone rang five times without an answer. “The wireless customer is not available. To leave a message wait until after the beep or call again later.”

“Matron Macintyre, Dave was talking to me on the phone when I heard his car crash. 911 thinks I’m a prankster calling. I can’t leave my apartment. What am I going to do? I know he needs help.” She set the receiver back in its cradle and stewed.

Then she picked up the phone and dialed zero. Nothing happened, so she punched in 911. “Ma’am, I’m calling to report an accident. A friend of mine just left the government apartments in his car to go home. I was talking to him on his cell phone. I heard tires screech, a crash, and the tinkling of breaking glass.”

“Is his name Dave?”

“Yes!” Hope flooded through Bailey’s veins. “Is he all right?”

"A squad car has been dispatched to the area. No report has been received. Thank you for calling." Again the line went dead.

The lights in the apartment flickered. The next time Bailey raised the phone to her ear, no dial tone pulsed in the receiver. As she set it down, her lights went out. She heard a siren and saw flashing lights pass the apartment building below. She stood wishing she could see what was going on beneath her. Dave had become more than important in her life. He was a necessity! The wind continued to blow and moan, and the flurries whirled and swirled like fast footed dancers. The window frosted over, and she realized no heat came from the vents. She shivered. Her battery operated clock told her she had been keeping watch for over an hour. The window frosted over. She shivered. Again she picked up the dead phone and replaced it.

"Oh, God, I'm helpless. Please be with Dave. If that was the ambulance, get him to the hospital safely." She wandered around in the dark apartment. Then the street lights quit, and the world plunged into the blackest of nights.

She dragged the settee next to the phone and carried all her bedding out to the living room. The room lost its heat, and she buried herself in the comforters. As she waited for the electricity to be repaired, she fell asleep.

Her dreams contained a pounding on her door. She remembered Dave's drum beat and smiled. He must be all right. He had returned. "Dave? Is it you?" There was no answer, and the hallway like a black cave concealed her visitor through the peephole. Again the pounding vibrated the door, and she stared vainly through the tiny glass. "Who is it? I can't see you."

"Security! Open up."

"I'm not supposed to open to anybody."

“Then freeze to death, you dumb female.” Steps thudded down the hall.

Bailey tried her phone. Neither it nor the lights worked. She padded into the kitchen to try her stove. The gas burner came on with a cheerful blue light. She went to the sink, but the faucet refused to give water. In the refrigerator she found milk to heat to make cocoa. Then she crouched in the warmth of the comforters to watch the dawn break over the top of the town. Was Dave all right? She set the mug beside the phone and snuggled down into the bedding.

Midmorning she awoke. The sun in total glory reflected from the solid white surface a blinding glow and made the ice coating the branches of the trees and bushes twinkle in iridescent colors like a fairy palace-world. The restored electricity glowed through her lights, and Bailey rose to turn them off, take the dirty mug and spoon to the kitchen, and restore the bedding to the bedroom. She was pushing the settee in place when her phone rang.

“Bailey, how is Dave?”

Bailey recognized the Matron’s husky voice. “I don’t know. Your call is the first that I’ve had this morning. The electricity just barely came on again.”

“I’ll call the hospital to see if he was admitted. You call his cell phone or home.”

The cell phone didn’t answer, but the matron returned her call. “He was released early this morning from the hospital. He took a cab to work.”

“Oh.” Bailey turned on her computer and typed an e-mail to Dave. “Matron Macintyre said you were in the hospital last night. I heard the crash through your cell phone. Are you all right?"

His e-mail read, "I've a bump on the head and bandage to cover it. My car is in the shop for the next two or three weeks. I'll be riding my bike."

Bailey remembered the motorcycle in his garage. "Brrr."

Teddy's mom, Tonia Sue Sommers, came in her old Ford to get Bailey for Sunday school. Then she swung by for Dave.

"We can't have our teachers spaced out like the pepperoni on frozen pizza." Tonia Sue's hearty laughter almost drowned Teddy's chatter in the back seat.

"Bennie isn't his old self, Bailey. He greets me at the door, but then he goes over to his bed and drops in like an old lady." His concerned face held frown lines above the brows. "I can't understand it. We feeds him good, but he don't dance around no more."

"Maybe he feels the cold weather like we do. It's hard to stay cooped up all the time." She stared out at the white world whizzing past. Again the desire to build a snowman, fall into a drift to make an angel, and crunch balls enveloped her. She wanted to be free to do more than pace back and forth in the apartment. Even in prison she had been allowed to jog outside and watch the puffing clouds from her lips.

"I don't know. I thoughts that, too, and wrapped him up like a baby. The next time I look he crawl out and lay on top." Teddy touched her hand to get her attention. "You think he missing you and your mama?"

"Maybe so." She laid her head back against the seat. "I can't come and visit yet." She wondered if she would ever be free.

The car turned into a driveway, and she recognized Dave's house. Her heart began to beat faster as she watched him come down the sidewalk that had been shoveled and swept clean. He smiled at her, and she wanted to sing.

"You got one big shiner!" Teddy examined Dave's face after he slid into the back seat.

"I was thrown sidewise into the window. It probably saved my neck from being broken because the air bags deflated too late." His eyes searched Bailey's face.

She nodded. The bandage covered his left temple. "How are you feeling?"

"Much better every day. The doctor says I'm on the mend."

"Good." Teddy was squeezed between them; however, the man's arm crept across the boy's shoulders so his fingers could twine itself in Bailey's hair. They rode listening to Tonia Sue and Ma'am Kuhn discuss the storm.

"Where's the Kuhn children?" Dave nudged Teddy.

"They's with the dad." Teddy whispered. "You knows they divorced."

Dave nodded.

As they entered the church, Stella Brown approached Bailey. "Would you like to come to our ladies' prayer meetings and Bible studies on Tuesday mornings?"

"I can't. I'm under house arrest." She raised the cranberry leg of her pantsuit to show the ankle bracelet. "Maybe some other time." Bailey turned to follow Dave down the stairs to his room. The continual embarrassment of incarceration burned within her. Would she ever live it down?

Dave kicked the door shut and pulled her into his arms. "Honey, this has been the longest three days of my life." The creak of the door handle shortened his kiss, and Bailey drew away. Teddy bounced in to help.

"That little Bennie ain't doing so good." Teddy looked up at Dave while they held a banner in place so Bailey could staple it to the bulletin board. "He don't eat much, and he sleep a lot."

Dave's glance at Bailey contained a frown. "Are you feeding him the same stuff he was eating before?"

"No, all he got were scraps. I feed him dog food, the kind with lots of protein and vitamins." Teddy's frown deepened. "He sniff and walk away."

"Is he getting skinny?"

"Oh, no, he look good, but he don't dance around no more. He curl up and sleeps all the day."

Dave laid a hand on the boy's shoulder. "I think he's just slowed down like a hibernating bear. Besides he is such a small dog, he probably doesn't need much to eat." He winked at Bailey. "I know somebody who doesn't eat enough to sniff at. She's small, too."

"Bailey!" Teddy whooped. "You and that dog is just alike."

Two children came into the room, and Bailey slipped out to find her own Sunday school class. After the morning service Stella

Brown caught the sleeve of Bailey's coat before she could slip out to the waiting car. "I've been thinking. You can't come to our Bible studies, so could we come to you?"

"What do you mean?" Bailey's eyes focused through the glass foyer doors to the Ford filled with her friends. Did the pastor's wife think she was in prison?

"Do you mind if we come to your apartment and have the Bible study there?"

Bailey's attention returned to Stella. A wonder glowed inside of her. Even as a child when school mates visited their friends' homes, she had never been allowed to go or invite anyone to the bar. "You would come to my place?"

"If you don't mind." Stella's intent gaze came from a serious countenance.

"You really mean it?"

"Bailey, we have our studies in various homes. Once when Tonia Sue broke her ankle and couldn't get out, we went to her house every Tuesday. It would be no inconvenience to come to your apartment."

"I'm on the top floor, and there isn't an elevator."

Stella grinned. "All of us could use the exercise, especially me. It's so cold out that I haven't been doing any walks around the block."

Joy zipped down Bailey's spine. "I'd love to have company. Let's do it. What about Tuesday morning at what time?"

"Ninish?"

"I'll definitely be waiting for you."

Tuesday morning Bailey set out glasses on the kitchen table with fresh cookies. Then she paced the floor of both rooms, not knowing what to expect.

The doorbell rang. "Come in and make yourselves at home." Tonia Sue, Ma'am Kuhn, and Stella chose the settee that Bailey had arranged to face her four kitchen chairs. Another three were rapidly introduced and seated.

"Your place is very open and fresh," said Tonia Sue. "I've been in the apartments before, but I've never seen a place so attractive. You have the gift of decorating." The three women sat elbow-to-elbow on the settee, trying to balance their Bibles, devotional books, and prayer lists.

A pleased Bailey beamed at the group and thought about the next time. She'd have more chairs and a bigger table. With the Matron's help she would purchase a set, and the store would deliver.

Stella as leader of the group had another idea. "We have a jail ministry every Tuesday after our Bible study and prayer time. I know that you have spent time in prison and found the Lord there. Would you be interested in joining us and giving your testimony?" She turned to the other ladies. "We feel that you would know how to talk to the women since you have experienced what they are experiencing."

"I am under house arrest." Bailey felt no embarrassment this time, but the inconvenience of constraint chaffed.

"But there are times you are permitted to go shopping or come to church, right?"

"I must notify my probation officer so that she knows exactly where I am."

The women nodded.

"I'm not a runaway, but there is a reason." She bit her lip wondering how to tell them about Clark and yet not mention Clark at all. She cleared her throat. "I am in possible danger unless accompanied by police or in their custody." She decided not to tell them about his kidnapping attempts.

Their eyes riveted upon her, and the silent observation bothered Bailey.

She rose. "Would you like something to drink and a cookie? I baked early this morning."

"You must be an early riser." "I could smell those cookies the minute I stepped in the hall." Tonia Sue's compliment broke the spell, and the tension drifted away.

Chapter 15: Thanksgiving

Matron Macintyre showed pleasure in Bailey's attending the Bible study, but her brow wrinkled at the thought of the jail ministry. "It can be done, but there are so many security measures. If you do go, I would have to request that I be present, at least the first couple of times." She chuckled. "Bailey, I don't know what you are going to try next."

"What do you mean?"

The Matron's head tilted. "You are not in the category of the normal parolee."

Bailey looked out of the big window, wishing she could enjoy the snow first hand. If she had Bennie, she would have to take him out for his little walk. “The rules have changed. Dogs are not allowed in the apartments.”

The Matron showed surprise. “When did this happen?”

“I don’t know; however, I have enough money to purchase my own property, and there’s a place across town in a cul de sac. I’ve seen the picture on line. I’d like to move.”

Matron Macintyre turned from the window to look at Bailey. “How does Dave feel about this?”

Bailey hung her head. “He wants to get married so I would move into his house, but his asthma won’t allow pets.” She stamped her foot. “Teddy said that Bennie is pining away. I can’t allow him to die. I need him.”

“I don’t think Bennie is in danger. However, Clark is still on the loose. If you start walking a dog down these stairs and outside every morning and night, I can’t guarantee your safety.” She touched Bailey’s shoulder. “It won’t be long now, and you’ll be really free from all restraints. Trust me. Things are moving in your favor.”

Bailey wasn’t sure if she could believe her friend.

“You need to see James more often, too. I’ve been talking with the social worker who is in contact with Serine. Now that he knows who you are, James is becoming problematic. We need to act before something is done that we’ll regret later.”

“But Clark is the problem.”

“If you and Dave would marry, I think we could get around Clark. He has no real interest in the boy. What I mean is that we could have his parental rights terminated. Serine is dragging her feet because you have only seen James once. If you are really interested, she thinks you should be more involved in his life."

"How can I?" Bailey reached down and tugged on the ankle bracelet. "This is worse than being in prison."

The Matron glanced around the room. "I know a lot of prisoners and parolees who would love to trade places with you."

Bailey swallowed the lump that had been forming in her throat. "You're right, but I need help. I can't do this alone."

"You're developing a small case of the jailhouse jitters, but you're doing fine." The Matron went to the door, her visit essentially over. "But we must be sure of your safety. Talk to Dave, but don't purchase that house." Again she glanced around the apartment. "You're very safe here. Clark has ventured into the shadows. If this were the big city, I'd say we lost him, but Lakeside is too small for even a cat to hide very long."

"He knows where I am. He's biding his time."

"Let's show him two can play that game. Stay safe." The Matron stepped out, shutting the door behind her. "Slide that dead bolt, Bailey."

The days seemed long, but Bailey put her time and energy into writing. Long hours at the computer began to pay bigger checks. She should have been satisfied and thankful, but Thanksgiving was just a week away, and her dream contained James.

"Matron Macintyre, is there any reason I can't keep James over the holiday? I have a place for him to sleep."

"Where?" The Matron's question came almost sharply.

"Why, I'd give him my bed and the bedroom. I could sleep

on the settee." She watched the matron's face closely. "It would only be for three nights."

"Let's talk to the social worker and make some arrangement with Serine." When she returned, she seemed extremely brisk. "Serine wants him for Thanksgiving, but she would not be averse to his staying with you on Friday while she goes shopping. The social worker agreed. You haven't really known him for over five years. An overnight would be stretching your relationship as you have never worked with children."

The idea that they thought she couldn't handle her own son nettled Bailey.

Matron Macintyre waited until their eyes connected. "Bailey, my husband and I would like to invite you to our house for Thanksgiving."

Surprised, Bailey studied the matron's expression. "You would invite me to your house?"

"Would you like to come?"

"Yes."

"Well, I have never taken any other parolee home with me. Unless Dave has other plans, we'd like to invite him along with you."

"I'll ask and let you know."

However, Thanksgiving Day seemed unimportant compared to the coming of James' visitation. Bailey triumphantly began to plan. She would show them that she was a real mother. She cleaned her apartment from corner to corner. She baked cookies. The Matron took her shopping for some toys and video games that would work on her computer. Dave entered the preparation with his own ideas.

"Transformers." He grinned.

"What?"

"Remember all those moveable plastic toys that could be changed from a plane or vehicle to a person?"

"I was never aware of anything like that." She turned away. To admit her deficit childhood always made her vulnerable, but she remembered a children's advertisement she had seen on TV at the halfway house. Inside her kitchen cabinet rested tubs of Pla-Doh and all the plastic tools that could mold it.

Thanksgiving morning Dave arrived in a rental car to take her to Matron Macintyre's home. "Have you ever been there?"

"No." Bailey remembered her grandmother preparing tons of dressing and baking turkey after turkey for the customers at the bar. The day had never been one of celebration. Rather she worked from dawn and into the evening serving and cleaning tables. There were never any accolades for the labor, but the minutest mistake would bring her grandfather's criticism and her mother's wrath. Her body trembled.

"Bailey, what's wrong?"

She forced a smile. "Nothing." Outside the snow had gone leaving bare brown branches and earth as glum as her memories. She pulled her coat closer.

"You're cold. I'll turn up the heat."

The simple action, his concern, and the love that prompted

his notice of her comfort began to warm her heart. Dave was so different from the members of her family. She relaxed and the smile became genuine as was the song on the radio that began to soften her heart.

As Dave drove, he fiddled with knobs and push buttons on the instrument panel. "Bailey, when we get you a car, let's make sure that it has this gas mileage indicator on it."

"I don't think I'll purchase a new model."

"But we'll find a nice used one that has options like this one." He showed her how the seat would heat at the push of a triangular button on the door arm. They played with the seat adjuster and the movable steering wheel. Bailey reached across him and twisted the turning signal handle. The window wipers swished across the windshield.

"Why did you do that?"

She laughed. "Because I knew what would happen if I pushed that button. I'm afraid that if I touch anything else, I'll eject like Batman."

"That's an old movie."

"I know, but I used to watch it on TV at the bar after I mopped the floor." Suddenly her laughter stopped. Grandfather had not known of her simple act of defiance. The TV was for customer use only, but she turned out the lights and the volume down low because he had already gone to bed with her mother and grandmother.

"Bailey?" Dave's eyes showed concern. "What's the matter?"

"Oh, nothing." She tried to laugh, but it failed.

They turned a corner, and Dave brought the car up to the sidewalk. Stan Macintyre met them at the door, ushered them inside, and took their coats. His head, a bald ball, had tufts of grizzled grey hair behind his ears. The wire rim glasses perched on his nose almost hid a hint of mischief and wisdom.

“Mary’s in the kitchen cooking up a storm. Why don’t you make yourselves at home? The Pasadena parade is on television in the den.” While Stan hung their garments in the closet, Dave led Bailey through into a warm room with an artificial fireplace. She sank into soft bliss of the thick, deep couch with Dave’s arm drawing her close.

“We don’t have many visitors.” Stan settled and leaned back in his chair before the TV. Heavy drapes hung on the walls behind the couch, and a small spinet organ nestled in the corner behind them. “I hear you two just might be getting married.”

A startled Bailey glanced over at Dave whose smile showed every white tooth. He nodded. “Quite soon, right, Bailey?”

“The meal is ready.” Matron Macintyre whisked off her apron to reveal a colorful print dress. They moved into a dining room with a table set for four. Within reach was a side table loaded with the Thanksgiving Day spread. “Stan and I are delighted that you could come. Our family lives half across the nation and couldn’t make it home for the holiday.” Her gaze rested on Bailey. “I want you to call me Mary today. Otherwise, I’ll think I’m on the job.” Her laughter tinkled with theirs. “Now let’s say grace and eat before the food gets cold.”

Stan carved the turkey while Dave helped Mary serve each of the four plates with generous helpings of dressing, green beans, mashed potatoes, and turkey gravy. They began to eat.

“Do you think Bailey could come with me to the homeless

shelter tonight?" Dave reached for another serving of turkey. "Our church always serves, and I volunteered, but I know another pair of hands is always appreciated."

Stan winked. "Especially if they're your girlfriend's, right?"

"I don't see any problem with it." Mary offered him some more potatoes. "I just need to know where she is at all times, and I trust you'll get her home early and safely."

Bailey and Dave helped to clear the table, but the couple wouldn't agree to their washing any dishes. "You go and feed those unfortunate people." Stan winked at Bailey. "I think you'll get your full share of washing dishes and then some."

"I'm getting her in practice for when we get married." Dave handed the towel to Stan and guided her out to the car. "They are such wonderful people."

"The best." Bailey waved at the couple standing behind the glass of their living room window. "I was so fortunate to get her for my probation officer. I would never have made it without her."

She watched afternoon sun hide behind a row of grey clouds. Branches of leafless trees swayed in the wind like the flowing hands of Hawaiian dancers.

"Do you think we'll get more snow?"

"It's predicted." She delighted in the white stuff. "Inside the jail we couldn't tell if it were summer or winter."

The workers welcomed Bailey with good cheer. Teddy's mother found a bibbed apron for both of them, stretched the net over Bailey's hair, made them wash their hands, and helped them slip on the latex gloves.

"You're not allergic, are you?"

"No."

"You can serve peas with one hand and mashed potatoes with the other."

Bailey stared at the long line of men gathering and silently waiting to be served. Their patience and lowly demeanor reminded her of the prisoner lines. At least they didn't wear the orange garb or zebra stripes. Other women positioned behind the table also held a large spoon in each hand. Beside her Dave picked up metal tongs to handle the turkey pieces and a ladle for gravy. Pastor Brown said grace, and the line moved forward. Behind her, Tonia Sue watched and replenished the pans of rapidly disappearing food. Teddy filled paper cups with coffee, tea, or punch. Bailey could feel the perspiration dripping from her chin.

"Hello, Bailey."

She looked from the food platter where she was putting in a half spoon of peas in the corner and mashed potatoes beside it. Clark's small ferret eyes watched her. His thin lips smirked, waiting for his tray.

"You didn't plan on seeing me again, did you? Well, you can't get rid of me that easily." He glanced around the room behind him. "How about taking a little recess and coming over to keep me company while I eat?"

"Leave her alone." Dave's gruff voice cut like a machete.

The spoons trembled in Bailey's hands.

"I was talking to Bailey."

"Move on." Dave shoved a piece of turkey on the tray and

emptied the ladle of gravy over the potatoes and meat. “She’s busy.”

“I need more potatoes.” Clark shoved his tray back into Bailey’s area. She added another spoonful. “I said more.”

Reverend Brown appeared at Clark’s elbow. “If you need more, you can return for seconds.”

Clark pulled the tray back and moved on down the line.

Tonia Sue came up behind Bailey. “Your shift just ended. It’s time for Dave to take you home.”

“Thanks.”

The cold gale struck with millions of icy needles. Dave helped her into the car, and they began to pull out of the parking lot. Thudding blows to her window made Bailey look upwards.

“I know where you live.” Clark stepped back.

Dave accelerated. “That guy never gives up.”

“I don’t know why. I’ve never encouraged him from the beginning.”

“You were nice to him--once.”

“That was a long time ago, and you know why and how he rewarded it.” She looked into Dave’s eyes. “Am I always going to be running from him?”

“I don’t think so, but we have to be very careful. We never know what a twisted mind will do next.” He drove up to the front door of the apartment building. “Bailey, get into your apartment quick. I’m going to park the car.”

She raced up the stairs, opened her door, and closed it. Leaning against the inside, she waited for Dave, her breath coming in fast and hard rasps. She heard rapid steps on the stairs that continued to her door. Before he could ring the bell she opened it.

Clark's grinning possum face leered at her. "Aren't you going to invite me in?"

"No!" She tried to shut the door, but his strength overpowered her.

"Clark, let me go!"

He twisted her arm behind her back. Pain shot from her wrist, to her elbow, and up to her shoulder. "Move."

"Clark, let me go!" She couldn't scream. His arm clamped around her diaphragm until she could hardly breathe. "You're a fool. Let me go."

"We have things to discuss." He pushed her forward. "Now down those stairs."

She went limp, but he continued down. "Clark, I warn you."

Suddenly he swung her against the wall. Everything turned black.

Chapter 15: Abduction

She awoke. Her head ballooned into the size of the universe, and she couldn't count the stars. Something like feathers touched her face as she pulled herself up from the carpeted floor. Her hands reached upward to prevent the tickling sensation, and felt the thin cotton material of shirts. Her mind cleared. She was in a closet. Slowly she rose, and clothes hangers tinkled around her head. She groped for the door knob and twisted. It held hard—locked. In one corner she found a couple of stacked suitcases. Inside was a flashlight. Heavy like a cop's night stick and almost as stout, she turned on the switch. The dim beam showed her Clark hadn't unpacked, or he had plans. Quickly she shut off the light to conserve the battery.

Her fingers squeezed the flashlight like it was his neck. The ferret! What did he think he'd gain? She waited, sitting on the top of the suitcase. When the door opened, she'd launch conk him as hard as she could. Her eyes became accustomed to the darkness. The overhead hangers could also be a weapon. If she dumped the shirts on the floor, she could attack like Captain Hook. A click and a crack of light under the door warned her. She heard him slam a door and the steps approach across thin carpet. She drew herself flat against the wall and waited as he fumbled with the knob. As the door opened, she could smell the alcohol. He was drunk. With one downward motion she whopped him behind the ears. He fell like a tree face forward.

Bailey ripped a sleeve out of a shirt and shoved it in his mouth. Then using the rest of it she bound his face. She tied a shirt around his wrists, another around his elbows, another around his knees, and the last one around his ankles. "It's a shame you don't have any more clothes." Then she twisted an unwound clothes hanger around his wrists and another around his ankles. "That ought to hold you awhile." He was too heavy for her to push into the closet, but thankfully he didn't move. She fled out the door and into the hallway of the apartments.

At the stairs she started down. Dizziness made her grab the handrail. Her body swayed. She felt herself losing consciousness and crumpling.

"Can I help you, ma'am?" A child's broad nose with a lined

brow and brown cheeks touched her face.

Bailey slowly pulled herself up by holding the railing. “I was dizzy. I must have fallen.”

“You don’t fall. I saw you sag like a balloon losing air.” The girl’s multiple pig tails flopped as she nodded vigorously. The beads woven into each braid glittered in the light and hit another with a tiny chink. “I’ll help you up. Where do yous live?”

“Top floor.”

“But yous was going down.”

“I changed my mind.” Each step took all the strength Bailey possessed. Her door was ajar, and she made it to the settee. She looked up at the child. “Dial 911, please?”

Before her new friend could touch the phone, Matron Macintyre entered. “Bailey, why did you cut off your ankle bracelet?” She turned to look at Dave who came in behind her. “What does this mean?”

Bailey shook her head.

“What happened Bailey?” Dave held her other hand. “I came up the stairs. You were gone. The door was wide open.”

“Clark.” Her throat could barely allow the word to escape.

“Clark!”

Matron Macintyre entered the room. “You shouldn’t have gone to the shelter. He followed you back. Where is he now?”

“The second floor of the apartments. I hit him with a flashlight and tied him up.” Her eyes met those of the Matron. “I was foolish when I opened the door. I didn’t think there was any danger."

"How did he get past me? I was coming up the stairs." Dave paced the apartment in front of her window.

"I'm sorry. It all happened so fast." Her tears came without warning. Bailey didn't want to talk about it. They left.

The next morning she kept the curtain pulled back against the wall to watch for James. Outside the large picture window more snow filtered down. The large flakes reminded her of feathers, floating like dandelion seeds or tiny parachutes.

She arranged the toys on the table, and found a plate on which to arrange the cookies. As she finished, the phone rang.

"Hi, Honey, how do you feel?" Dave chatted for a few moments.

"I'm fine. Did they apprehend Clark?"

"I haven't heard."

As she hung up the phone, Matron Macintyre arrived. "Bailey, a child has energy and needs attention. You aren't up to it, yet." She wandered to the window and looked out over the white, white world. Then she turned and squared her shoulders. "Bailey, listen to me. This is for your good. I've been thinking that it would be great for you to get married, but!"

"But what?"

"James." The woman turned and stared out the window again. "You and James need to live together, get to know each other again, before you marry. You were right when you said this place was no good for a child, and I believe you need Bennie, too."

"So what am I going to do?" Bailey was sitting up and

waiting.

"I think we are going to find you a house or an apartment to rent."

"But we looked and looked." Bailey threw her hands up in despair. "There's nothing out there. Nothing!"

"You said you had found a house."

"I called, and it's no longer available."

"Well, we'll just have to find something else." The Matron pulled a chair close to the settee. "I've been praying about this and also talking to Stan. We didn't have children of our own. We adopted a couple the age of James. Getting to know each other takes time. It's not impossible, but there's stress."

Bailey reached for a tissue.

"Your situation is different now from the first time you went house hunting. You have a good recommendation, and I'm not going to put another ankle bracelet on you." The matron smiled. "It's time to let you go."

"What about Clark?" Bailey couldn't suppress the fear that had crawled into her belly. She clutched her arms above the elbows and pressed her forearms hard against her abdomen. It didn't help much.

"We'll get him, and you'll have Bennie."

When Bailey tried to explain it to Dave, he couldn't understand the Matron's attitude. "She says I need to live with James and get to know him first. She says marriage is adjusting to another person, too. She says it would be easier on you and me if we do this in stages and not all at once."

"And she's taking off your protection." Dave stomped around the room. "You'll get hurt. I can't allow that."

Bailey nodded. The plan to marry and move in with Dave seemed so simple. Then she could sever Clark's rights easily. Dave would make a wonderful father. "And, Dave, I can have Bennie, too."

Dave whirled. "What about me? You get your son. You get your dog. Don't you want me?"

"Yes, Dave, I want you very, very much, but I also want our marriage to be beautiful and holy. Matron Macintyre said a child makes a strain on a marriage, and I don't want ours to fail." She watched him stop. His face held disbelief and anger. He had been so strong through all the frustration of the situation—and patient, but now she saw the hurt. "Dave, come here. Don't be distant with me."

"I can't believe you. You are cold, then hot, and then cold again. Bailey, what am I to believe?"

"That I love you with all of my heart."

"No, your heart is divided. You want James. You want the dog. You throw me the leftovers." His head bowed. "Oh, Bailey, I love you so. Can't you love me that much, too?" He dropped to the couch beside her.

"I do love you. I love you so much that I'm willing to wait." She swallowed trying not to cry. Her arms circled his shoulders and drew his head to her bosom. "Dave, I care so much for you. You are the finest man in the world. Please, please understand."

The narrow settee hardly held one prone person, but Dave and Bailey managed not to fall to the floor. He lay beside her and held her tightly, and her arms wound about him. “Oh, Honey, I wish we could fly to Las Vegas and just get married.” His face grew serious. “Bailey, I can hardly wait.”

After he left, the doorbell rang.

Chapter 17: James

James’ eyes strayed from his foster mother to the transformer toy on the table beside the Pla-Doh. “Yes, Serine.” His body twisted.

“Hold still. This one button is stubborn.” Serine pulled him back to her. “You know the rules.”

“Yes, Serine.” His head swiveled to the toys. “Now can I play?”

The woman let him go, but her hands trembled as she faced Bailey. “Don’t let anything happen to him, understand?” The unspoken threat did not escape either of them. Serine walked around the front room to stop at the big window. “It’s better than I thought.”

Bailey knew exactly what she had thought and grinned inwardly. “I thought you were going to leave him so you could go shopping.”

Serine whirled. “Oh, I changed my mind. I’ll do the shopping later.” She glanced at her wrist watch. “We’ve plenty of time before Christmas.”

“Well, make yourself at home. Would you like a cup of coffee, tea, or a soda?” Bailey stared at Serine’s eyes. They were green like hers and James. She wanted to talk to the woman about them, but James stood at her elbow.

“I’m just a little nervous about leaving him with a

stranger."

The barb hurt, but Bailey managed a smile. "He is safe with me. I'm his mother." Bailey opened her computer to a popular game.

James settled down in the chair. His fingers were already sending his race car around the track. Without raising his eyes, he asked, "Do you have pop?"

"Now, James, I'm not going to allow her to load you down on sugar." Serine stared meaningfully at Bailey before she stirred two packets of sweetener into her orange pekoe tea.

Bailey opened the refrigerator door. "I have diet root beer." Again she studied Serine's face, but Serine had frown lines above her eyes. The woman's fingers nervously rubbed the napkin like it was fabric being considered for purchase.

As Serine sipped her tea, Bailey opened up the Pla-Doh kit. James had already scooted off the chair before the computer and picked up the transformer to lay it aside to show Bailey how to make the dough press squeeze out layers and strings of colored dough. The two of them tried out every cookie cutter before James tired of it and went back to the transformer toy that roared into the living room and across the back of the settee. It flew to the window sill and rolled along the edge before coming back into the kitchen. Bailey boxed up the Pla-Doh. "James, would you like to play another game on the computer?"

"Yeah!" He was beside her immediately. "What games do you have?"

Serine stood. "We do have to go. It's Sunday tomorrow and my husband and I go to early mass."

"Mass?" Bailey stepped back from the table. Once again she

remembered the stained glass windows, the coolness of the church, the empty pews, and the priest. "You are Catholic?"

"Yes, we go to church." Her chin rose in defiance. "I'm proud to have been a Catholic all my life." She faced Bailey. "There's nothing wrong with going to church. It just might help you." Serine slid her arms into the brown trench coat. "James, put your coat on."

"We were going to play a game." He looked from Serine to Bailey.

Serine won. "Next time. Here's your hat and one glove. What did you do with the other one?"

Bailey found it and laid it on the Pla-Doh. "I hope you had a good time."

"Can I come back?" The little face pleaded as James tugged her shirt tail. "Then we can play the video games."

"Yes." She smiled and knelt down to his level.

"And stay forever?" His arms had wrapped around Bailey. "I love you, mother."

"I love you, too."

"James, we have to go."

Bailey handed him the transformer and the Pla-Doh. "Here, this is yours."

"Leave that Pla-Doh." Serine took the box from his hands and laid it back on the table. "You'll need something to play with *if* you come again." Before Bailey shut the door, she heard Serine say, "Pla-Doh is so messy, don't you think?"

James' vocal cords zoomed the transformer down the stairs.

"Why doesn't Clark leave me alone?" Bailey had thought about the question for so long that it popped out of her mouth.

Matron Macintyre maneuvered around a corner and pulled into the parking lot of the real estate office. "I don't really know, but this quote from the Russian novelist Fyodor Dostoevsky was drilled into us during officer training, 'Nothing is easier than to denounce the evildoer; nothing is more difficult than to understand him.' Now what do you think?" She stared into Bailey's eyes. Slowly her mouth curved into a broad smile. "I think it could be that the man was never shown any kindness until you served him in your grandfather's bar. Kindness produces strong cords."

"But I didn't want to be kind. I just did what grandfather made me do."

"Clark doesn't understand that. We don't know his background, but we know that you're a pretty girl and kind. Deviant mindsets follow different paths than the normal. There are men who become very obsessive with their girl friends or wives. Clark may have this wanton behavior. He has been able to stay out of jail for the most part, but that doesn't mean he is a stable part of society."

"Why did he rape me?"

"He was drunk. His inhibitions if he has any were gone."

"Why did he stick me in the closet?"

"Probably in his desire to control you, he was going to force you to be with him."

Bailey shuddered.

"Let's find you a home that will be safe." Matron Macintyre had already opened her side of the car.

"Here are your choices." The real estate agent spread pictures out on the desk for viewing. "This bungalow can be rented with the option to purchase. I have a salt box over on Riverside Avenue for sale, but it's a fixer-upper. The owner died and the heirs wish to sell it quickly. I can show it to you for a reasonable price."

The Matron looked at her watch. "We have time to see one."

Bailey's curiosity chose the salt box. She wanted to know how much fixing it would need to be livable. Riverside Avenue followed the river. The branches of age old trees curved over the vehicles, giving her an enchanted feeling of fairies and castles, but a sad little house sat on a bluff above the water. "It would make a wonderful summer cottage." His boots crunched through frozen snow to the front, as the real estate agent made the first tracks on the sidewalk. The flooring of the porch creaked and bowed under their weight.

Bailey turned to view the yard as she waited for him to unlock the door that overgrown bushes hid from the street. They stepped across the threshold, and the musty smell reminded her of stepping into her mother's house. The rooms contained the same sad appearance of torn upholstery, litter, and needed repair.

The man led them through the trash in an apologetic manner. "I'm sorry. I hadn't been inside. They told me it would require cleaning, but I had no idea."

Matron Macintyre turned to leave. Bailey followed her. In the car she said, "That isn't a good place for a child. The river is too close. They want too much money." She took Bailey back to the apartment. "Keep your door locked. Clark is still on the loose."

Inside Bailey opened up her pictures taken during James' visit and developed at the pharmacy. She scattered them over the table: James flying the transformer, James and the Pla-Doh, James sipping his root beer. The prints brought him back into the apartment. She chose her favorites and propped them up around the computer. Then she began to search the internet for the right place to live, glancing often to remind herself of her motherhood and her goals.

Dave came, and they took a drive out Riverside Drive so she could show him the salt box. "What a dump." He ushered her back to the car. "Bailey, I forbid you to live in anything like that." He turned the car toward his own home. "I have a surprise for you." He pulled into the driveway. Then he came around to help her out of the car. "Look across the street."

A real estate For Sale sign decorated the snowy yard.

"My neighbor went to Florida with her daughter for the winter. She fell and broke her hip. The daughter decided she wanted her mother to stay with her and to sell this place." He took both of Bailey's hands in his. "Do you want to buy?"

"Oh, Dave, it's perfect." She moved close for a hug and kiss. "I'll buy a pair of binoculars and check you out every morning and evening."

He laughed. "I just might buy a pair of my own."

Bailey enlisted Dave and Teddy to help her move the week before Christmas. After they delivered her furniture and boxes in the new house they went to Cindy's Cup to eat.

"You never had that much stuff before." Teddy bit into his hamburger.

"I didn't realize how much could accumulate in such a short time." She leaned across the table. "Say, can I have Bennie back?"

"Yes, he's been missing you."

"We'll get the dog when we drop Teddy off." Dave stirred a French fry in catsup. "Bailey, you're going to need a car. Mine will be back sometime this next week. I've been thinking it would be wise to buy this loaner that I've been using." He popped the fry in his mouth and swallowed. "You like it, don't you?"

"Well, I guess so." Bailey did some fast calculating. "If I don't have enough to purchase it, I could buy it on time."

He nodded. "We'll talk about it later. What do you say we go Christmas shopping?"

"And spend more money!" Bailey laughed. "Let's get a tree and the trimmings. James is coming this evening for a few hours. He could help decorate."

"You know I'm not too good at it."

"That's why I'm getting help." They had pulled the Scot pine out of the box and assembled the parts so that it resembled a tree when the door bell rang. Bennie ran to the door barking.

"A dog!" James wrapped his arms around the black and white terrier. "Is it yours?"

Bailey nodded. "Bennie is ours."

"We can keep him?"

"We are keeping him."

The boy and dog ran into the other room, but Serine stood at the door.

"So you're actually going to take James away from me." Serine's temper blazed.

"I'm not taking him away. He's already mine."

"How can you say that? I've had him longer." Tears ran down Serine's square chin while her thick fingers intensely clutched her gloves. "My husband and I love this boy. We wanted to adopt him the minute he came into our home, but you wouldn't sign the papers. Now you are jerking him back." She wiped the tears away with a tissue pulled from the pocket of the tan trench coat. Then she glared at Bailey and stepped menacingly closer. "What's going to happen to him if you discover you really don't want him?"

Bailey stood her ground. "I've always wanted him. I didn't have an abortion, because I wanted him, Serine. I went to prison because I needed money to raise him properly and chose the wrong way to get it."

"So what are you going to do if you run out of money?" Serine's lips pursed which made the square jaw jut out like a bull dog's. "Steal or deal drugs?"

"I don't do drugs, and I am not a thief."

Serine left James in a whirlwind of anxiety. "If you have any problems, here's my cell phone number." She knelt before the little boy and removed his coat. "Now, be nice. She's your mother. I'll be back later this afternoon. Understand?" Serine whipped around and stomped out the door.

Bailey could hear her car roar from the driveway and careen around the corner. What could she do? James was hers and hers alone. She remembered the passage in the Bible where the two women brought a baby before Solomon. The mother had wanted what was best for the child even if it meant she didn't get to keep the boy or raise him. Bailey's eyes rose upward. "God, I need a Solomon to tell me what is best for James."

Matron Macintyre had devoted several sessions to talk about James, and Bailey thought they searched out every angle concerning the boy. But neither one brought up the subject of Serine, the foster mother, unwilling to give up James. Bailey turned to see her son racing into the room.

"Dave says to come quick. He needs both of us to get the star on the top."

Bailey allowed the scene with Serine to fade into the background of her mind for the vivid present. Dave wavered on top of a stepladder with tinsel rope coiled around his neck and lying in layers on his shoulders. He held the star in one hand and reached for the top of the tree with the other. Everything seemed to be swaying. Bailey grabbed his legs just in time.

Before the three finished, Serine came for James.

"I don't want to go home." He clutched Bennie around the neck.

Bailey knelt down to look him in the face and button his coat. "James, this will be your home. Bennie is your dog as much as mine, but we have to go through the legal system."

"The courts?"

"Yes, it won't be long. I love you."

Dave came up behind her as she watched the car roll down the driveway, and the red tail lights fade down the street. "Honey, come over to my house for some hot cider."

They locked the house and walked across the street. Before she entered, Bailey looked back at the blinking tree lights. "It's wonderful, Dave. God has been so good to me."

"And me. Come. It's cold out here." He served the instant hot cider in heavy mugs in the living room. After setting them on the end table, he settled down beside her on the sofa. "We never did finish that movie." His arm came around her. "Actually I don't feel a need for it." The kiss began slowly, but it deepened, and Bailey could feel her heart pounding harder and harder.

She pulled away.

"Um." Dave reached for her again. "That was just a starter."

"Dave?"

He straightened. "I wish we'd gotten married instead of moving you into that house." Then he smiled. "But it has its good points." He reached under the sofa and pulled out two pairs of binoculars. "One for you, and one for me."

She laughed. "I didn't think you'd really do it."

He set them aside. "We do have to talk. My folks have invited us for Christmas and want to meet you. I am off from Christmas Eve to January 2. Do you think you could come?"

Chapter 18: Visiting Jail

Bailey sat on the sofa of the parsonage living room. Stella set a cup of coffee and cookies in front of her on a napkin.

"Now back to this Christmas party." Stella settled herself in a chair close to the small coffee table and picked up her cup. "We have to be careful about how and what we do."

"Have you contacted the jail?" Tonia Sue reached for a cookie.

"Yes, the ladies can receive gifts, but it has to be soft stuff like socks and such."

"That doesn't sound like much of a gift."

"But we can give Christian literature, home baked cookies, and candy. The warden said not to get extravagant or leave anyone out. What do you think, Bailey?"

Bailey stirred sugar into her coffee. "I've never done anything like this before."

"But you were in jail. What would you have wanted for Christmas?"

"To get out." The others chuckled, but Bailey's face didn't loose its serious tone. "Holidays were only celebrated on TV or with meals. I would have given so much to get a letter from my family, a picture of James, or a phone call." By now she couldn't hold back the tears. "Most of us didn't even get a visit from someone we knew outside the walls." She swallowed back her emotion. "I'm sorry. I didn't mean to unload." She dabbed her face with the napkin. "I think you are doing something marvelous, but no one ever did anything like this for me or the ones around me. It was like I had been buried in a living tomb away from society."

Stella wiped her face with her napkin. She heaved out a huge breath and stiffened her spine. "Okay, let's write personal letters to each and every inmate. We can put them in Christmas cards. Then we can put a pair of socks, a bar of special soap, and some wrapped candy or cookies."

"Both," said Tonia Sue dabbing her eyes. "I'll make several kinds that can be wrapped individually."

"Let's bake and wrap them together." Stella's excitement bubbled. "We can get together at my house."

"Bailey, I can't make it to go with you to the jail." Matron Macintyre heaved a sigh. "I have a new batch in the half-way house, and I can't leave them. Do you think you can handle this alone?"

"I won't be alone. Stella and Tonia Sue will be there. Besides the guards will be around, too."

"Well, watch out for Rosenbaum. She's blaming you for being back in jail."

Bailey winced. Rosenbaum wasn't someone to joke about.

Bailey carried a box as she entered the jail. Rosenbaum's hard face leered through the glass. Stella and Tonia Sue dropped their boxes on a cart. A jailor began to poke through their gifts."No ribbon." His hands tugged at the pretty strings and tore off the decorated paper. "I'll get a trash bag."

As they waited for him, Stella, Bailey, and Tonia Sue began to remove the gifts from the boxes onto the stuffed chairs in the foyer. By the time the jailer returned with the garbage bag, the gifts were out in plain view. Quickly the three women shoved the holiday ribbon and gay paper into the black sack and left it in the foyer to pick up on their way out. Bailey looked up. Rosenbaum's hard face wore expectancy and the trace of a smile.

"You may enter." The jailer punched the code buttons of a small square box fixed to the frame.

As the heavy metal slid open, Bailey's heart began to pound. He stood to one side of the opening, and she stumbled inside. Vainly she tried to force one foot ahead of the other, but she stood inside a short, secure hall, and the screeching steel closed with a clank. Cold tremors crawled down Bailey's spine. Her arms broke out in goose bumps under her heavy sweater. Her legs buckled, and she felt herself sliding down a hill into the deepest black pit.

"Bailey, wake up!"

A thick fog glazed her sight, and Bailey saw the human forms above her like enormous animals pawing her body. She screamed. "Don't kill me. I won't tell!" Her flailing arms pushed them away. She felt the cold concrete beneath her palms and sank back on the icy floor. She heard the man's voice.

"We'll have to get her out of here."

The screech of the sliding door made Bailey open her eyes. "What happened?"

"You fainted." Stella reached down and helped her get to her feet. Then Bailey leaned on her for support and came back out into the foyer. She set Bailey in one of the stuffed chairs. "Are you going to be okay?"

"I think so."

"Tonia Sue and I will go back with the jailer to distribute the gifts and hold a Bible study. Will you be all right out here?"

"Yes." Bailey watched them disappear in the short hall way. That one day Matron Macintyre had brought her into the jail to take a shower, Rosenbaum had threatened her, but the woman's presence assured her every step of the way. She looked through the wide windows. They were entering the next locked hallway that connected the cell blocks. The jailer opened the women's area. She saw the women collect around them and receive their gifts. Rosenbaum ripped hers open. She forced her fists into each sock and turned in rage to pommel the glass.

"Where's my sugar? You forgot my sugar!"

Quickly a second guard ushered Stella and Tonia Sue out of the room, pushing the cart with the rest of the presents through the open door. The door locked behind them, but the jailer and guard grabbed Rosenbaum's arms and forced her into an individual cell. The prisoner continued to rage about "sugar." After she was locked inside, the other inmates were ordered to their cells. Then the jailer and guard came out to Stella and Tonia Sue.

The four disappeared around a corner, but Bailey could hear the muffled ranting from Rosenbaum.

Bailey closed her eyes and saw the dead body of her cell mate. Rosenbaum dragged the body out into the foyer where everyone had disappeared. The hard face had appeared once again in Bailey's cell.

"You don't know what happened, hear me?" Coarse hands had gripped her shoulders. "Listen." Shaken like a rag doll, Bailey sagged to the cell cot. "You rat, and you're dead."

The sound of the scraping metal door startled Bailey, but Stella and Tonia Sue emerged with the jailer. "We have to leave the gifts for the guards to distribute." Stella reached Bailey first. "Are you all right?"

"Yes, I don't know what happened to me."

"You fainted. We didn't realize how emotional it would be for you."

That night Bailey's dreams held the sneering, triumphant face of Rosenbaum. Her feet and hands were so cold that she rose from her bed and turned up the thermostat. A glance out the frost crusted window didn't tell her more than her ears had already heard. A howling northerner bent the trees on the edge of Dave's sidewalk to a bowing position. A plastic grocery sack swept down the street and blew out of sight like a balloon shaped bird seeking refuge. Shivering, Bailey returned to her bed to close her eyes and heard the evil woman's voice. "You rat, and you're dead." The lifeless form of the Christian girl who had prayed her through to Jesus lay on the cold, cement floor.

She awoke, feeling sick, but she didn't have any desire to go back to bed. The temperature had risen, but she couldn't shake off the feel of a chill. Even little Bennie shivered and curled up over a furnace vent in the living room. First she donned every long sleeved sweater in the closet, her wool pants, and her coat. Then she sat in front of her computer in her boots, stocking cap, and cheap, stretchy gloves advertised to fit every size. Her head ached like the sinus pockets were rammed with cotton, and she began to cough.

The gloves made her typing clumsy, but she e-mailed Dave. "Don't come today. I have a cold."

His reply came quickly. "Go to bed. Drink lots of water and juice. Do you have plenty of juice? I'll drop by with some over-the-counter stuff."

She didn't want him to see her like this. She rose from the chair and wandered past the Christmas tree for a hot shower. The steam opened up her head and warmed her body. She let the hair drier run over her hair and face. The heat felt heavenly. She didn't want to leave the small space of the bathroom with the sauna atmosphere, but her doorbell was ringing. Bennie ran from the door to the bathroom yapping.

Dave came and brought the frozen north wind into the room. The blast hit her and made her a shaking leaf. His arms came around her body, but the outside temperature of his coat and gloves was below zero. She pulled away, backing half way across the room, and Bennie growled.

"Honey, what's the matter?" His face lost its delight and frowned as he studied the dog.

"I'm sick. I've got a bug. I don't want you to catch it." Her teeth chattered, and she folded her arms across her breasts. Bennie stood at her feet.

"I'm sorry." He picked up the sack he'd dropped as he came in the door. "I brought you orange juice, Kleenex, mouth wash, aspirin, and a cold remedy. And the pharmacist suggested these lemon swabs." As he talked, he unloaded the sack and spread the contents over the couch. "Are you warm enough?" He glanced down, and his face showed disbelief. "Bailey, you've got to get those feet off the floor. Before she could stop him, he had picked her up and deposited her on the couch beside everything he'd brought in with him. He stripped his coat from his shoulders and wrapped her with it.

His aftershave tantalized her senses as he kissed her forehead. "Is that better?"

"Thank you." The coat's warmth seeped into her bones. She curled like a cat in the sun and closed her eyes. Bennie jumped on the couch, lying at her feet which lost their chill. It was so warm, so comfortable.

Immediately he stepped to her thermostat. “It feels cool in here. Is your furnace working?”

“I think so.” Her eye lids were drooping.

“Let me check it.”

She watched him open the tiny space to the furnace.

“Where’s your sweeper. There’s so much dust in here that it’s a wonder you haven’t had an explosion.”

Totally relaxed, she knew no more until she woke hours later. The sleeping Dave sprawled in the stuffed chair. The remains of pizza lay between him. Bennie jumped off and sniffed at the boxes. He whined.

“You need out. Just a minute.”

Dave woke as she closed the door. “Come here, Honey.” He patted his lap. “How are you feeling?”

“Much better.”

“Good. You sound better.” He cuddled her close to him and bent to kiss her.

“I still have germs.”

“Let me share a few with you.”

She jumped from his lap and picked up the pizza box as she headed for door to allow Bennie back inside. Inside the kitchen she allowed Dave to kiss her again. “Don’t you think it’s time for you to go home?” The clock showed 11:30 p.m.

“That’s a real thanks.” He picked his coat up from the couch and headed to the door. “I’ll see you before I go to work tomorrow morning."

"I'll have breakfast ready."

Matron Macintyre arrived the next afternoon. "I heard you were sick, and what happened at the jail?"

"I fainted." Bailey twisted her hands. "I think I was already on the way to getting sick. I don't think it will happen again." She studied the Matron's face. "Honest, I think it will be okay."

"You plan to go again?"

"I have to do it. Don't you understand? I have to face my fears. It's the only way I can be at peace with myself."

The Matron shook her head. "I don't think you have to do this."

"But I want to."

"Okay, you have my blessing." The Matron looked at the tree. "That's nice."

"It's the first tree I have ever had." Bailey was pleased. "I think it's beautiful." She knelt to show the crèche below. "I love this, too."

"James helped you?"

"Yes! When can I have him? Haven't I passed all the tests?"

"All but one—Serine."

Bailey turned away. That had stabbed her heart. "I'm the mother."

"Don't worry. It will come in time." The Matron rose to go to the door. She stopped to face Bailey. "Stan has been working on who your father is. The priest didn't do it. The priest is one of the resulting children."

"But mom said."

"I know what your mother said. Stan thinks there may have been another priest with those green eyes, an older priest, but no one seems to know where he went." Her hand touched the door knob, but she turned again to face Bailey. "By the way, when do you and Dave leave to visit his folks?"

"I can go?"

"You can go."

Bailey's joy lasted just a few minutes. "What about James?"

"You are going to have to make a choice. Dave can go alone, or Serine will have James for the holiday."

Chapter 19: Florida

"Serine, I'm trying to be diplomatic." Bailey held the phone away from her ear to avoid James' foster mother from breaking her ear drums. Then she spoke as quietly as possible. "I understand that you have plans for my son, but I need to take him to Florida with us to meet his new grandparents."

"You can't take the boy out of the state. Ask the agency. That's one of the rules."

"Has he ever been out of Indiana before?"

Serine paused. "Yes, but I received permission. We went to Kentucky last summer."

“If you can take him out of state, so can I. I’m his mother.”

Bailey didn’t feel good about the call when she hung up the receiver. Serine blocked every avenue she could, but James didn’t belong to her.

“Did you ever think you might win this war with kindness?” Dave slid his arm around her shoulders and pulled her close.

She laid her head against his chest to listen to his heart. “I didn’t think I was being unkind. What do you suggest?” She lifted her head, and he kissed her. She leaned into it. Dave was so sweet.

“Um, maybe going half-and-half with Serine. We have three days before Christmas Eve when we fly down to Florida. Let her have James for Christmas. We can come back early and have him for New Years.” He kissed her again. “This is getting dangerous, you know?”

“I know, but I like it.”

“Me, too.”

She came up for air. “But James wouldn’t get to go with us. He wouldn’t meet your parents.”

“Save that for Easter. Just go with me, okay?” He rested his chin on her new curls. “I don’t really like the smell of your permanent.”

“The beautician said it will go away after two or three shampoos.”

“Shampoo it every day before we leave, okay?”

She pulled away. “I still want to take James with us.”

“Honey, I think Serine is afraid that you will run away with him. Give her some slack. We'll have a great time in Florida and share him with the family at Easter, okay?" His arms were reaching for her, but she slid away.

"Okay, I'll call her back. We'll leave on Christmas Eve and come back on the twenty-seventh. Then I'll have James over New Years." She reached for the phone.

Bailey purchased two summer outfits for Florida. She entered the air terminal and her nervousness grew as the well dressed passengers milled around her. Dave rented a locker-storage unit to leave their winter coats. Then they submitted their luggage and paid for the tickets.

"This seems like a honeymoon," he said with a grin as they boarded the plane.

"We're not married yet!"

"I'm sure that could be solved easily when we get to Florida."

"I don't have the proper clothes." Again she realized that the other women had paid far more for their silk suits and dresses than the cotton print with the spaghetti straps she was wearing. "I just don't think I brought enough clothes."

Dave sat next to the window and stared at the runway. "Don't worry about it. We're going to walk the malls down there and dress you like a doll."

"Fasten your seat belts." The hostess mimed the action of the breathing cap and tube coming down from the ceiling. She pointed to the overhead compartments and demonstrated the cushions as floats or life preservers. Bailey found herself clutching the edge of her seat with both hands and wondering how she would ever remember all of the information if there were an emergency.

"Smile, Honey. This is fun." Then he grinned. "We're not going over the ocean."

He was laughing at her. She unclenched her fists. The plane began to move. The vibration of large wheels rumbled underneath her. The engines screamed louder and louder as the plane picked up speed. Suddenly there was a little bounce, and they were in the air.

"Are you all right?" His arm slid around her shoulder. "Come here. I need the company."

Her head found the perfect spot near his heart as his hand pressed her curls closer to him. She closed her eyes and counted his heart beats.

"Um, I like the smell of your shampoo. Strawberry?"

"I don't remember." She closed her eyes, relishing his nearness, and relaxed.

"Wake up, Honey. We're here."

She roused to discover the activity of the other passengers pulling their seats into rigid uprightness and the clink of seat belts.

"Prepare for landing."

"Don't look so scared."

His smiling face increased Bailey's anxiety that continued to grow as the plane landed with a lurch, and the screaming motors coasted the bulky vehicle to a stop. What would Dave's parents think of her? Her hand reached down where the ankle bracelet had been. What would they think when they discovered their son had asked her to marry him? Would they reject her when they found out she was an ex-con?

"Come on, Honey. Grab your purse." Dave gave her a gentle nudge into the aisle.

From the crowded aisle to the long, tunneling corridor, Dave's hand in the middle of her back continued to push. As soon as she stepped across the threshold of the terminal, he dropped his hand and charged ahead. She had to trot to keep up with his long strides. They mingled in the throng surging through the hall way like driven cattle to emerge into the food court.

"There they are!"

Bailey stopped and stepped back as a crowd circled Dave who leaped forward, grabbing a stylish woman. "Ilene, did Jim make it?"

"He's in Iraq."

"I knew, but I thought."

"Another eight months."

Then the group circled Bailey. She cringed as if wolves panted for the kill. The stunning women and worldly men out-classed her. Dave shoved his body up against hers.

"Meet my fiancé." He smiled down into her eyes. Bailey could read the pride and love, but she could also see the skepticism of his siblings. "This is my mom." He moved Bailey in front of a plump lilac suit with a flowered blouse.

As she raised her eyes, Bailey saw a welcoming smile. She reached out her hand. "I'm Bailey Berkley."

Dave squeezed Bailey's hand and pulled her closer to him. "Isn't she wonderful, Mom?"

The terrible spell broke, and the girls--Ilene, Donna, Madge—reached out open arms. "We thought he'd never bring a girl home."

"You're so pretty and petite!"

"He hasn't told us anything except your name."

Then they turned on Dave. "You're going to have to tell us all about her."

"It's not fair to keep us in the dark."

Bailey hugged them back and looked to Dave for instructions.

"Let's get your baggage." A leaner, taller Dave herded them toward the escalator.

"Hi, Harry." Dave shook his brother's hand and turned. "Where's dad?"

Faces became sober.

"Mom?"

The little lady breathed deeply. The single button on her jacket showed strain. "Your father is playing tennis in Memphis." Her lips clamped shut into a firm line.

Bailey saw the eyebrows of the family.

"Come on." Harry hustled them down the moving steps. "Let's get that baggage before someone else claims it."

The condominium awed Bailey. As large as a church, the foyer led into a kitchen of gleaming, stainless steel appliances on the left and a grand arch on the right aced a chandelier glowing over a mammoth table. The places were set with linen napkins, china, and silver beside crystal goblets. She felt so small, so out of place. The others pushed past her. Dave's feet were pounding up a carpeted staircase, and he held a suit case in each hand.

"Come on, Bailey. The bedrooms are up here."

She followed to arrive at the top of the curving rail out of breath.

Dave stood at an open doorway. "This is your room. Mine is across the hall." He dropped her luggage on the floor and walked to the drapes that reached across the entire wall. "The girls always have this room while Harry and I share the other one." His nod indicated across the hall, but he was looking outward and downward. "Hurry and get into your swimming suit."

Bailey walked past two queen sized beds and glanced down to see the pool. The clear, shining aqua waters revealed the steps at the low end and coins lying on the bottom. A slide with running water stood at one side, and a small diving board at the other. Drying towels covered four lounge chairs, and various goggles, fins, and snorkels littered the area.

"Dave, I can't swim."

"I'll teach you." His arms came around, and his lips met hers.

"A-hem!" Harry stood at the door. "Remember mom's rule?"

Dave nodded. "No boys in the girls' room." He paused at the door. "Hurry. I'll meet you in the pool."

Tension built when Dave wasn't around her. Bailey didn't know how to carry on a conversation with his sisters or his mother. Their interests lay outside of her experience and knowledge. Married Ilene spoke rapidly, and Bailey had to listen closely to understand what she was saying.

"Fred's returning from Europe on New Year's Eve. We'll be going to a masked ball held by the Westchester Fire Department." She described her gown of real silk and pearls, but Bailey could add nothing to the conversation.

Donna in comparison was a sleek Persian kitten. Her speech purred about a career in engineering that was remaking an old company into a marketing magnate. "I'm designing the masks patients wear when using oxygen tanks."

Bailey could only stare. Her admiration for Donna soared, but her inferiority bit a deadly hole in her ego.

The flashy Madge with her oversize dark glasses and short shorts brought Hollywood into the house. Bailey envied those tanned and lengthy legs and stayed in the sun too long near the pool. That evening Dave applied lotion to almost her whole red body.

Harry in his trunks walked and swam like the Greek god Thor. When Dave wasn't present, he offered her swimming lessons.

"Don't do it," said Ilene, "unless you enjoy a man's hands all over you." She picked up her towel and sauntered into the house.

"Honey, Harry wouldn't hurt yah a'tall." Donna sat on the pool edge and flipped water in his direction. "He taught me to swim."

"Tried to drown you, you mean." Madge adjusted her sunglasses.

Harry laughed. "Sure, all it took was throwing her in the deep end. Sink or swim. She swam."

Bailey pulled her towel around her and went to find Dave. "When are we going shopping?"

"Whenever you're ready."

After meeting his sisters, Bailey didn't know what to get them for Christmas.

"Don't worry about it." Dave had already shopped, and the boxes in fancy paper sat under the tree in the massive living room. Garlands looped around the walls, and a stocking for each member was stuffed and hung on the mantle.

"But I know your mom has something for me, and it wouldn't be right not to get her something."

"Bailey, not a one of my family needs anything. Save your money." He took her to a women's shop. "Let's find you another swimming suit or two."

"No, I'd rather get some real clothes." She found a couple of cotton shirts and shorts to match. "Now let's look for gifts."

They walked the mall, laughing at the silly stuff and enjoying the Christmas decorations. Dave wanted her to sit on Santa's lap for a photo, but Bailey refused.

"I don't want any man touching me, except you."

He grew sober. “Honey, that is wonderful.” His eyes glistened, and he pulled her close for a hug and kiss on the top of her head. “I value that trust.”

When they found the candy shop, Bailey got a box for everyone.

“Satisfied?”

“They’ll melt before we get back.”

“Not if we go now.”

That evening Dave blew up a rubber raft that would have fit over a king-size bed. He positioned it beside the pool so he could lie beside Bailey. “The stars are so bright tonight.”

“Because it’s Christmas Eve.” She felt his hand find hers and lay touching her thigh. To subvert the tingles running up and down her leg, she pushed it just an inch away. “I wonder which star led the wise men to Jesus.” She turned her head to study his profile pointed upward.

“I don’t know, but God is up there, Honey, and He’s watching us.”

“I know.”

“Last year I asked Him to give me somebody special.” His body twisted to lay on his side propped up by an elbow. “He brought you into my life.”

“I remember that day in the library. I didn’t have a card.”

“I wanted your name and address. When you walked out, I thought I’d never see you again.”

Bailey traced his nose with a finger.

"Then I went to find you at the halfway house, and you were gone."

"When did you do that?"

"Just after Matron Macintyre moved you out."

"I didn't know."

"But remember the day I tried to get your address?" He laughed. "I feared you didn't like me." His face only a foot away moved closer. "You looked so lost and venerable."

"I was." Bailey could feel the warmth of his breath brushing her face. After the sun went down the air had cooled, and a breeze was raising goose bumps on her damp skin. His nose, chin, and lips bent over hers.

"I love you, Bailey." He kissed her. "Let's go in. You're cold."

Christmas morning Dave's father arrived with a whole suburban filled with Christmas. The slender tennis player moved as though chasing a ball and preparing to lobby it over the net. Bailey and Dave followed him to the garage to help him unload, and he looked her over thoroughly. "Play tennis?"

"No."

"You're the size of Chris Earhart. I'd think you could really move on the court."

"I never had the opportunity."

"Well, we'll teach you." He winked at Dave.

"Oh, Dad, hands off. She's mine."

Dave's father reached out to cuff his son lovingly on the ear. "Come on. The family awaits, and Christmas won't last forever."

They sat in the big living room in a circle. Harry passed the gifts to everyone, making a pile beside each chair. Bailey couldn't believe the pile forming at her feet, but as she looked around the room and realized the piles beside the other chairs were just as large.

"Who wants to read Luke 2 this year?" Dave's mom held an open Bible.

His father accepted the Bible, and his gruff tones began, "In those days Caesar Augustus issued a decree."

Bailey watched Harry stare at his sandaled foot and trace the ceramic tile's edge with the thin edge of the toe. Irene's body bent forward intent on her father's face. Donna's eyes were closed, and her hands lay on the purple shorts just above her knees. Madge stared out the window into the pool area, and her mother smiled with clasped hands. Dave turned to Bailey and winked.

"Today in the town of David a Savior has been born to you; he is Christ the Lord. This will be a sign to you; you will find a baby wrapped in cloths and lying in a manger." Dave's father looked up at the group. "Let's pray. Father, we thank you for this season and for bringing our family home. Bless Jim in Iraq and keep him safe. Amen."

When Bailey opened her eyes, she saw Madge's finger dabbing at her eye, Dave's mom with a tissue, and Donna reaching for her purse.

ime for presents." Harry grabbed his top gift.

"Don't you think we ought to let our guest go first?"

Harry shrugged his shoulders. "Okay, but be quick about it."

They tittered, but Bailey knew she was in the spot light. If the phone hadn't rung at that moment, she thought she would have melted.

"Dad! It's Jim calling from Iraq!"

Chapter 20: Holiday Cheer

Once again in her own home Bailey admired her ring as she unpacked the new suitcase full of new clothes. Dave's sisters and mother played with her like a Barbie doll after the unwrapping of gifts. The boxes she opened contained just the accessories. They took her into the girls' bedroom and had her try on two party dresses.

"Oooh, how sexy!" The girls laughed in glee, and Bailey looked down at the black sequined, v-necked dress that clung to her body like the skin on a seal. "You'll have to find some heeled sandals to match—any color, as long as they're shiny." The red, mandarin collar of the other dress also was form fitting, but they said, "Bailey, you look like a little girl. Be careful where you wear it."

"The truant officer will be after you." They giggled, but the mirror didn't show the real Bailey. Dave had not told them of her prison record. They didn't know she had a son. How would his family react when the bomb hit?

She had wanted him to be honest, but he had shushed her fears.

"It's not their business. You've paid your debt. Forget it."

"But they will find out in time. What then?"

"Don't worry about it."

But Bailey did worry. No matter how the information came, they would not be happy hearing it from another source than Dave or her. She shuddered.

She hung up the power blue suit and its flowered silk blouse, but the new swim suit from Dave, she lay on the bed. He had been almost apologetic. "I saw it and knew only you should have it."

"Should I put it on so we can go swimming?"

"No, we're going out to eat."

Bailey wore the sequined dress.

He chose a restaurant with linen table cloths, silverware that glistened in the candle light, and music that hovered around them. The waiter took them to a private nook overlooking the ocean. The crying gulls swooped over the rippling waters or stood like statues on the dock posts. Boats rode the gentle waves like they were being rocked asleep.

Dave seemed unnaturally nervous as he drove in the darkness beside the sea lying like rumpled silk under the full moon. The beach glistened and beckoned, but she was wearing heels. Nevertheless, he led her down a sandy path and set her on a smooth rock facing the Gulf of Mexico. "I used to come out here to sort out my thoughts."

"It's perfect." She watched him go on his knees before her.

"I want you to marry me." He opened a little box, and the

diamond sparkled in the mellow natural light. He pulled out the ring and turned it to watch the glistening facets.

She was overwhelmed. “You’ve already given me a bracelet.”

“This matches.” He slid it on her finger and kissed her palm. “I want you to be my wife.”

“I will.” She could barely whisper the words for the lump in her throat. “Never have I been treated so royally.” She couldn’t hold back the tears. “Oh, thank you, Dave.”

He had cocked his head. “Bailey, do you love me?”

“Yes.”

“Say it.”

“I love you. I will gladly marry you.”

“Let’s get married tomorrow.”

She laughed. “Our plane tickets.”

“There’s always another flight.” He was kissing her neck, her lips, her mouth. An urgency, a forcefulness, and a demand underlined his words. “I can’t wait, Honey.” His arms had pulled her close to his body while his hands kneaded her back. He came up for air.

“Dave, what about James?”

“James?” He pulled back. His eyes like obsidian glistened in the moonlight. She saw his mouth quiver.

“My son.”

“He’ll be our son, but can’t he wait?” Dave pulled her back into his arms. His breath brushed her eyes as he kissed her forehead, bringing kisses down the bridge of her nose. "I need you to myself."

She allowed him to kiss her mouth and send her senses to the moon and back before she could slide away and walk to the car. Matron Macintyre had urged her to wait. She could hear the words.

"Bailey, get James first and learn to live with him before you marry."

Dave opened the door for her, and she slid onto the seat. "I have the marriage license in my billfold. I know where we can get married tonight." Before he started the motor, he pulled her into his arms. "Bailey, I'm serious." Again his kisses were hot, and his hands slid down her back to her waist. He pulled her into the driver's bucket seat. "Please, don't make me wait, darling."

She closed her eyes. Her arms circled his neck, and she couldn't stop kissing him.

Suddenly, his head jerked up. He turned the starter key, pressing her waist with his arm closer to him. He guided the car out onto the highway, turning it toward the city. "There's an all night chapel on the north side of Tampa Bay. We can be there in ten minutes."

"Ten minutes." She mouthed the words, but again her mind played with the matron's admonition. "Oh, God, help us!"

"What did you say?" Dave's arm relaxed.

"I asked God to help us."

"God? Oh." His balloon punctured. "Bailey, should we do this?"

"I don't think so." She slid over into the passenger seat and hugged the door.

Dave muttered, “Let’s go home.”

She glanced over at his stoic face that stared straight ahead into the darkness speared by the headlights. His fists, clinched like a fighter’s, never moved from the steering wheel. Once he reached over to flip on the radio which he turned up to maximum volume. When he stopped the motor of the car in his folk’s drive, he stepped out, slammed the car door, and headed for the front entrance.

“Come on.”

She opened the door, but he had already entered the house. The sound of his shoes stomping up the stairs greeted her at the threshold. She softly closed the door.

“Did you have a nice evening?” Harry leaned against the kitchen doorway with a glass of liquor in his hand.

Bailey fled like a frightened deer up the stairs, but Dave had already closed the door on the boy’s room. She wandered over to the window and drew back the curtain to watch his sisters draped around the pool. His father swam laps. She turned away to pack.

Dave had been distant on the plane although he sat in the seat beside her. She laid her hand with the ring between them and caught him glancing down many times. Once he touched her bracelet and pulled it around her wrist to straighten the chain. Then he jerked his hand away.

She walked around the bed and into the living room to plug in the lights. Several gifts for James lay under the tree, but he wouldn't come for another two days. She opened the drapes. The dull, grey skies held promise of more snow, but Dave had cleaned his sidewalks and left. She played with the binoculars. He hadn't told her where he was going, but he didn't have to go to work.

Her computer hadn't been turned on for over a week. She pushed the button and stepped back. As she waited for the screen to clear from all the preliminaries, she wandered back into the kitchen and fixed some instant coffee. By the time she came back with the steaming cup, the computer was ready for use.

"Ding-dong." The door bell brought her back to the present.

"Coming!" The excitement of seeing Dave moved her heart into a faster beat. She peeked through the hole and opened to Matron Macintyre. The police woman came in with a smile.

"Wow, that's a ring." Her eyes studied the diamond whose facets created rainbows on the walls. "How was your trip?"

"Marvelous!"

Matron smiled and nodded her head. "Can we sit down?"

Bailey led her to the sofa and chose the opposite chair. "What's up?"

"James. Serine and her husband wish to adopt him. They have a court proceeding that will take him away from you. According to the paperwork, you are described as an unfit parent."

"Unfit?" Bailey's past flitted through her mind. Her body sagged. "Do I still get to see him this week?" Bailey's hands began to nervously twist as she stared at the gifts under the tree.

"I am not sure. Part of the stated law suit reads that you chose going to Florida with your boyfriend over having James at Christmas."

Bailey sat up. "Serine wanted him for Christmas. She said I could have him day after tomorrow and through New Years."

"I think you need to speak to the social worker, face-to-face."

"Will you go with me?"

"I'll take you." The Matron rose and headed for the door.

The social worker smiled a lot at Bailey and Matron Macintyre, but she shook her head. "I need proof. Serine has made quite a strong case with your prison record, drug dealing, and neglect of parental care."

"I am not a drug dealer, and I don't use drugs. I never have."

"Calm down, Bailey." Matron Macintyre laid a hand on her arm and turned to the woman. "Cheryl, I've come to know Bailey quite well. She is a hard working citizen who takes her responsibilities seriously. What do we need to do?"

The woman pulled a sheet out of her files. "Fill this out. I need three character references, and do it quickly." She looked at the clock. "Could you get it all together by three this afternoon?"

"We'll do our best."

"First we're getting copies of this made at the library. While you fill yours out, I will ask Dave to fill one out. I'm going to do one. Who do you think would fill out another?"

Bailey's mind went blank.

"Is there someone at the church?"

"Teddy's mother or the pastor's wife."

"Good. We'll get one to both of them just in case mine or Dave's is thrown out."

"Oh."

By a quarter of three they were standing again before the social worker's desk.

"Are these satisfactory?" Bailey quivered as she held the papers.

"Oh, you have four. Fine." The woman glanced through quickly. "These look good. I will present them to the parole office and the judge."

"The judge?"

"Oh, yes, this all has to go through the legal channels. I wouldn't be surprised if you didn't have to appear in person and answer questions."

Back in the car Bailey sat in the passenger's seat and held her head with both hands.

"Headache?"

"No, Matron Macintyre. I was praying."

The Matron nodded. "Very good." As she dropped Bailey at her residence, she paused. "I think my husband has some very interesting facts put together about your father, but he's not ready to disclose them, yet."

"My father?" Bailey opened her door and sagged against the car.

"Don't worry about that. Let's handle one problem at a time."

The car pulled away from the curb, and Bailey noticed that Dave was home. She ran across the street and rang his doorbell.

"Come in. The door's open." Dave stood in his kitchen in a chef's apron. "I'm fixing steak. Did everything work out this afternoon?"

"I don't know. The social worker has to take those papers to the judge and parole officer." She came over to look at his sizzling meat. "Is there something I can do?"

"Set the table and pour the drinks." He waited until Bailey was seated, and the meal was almost over. "Honey, I have some news."

She glanced up. His face didn't exactly look happy.

"This is either a celebration dinner or a going away party."

"What do you mean?"

"Remember how I wanted to marry you in Florida?"

"Yes."

"Well, I knew this was cooking." His eyes focused on her house across the street. "I have been transferred to another library. The state manager called me in this afternoon to review my credentials and work habits."

"Anything wrong?"

"Oh, no, actually everything was fine. It's just that I'm needed elsewhere." He toyed with the potato on his plate. "I asked to stay here, but my expertise is required in Indianapolis."

"Indianapolis!" She dropped her fork. "You're leaving?"

"Well, yeah. I have to move. It's too far away to commute and gas prices prohibitive." He rose from the chair and came to her. Gently he pulled her up into his arms. "I'm selling this placc. I posted it with the real estate office as soon as I left the library. There's a guy wanting it."

"Who?"

"I didn't get his name. The agent said this fellow came in trying to get your place just after you took it. He's been searching the town ever since."

Before she could stop them, the tears gushed out like a dam breaking.

"Oh, Bailey, I'm not going to walk out on you. I love you, but I have to follow my job." He was holding her in his arms and rocking her. "If we were married, it wouldn't be any problem."

"But James."

Dave pulled back from her. "Honey, I think this will be good for both of us. You can have James and see if you really need me."

Serine kept her promise to allow James to spend New Year's weekend with Bailey who was packing Dave's dishes in boxes. The boy stood next to her elbow and handed her pieces of newsprint.

"Why is Dave going away?"

"He has to work. His job has moved." She set a wrapped cup

carefully in the box and reached for another cup.

“Are we going to move with him?”

“I hope so.”

“Right now?”

“No, we have to wait on the judge’s decision.”

“Oh.” James crumpled a piece of paper and tossed it across the room, missing the waste basket. “My other mom said she was adopting me.”

“No body can adopt you. You are my son. Now pick up that newspaper you crumbled and bring it back to me. I need it.”

“I don’t want to.” James ran into the other room shouting. “I don’t want Dave to leave. I don’t want to be adopted.”

“What’s all this?” Dave came into the room. “Oh, honey, you’re doing a fantastic job.”

“James just ran into your bedroom.”

“I’ll take care of him.” He gave James a life preserver. “You put this on when we get in the boat.” He set the boat down on the garage floor for the boy’s pleasure.

“Look, mom! I can really paddle fast.”

She grinned from the doorway. “You sure can.”

“Are we going to take the boat out in the water?” James turned to Dave.

“In the summer time.”

Serine came for James on Sunday evening. The boy opened the door to let her inside the house while Bailey dried dishes in the kitchen. Benny barked until the boy picked up the dog.

"How's my munchkin? Did you miss mummy?"

"You ain't my mother." He brought Benny close. "This is my dog. I get to keep him."

Serine backed away. "The dog stays here."

"But he's mine."

Bailey stepped to the door. "Come, Benny. Time to go outside." She opened the door to let out the dog. When she turned, she saw Serine reach down to kiss James, but he pushed her aside.

"My mother is going to marry Dave. He's going to be my real father."

"Gary, get your things. You don't know what you're talking about." Serine's face lost its humor, and she pivoted on her high heel to glance around the room. Her focus remained on the Christmas tree. A frown crossed her face. "It's time to go home. Now scoot."

"That's not my name." James looked from one woman to the other.

"Get your things now." Serine's words came from gritted teeth.

"Do I have to?"

Bailey nodded. "For now. Soon the court will allow me to keep you forever. Be a good boy."

"This summer were going boating—Dave, mother, and

me." He winked at Bailey.

"When did you learn that?" Serine scowled.

"Oh, Dave taught me." James sauntered into the bedroom his head held high.

Serine stared at Bailey. "What else did he learn while he was here? How men and women make love?" The woman smiled viciously. "So you're going boating? We'll see about that."

"His name isn't Gary." Bailey went to the door to let Benny back inside.

Serine paused. "I don't approve of animals in the house."

"It's not your house."

On Monday Bailey watched the moving van back up to the door, and Dave work with the movers in loading it. He came to kiss her good-bye.

"When are you coming back?"

"I'm sorry, honey. It won't be this week end. I need time to find a house and get settled."

She nodded.

"Bye."

"Bye." She watched him climb into the truck. He waved. She returned the wave as it passed her window. Then the truck turned at the end of the street. He was gone.

Darkness settled over Bailey. Her mind floated away out of reach. She sat on the sofa, staring down the street, but didn't see the Matron's car pull into the drive. She didn't hear the pounding on the door or the turn of the knob.

Matron Macintyre held her by the shoulders. "Bailey, wake up. Are you on dope?"

"He's gone."

"Come on. Get your hat and coat." The Matron looked at the Christmas tree. "Isn't it time it came down?"

"I've been helping Dave pack."

"I see. Bailey, get in the car. My husband wishes to take your picture, check your finger prints, and get some DNA samples."

"He left me."

"Dave's coming back, Bailey. He loves you very much."

"He wanted to know if I needed him." She turned sidewise in the seat and laid a hand on the Matron's right arm. "I can't live without him."

"Bailey, snap out of it. Grow up. You're not a baby any more."

"I am grown up."

"James needs a mother. Now get with it."

Bailey sat back into the seat. James needed a mother. She was his mother.

Stan Macintyre sat behind a desk with papers piled around him like an editor. "Hi, Bailey, I think I have some interesting news. Your DNA matches that of Serine, the young priest, and possibly Ernest Brown from the description and pictures I've studied." He leaned back in his chair.

"Serine is my half sister?"

He nodded.

"Does she know?"

"Not yet." He picked up a paper. "I can give you a name, but your father passed away in prison. He was incarcerated the same year you were conceived. I understand he wasn't a full fledged priest, but a young novice."

"What's that?"

"A fellow just out of seminary, but he hadn't taken his vows yet." Stan's fingers drummed the desk top. "Have you seen your mother recently?"

"No, Narla committed her to a nursing home, but I wasn't told."

"Bailey, you need to find her. That's the only way we'll ever know the truth."

"She won't tell me anything."

"Ask Narla where she is."

Bailey shook her head. "I don't know how to get a hold of Narla either." She stared out the window. What had been so important to her years ago didn't seem to matter any more. "And the priest?"

"I have talked to the one you found in the church. He would like to meet you." Stan rose from his chair. "He knows more, but he thought he should be the one to tell you."

The news about Serine shook her more than anything else. No wonder Serine felt close to James. She was his aunt. She was relation. Would that make her claim in the courtroom stronger?

Chapter 21: Family Trouble

About bedtime someone began knocking, er, pounding on her door. Bennie barked like the whole world ought to know, and Bailey came out of the kitchen in her house coat and slippers.

"There is a doorbell." And then she saw her sister.

Narla stood with four suitcases, three children, and her superior attitude. "Well, it's about time you opened the door. It's freezing out here, and we're about to catch our death of cold." She marched in, dropping two suitcases at the door and the children as well. "Where's the bathroom?"

Bailey didn't have time to reply. The bathroom door banged shut. She closed the entry door. The three little girls huddled on the couch.

"I gotta go pee," said the youngest. Her arms and legs bunched together like sticks, holding her crouch. Her pinched features were covered with a cloud of brunette curls. Butterfly barrettes held the mass back from the pointed face. Large brown eyes stared at Bailey.

"Hold it, Sucker," said the oldest. Then she turned her woman of the world look on Bailey. "You gotta be Bailey. Mom's told us all about you, and we hate you."

"I gotta pee now!" Unable to hold it any longer, the youngest twisted her legs around each other, as the trickle going down her legs darkened the carpet.

Bennie sniffed it over while Bailey headed to the kitchen to get a towel.

Just then Narla charged out of the bathroom. “We got thrown out of the apartment because we couldn’t pay the rent. I knew you wouldn’t mind our coming here.”

The youngest tugged on the stylish cut skirt. “Mom’s, I gotta go pee.”

Without looking down, Narla snarled. “You know where it is.”

“Sucker peed on the floor.”

Narla looked down, and Bailey saw the trail headed into her bathroom on her clean carpet. She dropped the two towels she’d brought from the kitchen and stepped on them to pull the urine spot out of the rug.

“How did you know where I live?”

Narla smiled. “Lakeside isn’t Indianapolis, you know. Everybody knows everything.” She looked over at her two girls still on the sofa. “Angela, get that dirty thumb out of your mouth, and don’t stick it in there again, or I’ll slap yah.” She turned to Bailey. “I’ll sleep in the bedroom with the big bed, and the girls can use the couches.”

“No.”

“No? What do you mean?” Narla’s hands cupped her hips, and she glared at Bailey. “It’s cold outside, and we don’t have no where else to go. Ever since Mom went to the nursing home, a gang has trashed her house. Grandpa turned off the utilities. We can’t possibly go there.”

“Go home.”

"Home!"

"Mom's means we don't have no home no more." The oldest child sat quietly, holding her younger sister close to her side. "My daddy ran off with all the money. We gots kicked out."

The youngest came back from the bathroom. "My panties wet."

Narla shook her off like tree drops leaves in the autumn.

The child began to cry.

"Shut up."

"Come here, Sucker, before Mom's gets mad." The oldest child beckoned her to the couch and held her sister tightly.

"I don't like wet panties."

"Hush, and you might get some candy."

For the first time the middle child spoke. "That's a lie. You don' have no more candy. We ates 'em all."

Narla stepped between the children and Bailey. "We could use a decent meal."

Bailey stepped backwards, away from the horde. She had no desire to let them stay or to feed them, but a scripture flitted through her mind. "If your enemy hunger, feed him." A battle began in her mind. *"Lord, if I treat Narla nice, I won't get rid of her. She'll destroy everything I've worked to earn."* Tears leaked out of her eyes and ran down her cheeks. After all Narla had done, why did she have to come here?

"Bailey's crying." The oldest child continued to pull her sisters close on both sides of her.

Narla picked up the other two suitcases. “I’ll put these in my bedroom.”

“Oh, no, you won’t.” Bailey jumped between her and the hallway. “You’re not going in there. This is my house. That’s my bedroom, and you have no right.”

Narla’s eyebrows climbed her forehead, and her mouth smirked. “Drugs. I knew it. That’s why you don’t want me in there. You don’t want me to find them and report you. I’ll report you anyway. Where’s that phone?” She dropped the suitcases and marched across the room. Lifting the receiver, she punched the buttons.

Bailey stumbled into the kitchen. Narla had always gotten her way and bullied everyone. There were no drugs in her bedroom. If the police came, she knew Matron Macintyre would be notified. Could she force Narla to leave? She turned to watch the three girls huddled on the couch. What would happen to them? They were innocent, and yet victims of Narla’s greed and selfishness. Bennie sniffed the sodden towels, and Bailey grimaced. The strong odor of urine multiplied.

“Angela, couldn’t you hold it either?”

Setting the phone back in place, Narla strutted towards Bailey. “Well, that takes care of that. The police will be here in a few minutes to arrest you. I guess I’ll just have to house keep for you and watch your dog.”

Bennie growled.

“Maybe I’ll have to call the humane society to get the mutt.” She sat down in the only stuffed chair. “My, what a big tree. Don’t you think it’s time to put it away until next year?”

Bailey stormed into her kitchen.

The police came. Matron Macintyre came. Narla was taken to headquarters. Human services retrieved the three girls. Bailey locked the doors, picked up Bennie, and went to bed. The phone rang.

"Hello, Bailey."

In her sleepy state she knew it wasn't Dave, but the man's voice held a familiar tone. "Who are you?"

"I just talked to Narla, and she told me how lonely you are since that boyfriend moved out."

Clark!

Bailey hung up. She closed the drapes and checked the outside doors. Then she found a shadow and dropped into it. He wouldn't be able to see her. The phone's rings pierced the darkness like the prison buzzer. She shook with fear. Bennie's toenails clicked across the kitchen linoleum as he came to her. She held him on her lap, her face buried into the fur on his back. The door bell rang. Then someone began pounding.

"Bailey, open up!"

She crept to the phone and dialed 911. Allowing the receiver to hang to the floor, she crawled back into her shadow.

"Hello?" A woman repeated it several times.

Bailey heard the click. The dial tone and then the metallic operator's voice droned, "Please, hang up your receiver. This is a recorded message."

The repetition made Bennie whine, but she hushed him.

The voice turned to a guitar beat that grew louder and louder.

Bennie began to bark.

She set the receiver back on the hook. Then as it began to ring, she unplugged it from the wall. Quietly she padded back to her bed and slid between the sheets without making the springs creak.

She almost drifted off to sleep when the doorbell rang again. Sirens came down the street. Strobe lights flitted across the drapes. She heard heavy feet crunching the snow outside the house. Did she dare open the door? She stood to her feet and pulled the bathrobe tightly around her, retying the strings.

"Police. Open up!"

Dear Lord, I don't want to do this. Bailey stood before the door looking out the peep hole. A pair of uniformed officers conversed on the step.

"Did you find anything?"

"It all appears peaceful. There weren't any foot prints around the house except those of a dog."

"You think we ought to force an entry?"

They turned to the door as Bailey clicked the latch and slowly opened it.

"Ma'am, we're sorry for disturbing you, but someone just placed a call for 911."

"I did."

"Was this a prank call?"

"No, sir, Clark tried to gain entry."

"Clark?" The officer had opened a pad, taking notes. He glanced at his watch, recorded the time, and stared at Bailey. "Who is Clark?"

One of the officers aimed his light around the door jam. "No, sign of force."

"I don't like him. He looks me up. He wanted me to open the door. He wouldn't go away. I was afraid, so I called you."

"I see." The officer pulled out his pad and began to take notes. "Is there anyone inside with you?"

"Bennie, my dog."

"May we come in to check it out?"

"Yes, sir."

She stepped aside, and the two walked inside, flipping on the lights and peering into every room. They came back to the front door where she waited.

"Everything seems to be intact." He looked around the room. "Your phone is unplugged." He reached down and re-plugged it. "I guess you'll be all right. Call us if anything happens."

"Thank you. I will."

They left.

Bailey locked the door and headed for the bedroom. The phone began to ring. She stooped down and unplugged it. The cool sheets welcomed her, and she promptly fell asleep.

That night Bailey had nightmares.

"Recreation time!" The automatic cell doors rolled open, and Bailey, shoved forward, stumbled out of the cell block into the wide foyer that led to the fenced yard.

"Get outta my way."

Bailey hit the cement wall. Another inmate behind her grabbed an arm to assist her back into line.

"Single file!" yelled a guard behind them, and the jostling ended. The women--garbed like zebras, shoulders hunched, and faces downward--marched into the open area to be counted. As soon as the guards were satisfied and retired into the building, the prisoners broke ranks.

The same dirty blonde that had pushed Bailey circled her with a half a dozen other brazen women. "Lookee at what they brought in new today." Her long skinny arm reached out, and the woman grabbed a handful of Bailey's hair and yanked Bailey's face close to hers.

Bailey screamed.

"Shut up! Do yah want us locked up in confinement?" Wrinkles at the corner of the pale eyes and the sagging skin underneath emphasized the enlarged pupils that stared into Bailey's face. The nose like a dagger protruded above thin lips, the lower half a shelf of imperialism. "I'm the boss around here. Do yah understand?" Nicotine-stained teeth grimaced less than an inch away.

"Yes." Bailey closed her eyes to endure the excruciating pain, but she could still feel the breath and smell the unwashed body of the hard faced woman.

"And don't yah forget it." She shoved Bailey away and laughed with the others in her circle when the girl fell to the pavement.

Bailey waited until the circle widened, and she could stand alone without interference. The woman strutted away, her slender hips swaying in triumph, and turned slightly to look back and hoot louder than before.

A kind arm drew Bailey into another circle. "Beware of Rosenbaum." The whisper tickled Bailey's ear. "She's vicious."

"Like a grizzly that ran into a porcupine," said another. "Even the guards are scared of her. She runs the show around here."

"You don't dare challenge her."

"That Jezebel will stab yah in the back."

Bailey studied the group surrounding her. "How do you handle her?"

"Nobody----nobody handles that gal. There's rumors she's in for murder. Shot and killed a man—an officer."

Bailey awoke in a sweat. Bennie had crawled up on the bed and was breathing inches from her face. His doggy odor suggested a bath; however, the realness of the dream brought back old memories inside the jail.

One evening when the cell block was locked down, Bailey chatted with Ginger, the inmate on the bottom bunk. "What do you know about Rosenbaum?"

"Only the rumors. I heard she operated a still. When the revenuers came, she tried to run the law off with dogs and sawed off shotguns." The girl rolled over on her back to stare up at Bailey. "It happens all the time down in Kentucky. Moon shiners sell their whiskey, and the law comes after them."

Bailey stared at the ceiling. "How do you stay away from her?"

"Become a Christian. Rosenbaum steers clear of Christians."

The next day Ginger got a letter from home. "Bailey, mom sent me some money for some new pajamas."

"I thought they gave you what you needed in here."

"Two outfits a year. Things get kinda tacky and frazzled before the year is over." She held up one arm. "Both elbows are out, and the knees aren't much better."

"Tear them off and have short sleeves and shorts."

Ginger laughed. "How many pairs do I need?"

Rosenbaum met them in a corner of the yard that afternoon. "I heard you got a letter." She held out her open palm. "Ginger, hand it over."

"That's extortion. Mom sent me money for pajamas."

"Well, girls, I need some pajamas." She laughed, and her crowd jeered with her.

"You can't make me."

Rosenbaum stepped forward with a snarl, but one of her friends nudged her and nodded toward the advancing guard. "That money is mine." When the guard arrived, Rosenbaum was all smiles.

The next morning Ginger's body hung in the shower.

"I didn't know she was suicidal." Bailey shivered. Rosenbaum's face wore a sneer. No one else commented, and Bailey turned away, sick. About a year later while Bailey lay on the top bunk, Rosenbaum grabbed a girl by the throat, not realizing her own strength and the fragility of the other. The woman's neck popped, and the body slid to the floor of the cell—lifeless.

"Yah didn't see nuthin'." Rosenbaum stepped closer to Bailey.

"I was asleep." Bailey scooted up against the wall, and Rosenbaum pulled the body out into the exercise yard.

Who was to say the woman hadn't tripped over something, fell against a wall, and killed herself? The prison didn't even hold an inquest.

Bailey rolled out of bed and went to the kitchen. Benny's toenails clicked on the linoleum behind her. The full moon's light reflected against the snow until the outside glowed in violet, and the shadows streaked across the lawn like tall, skinny desperados. She looked at the clock--three. She shuffled to the picture window in the living room and peered across at Dave's house. No one had moved into the place, and a sign stood out front like a rotten spot on a tomato. She pulled the drapes and turned on the Christmas tree lights.

The tree should have come down and been put away days ago, but she reveled in the beauty like a child. The colors muted and the ornaments hung in a fanciful world. Why couldn't it be

Christmas all year long? Why couldn't people get along with each other all the time? Why was it so difficult to get her son back?

She knew the answer to the last question, Serine. The woman refused to believe they were sisters. Bailey couldn't understand the ruling. The judge agreed to her visitation rights, as well as Clark's, but he didn't show at the hearing.

"You're still on probation. Come back in September."

In September she would be free, but would she get James? The longing for a real family stirred within her. Dave would be the father, and she the mother, or had he left her world, too? She turned the ring on her finger. She was still his fiancée.

She padded to the computer. Maybe Dave sent an e-mail. He hadn't, but she found her blogs and began to type. The sun painted the sky in pinks and blues. It promised to be a good day. Bailey went for a shower.

Chapter 22: Visiting Jail

Tonia Sue Sommers and Stella Brown met her at the church.

"We ought to pray before we make that jail visit." Tonia Sue's suggestion took them into the sanctuary.

Bailey stepped down the carpeted aisle. The silence held an inaudible ring, and she searched the paneled walls, the colored glass of the windows, and the glossy pews for an answer. The piano surrounded by artificial flowers in the corner resembled a garden, and Stella dispelled the darkness with the flip of a switch. The three knelt at the altar railing before the pulpit. Bailey closed her eyes and waited.

Silently she prayed for James, for Dave, and for herself while the two women vocalized their needs. A presence, new to

Bailey, surrounded them. A joy purged her heart and brought tears to her eyes. Stella ended their prayers. "Thank you, Father, for hearing us. Help us to be a blessing to someone today. Amen."

They walked outside to the car in a spirit of anticipation. Bailey noticed their beaming faces and the spring in their steps. While Stella drove, Tonia Sue chattered, and Bailey watched outside the window the houses on the street. A man strewed salt on his sidewalk. A woman entered a car whose exhaust was a plume of white smoke in the frosty air. They passed the school. The play ground equipment vacant of childish play, but the windows glowed yellow behind the construction paper snowmen. James was there. He was safe.

This time Bailey didn't feel the oppressive heaviness in the jail. She followed her friends into a room where chairs surrounded a table. The women of the prison came in with their Bibles and sat quietly as they listened to Stella.

"Trusting God means we bring all our troubles to Him." Stella's eyes focused on Bailey. "We know He knows all about them, because He knows everything. But He wants us to talk to Him about them."

Bailey felt a stirring inside her. God was interested in her troubles. When they bowed their heads for prayer, she thanked Him for His concern.

The meeting didn't last long. As they filed out, Bailey saw Rosenbaum in the cell block, staring outward. Bailey raised her hand and waved. A smile brightened the face until the lost ness that soured the inmate's expression seemed to melt away.

"Did you know her?" Tonia Sue had seen the wave.

"Yes, Rosenbaum was in my cell block."

“We’ll have to pray especially for her.”

“Pray for her?” Bailey was shocked. “She was my enemy.”

“More the reason to pray.” Stella led them out into the January sunshine. “Christians are to love their enemies and pray for them.”

“She’s wicked and mean.”

As they got into the car, Stella laid a hand on Bailey’s shoulder. “Let’s pray for Rosenbaum right now.”

For weeks the three ladies visited the jail. Bailey continued to notice Rosenbaum and waved--sometimes as they walked in, sometimes before they walked out, and twice on one occasion. Then Rosenbaum entered the Bible study. Bailey could feel the juice draining out of her. It was something to wave when there was a heavy wall of glass between them but sitting beside her enemy gave her the chills. What if the inmate decided to reach over and choke the life out of her? She had seen it happen.

“Hi, Bailey.” Rosenbaum’s voice held warmth that seemed unnatural. Her lined face as watchful as ever appeared less tense and not as distrusting. The relaxed muscles didn’t smile, but they didn’t bite either.

“Hi.” Bailey’s tongue stuck to the roof of her mouth, and the air escaping to talk had been like the hiss of a cat. She looked over at Stella’s welcoming face.

“We’re glad to have a new comer today. Would you please tell us your name?”

“Rosenbaum.”

“ Welcome to our Bible study, Rose. Do you have a Bible?

No? Well, Bailey will be glad to share hers with you."

A few of the inmates snickered.

"My name is Rosenbaum."

Stella glanced up from the head of the table. "I'm sorry. I thought you meant your first name was Rose and your last Enbaum. Please, accept my apology."

Rosenbaum nodded. Her eyes shifted, but the hard face showed no emotion.

Bailey pushed the Bible on the table towards Rosenbaum.

The inmate stared. "I don't know nuthin' 'bout this book." She frowned at Stella.

"Bailey will help you find the passages." Stella didn't even look up. She turned pages and adjusted her notes beside her Bible. "Why don't you two scoot your chairs closer?" She paused. "That's better." Stella glanced at her notes. "Bailey, look up John 13:34. You read that verse, and Rosenbaum the next."

She had to touch Rosenbaum's skinny arm in order to flip the pages to the passage, but Rosenbaum didn't flinch. Bailey found the scripture. "A new commandment I give unto you. Love one another as I have loved you." She pointed to the words.

Rosenbaum read slowly, one word at a time. "By this shall all men know you are my…" She stumbled over the next word.

"Disciples." Bailey prompted.

"Disciples, if you love one another." Rosenbaum looked up. "I never read such in my life. What is this disciples?"

"Followers of Jesus."

"Oh, why didn't they say so?"

As Stella explained the verse, Rosenbaum's finger moved over the words again, and her lips formed the syllables. "Disciples." She looked over at Bailey. "Are we disciples?"

Bailey could only nod.

Stella heard the question. "We are disciples if we have Jesus in our hearts and live for Him. Rosenbaum, do you have Jesus in your heart? Do you live for Him?"

"No, I never give it much thought."

Stella smiled and continued the lesson that included loving enemies. Rosenbaum followed the Bible study closely. As everyone rose to march back to the cell block, she stood before Stella who was handing out tracts. "Could I have one of them Bibles?"

Bailey shoved hers into the inmate's hands. "You can have this one. I have another at home."

But Rosenbaum stalled. "Mark for me that place where we read about loving everybody."

Bailey found John 13 and showed her. Then Rosenbaum shoved her tract between the pages. Bailey watched her enemy pass through the door without a backward glance.

In the car Stella showed an excitement. "That's what prayer can do!"

"I'm not so sure. Rosenbaum wants out of jail, and she just might think this is her open door."

Chapter 23: The Conference—Meeting

Bailey entered the side door of the Catholic Church as Stan had instructed. The narrow hall had thick tombs on shiny walnut shelves half way down one wall and matching cupboard doors across the bottom half. A coat tree held three civilian hats and a couple of dark suit jackets. She studied the heads of thc various walking canes in a knee high canister. Three were rounded wooden tops of different colored wood. One was shaped like the head of an eagle. The closed orange-yellow beak and white head showed off the black beads under the frowning eyebrows. Below the handle, carved feathers ran down the cane like folded wings. She lifted it from the case to see intricately scaled legs painted like the beak and clawed feet beneath a wooden tuft of white feathers. She slid it back into place to touch the large emerald glass head on a scepter like stick. Jeweler's brass filigree attached it to the top.

"Interesting, isn't it?"

She startled at the man's husky voice and whirled to face the priest in a brown suit with a clerical collar. Laughter lines crinkled the outside corners of his eyes when he smiled, and the pointed chin broadened slightly. Soft hands in loose fists worked the hem line of the jacket.

"Good morning, little sister."

Bailey trembled with her life long distrust of priests. Only her conversion while in prison had opened her to believe the church could be good. She stared at the pallid face whose nose bubbled on the end like the emerald cane, but his expression held a warm welcome.

"Are you mute?"

"No, I just don't know what to say."

He chuckled and moved closer. His hand rose to her shoulder.

Bailey instinctively dodged and stepped out of reach.

“This way.” He motioned with his head toward the other end of the hall, allowing her to go first.

She turned half way around. “Where are we going?”

Again his smile broadened his chin. “Enter the next room on your left.” The door was ajar, and he reached his arm out to push it wide open for her. Padded chairs surrounded an oval table that filled the room.

She felt his hand in the middle of her back guiding her to sit down. Turning, she saw Serine and another woman slip through the door.

“Have a seat, Serine. Hi, Petunia. We’re glad you could make it. Did the library close?”

Petunia laughed. “No, I’m allowed a little time off now and then.” Her eyes focused on Bailey. “What are you doing here?”

“I’m not sure.” Bailey licked her lips. Her legs tensed, and she prepared to rise and run.

The priest’s smile hadn’t faded. “I think we’re all here now. Would either of you ladies enjoy a cup of coffee or tea? We have several kinds from which to choose.”

“No thank you.” Bailey’s hands gripped the arm of her chair. She watched Petunia and Serine stir cream and sugar into cups of coffee--not a hair out of place in their stylish coiffures, and their trendy suits fit perfectly. Bailey glanced at her cheap sweater and jeans. Bile began to build under her tongue.

The priest offered her a cup, but Bailey shook her head. She just wanted to get this over with quickly and run from the oppressing situation. Not a window broke the solidness of the walls and ceiling. The only opening was the door, just like a prison cell.

He settled comfortably in the cushioned chair between Serine and Bailey with his unsweetened tea. "I think we're all family. I understand that you girls went to school together. I was raised in a Catholic orphanage near the convent in Indianapolis." He raised his cup. "Tell me about yourselves. I have always wanted to be a part of a family."

Petunia gasped. "I don't understand." Her hard eyes focused on Bailey.

Bailey could also feel Serine's penetrating gaze but chose to study the wood grain on the table by tracing it with her finger. The table and room resembled the one where her parents and the social worker attempted to force her to sign the papers that would allow James to be adopted. She glanced up at Serine.

"I was adopted by a couple here in town when I was quite small. I don't remember seeing Bailey until we were in the same English class in high school." Serine completely ignored all but the priest.

"Oh, you were friends." The priest couldn't hide his excitement.

"Quite the contrary." Serine laid her spoon aside and blew on her coffee as she held the cup in front of her mouth. "We were raised on opposite sides of the track, so to speak." Her chin tilted upward, and her eyebrows dared Bailey to comment.

Petunia grimaced. "My parents lived in the best part of

town. I was a cheerleader, on the school council, and involved in many activities during my school." She set down her coffee. "I don't see how I'm related to any of you."

Bailey studied the grain of the table top. She wanted to get up and run, but she was trapped. She heard the door click behind her and jumped to her feet. The movement sloshed their tea and coffee. "Oh, I'm sorry." She looked from the priest who passed it off very easily to Serine whose face had hardened. Petunia wiped her cup and table area carefully with a napkin and reached for another. Bailey slid back down into her seat like a reprimanded child.

"Where did you live?" The priest turned to Bailey.

Her eyes wandered to Serine and Petunia. A knowing smirk grew across each woman's face. Bailey's hands began to sweat until she could feel the liquid in her palms. She came unprepared for this test. Stan had told her the priest wanted to talk to her, and that she would be safe, but she hadn't known of Petunia or Serine's presence. The silence made her feel she was positioned over a cliff without wings. She looked down at her hands that were clenched knots on her lap.

"I lived above a bar." She saw the priest's smile disappear. Ungodly fear raged inside her, and she turned on the other women. "It wasn't my choice. I didn't like living over a saloon, but my mother was a drunk, and that's all we had. My grandparents accused me of stealing from the cash register, but I never took one red cent. Never! I worked before I went to school. I worked as soon as I came home. I didn't have any time to study homework except at school. I wore my sister's hand-me-downs." The tears raced down her cheeks. "I wasn't on the honor roll or allowed a part of the in crowd. I loved school, but then I had to quit." She rose to leave.

The priest laid a hand on hers. “Don’t go. It’s all right.”

But Bailey saw Petunia’s disdain and Serine’s hatred. It wasn’t all right.

His body swiveled the chair, and he reached for tissues. “Here.” He pulled one from the box and dangled it in front of her. “We didn’t mean to make you cry.”

She knew he told the truth, but behind him Serine tipped her chin and held the cup to her mouth to hide a revealing smirk that she shared with Petunia.

“I don’t belong here.” She pulled away and pushed the chair from the table.

“Bailey, wait.” His mouth had softened. “I’m your brother. I want to get acquainted with you, Petunia, and Serine.” His eyes glanced to the other women. “I was raised in an orphanage with no real family. I am delighted to meet you.”

She could only move backwards. “I don’t know you or your name. I only came because Stan told me to.”

“My name is Joseph. My father impregnated our mothers.” He included Petunia and Serine as well as Bailey. “We are all victims of rape.” He rose from the chair to turn hers toward her. “Please sit down. Now can I get you something to drink?”

“No.” Again Bailey sagged into the chair. “Who was he?”

“Our father was a young fellow fresh from the seminary. He should never have tried to live in celibacy. He liked all the ladies.” The smile failed, and his face lined with strain. “It’s not a pleasant thought or one that I would like to dwell upon, but he gave me life. He gave you life. For that I thank him and thank God.” His eyes glanced upward.

"How do you know?" Serine leaned towards him.

"My mother was a nun." This time he bent his head, and Bailey could see the Adam's apple bob as he swallowed. "She visited me in the orphanage, but she never told me who she was until she had cancer. She knew our father well and his activities." He couldn't hide the grief. "All those years I wished for family, anybody, and she was there, my mother." He turned to Bailey. "And you were all here, my sisters. Please, don't go—not yet."

Serine's agitation grew. "So was my mother a nun, too?"

"I believe so. I've tried to search the records, but I really don't know. Stan has been quite helpful lately. I do know you were adopted. I wasn't."

"This is outrageous!" Petunia stood. "I have never been so humiliated in all of my life. My mother has always been faithful to my father."

The priest studied his tea, turning the cup with those soft white fingers. Slowly he raised his face to Petunia. "You were conceived out of wedlock. Your parents married, and you were born three months later in a Catholic hospital where my mother nursed."

Bailey turned away. The knot in her stomach twisted ruthlessly. She had always thought her father was a priest, a man of some character if not morals. Now Joseph claimed otherwise. She looked from his face to Petunia and Serine's. None had anything in common with her. Her mother was a whore. "I've got to go."

"Bailey, you were raised in your family's home. Tell us about it."

She swallowed, looking at the table top, and raised her sight and watched Serine's face. "No, my life wasn't pleasant—

isn't pleasant. My grandparents and my mother hate me—have always hated me. They lied to put me in prison—to get rid of me." She turned to Petunia. "I didn't deserve to go to prison. All I wanted was to love and raise James like I wanted to be loved and raised." She stood and reached for the door handle.

"Bailey, don't go. Who is James?" The priest's eyes brightened.

"My son." Serine's words were clipped and sour. "I've raised him in that loving home. Now she is trying to destroy it."

Bailey could take no more. She headed out the door with Joseph behind her. His arms encased her, stopped her, and led her back into the room. When he had her seated, he used a tissue to swab her tears, and she blew her nose in another.

"Now, tell me about James."

She recognized a change in his manner and his mood. No longer did his cheerful disposition rest on his face. The eyes seemed to absorb and control her. She pushed her chair away, but his concentrated stare bored into her defense.

"Tell me about James."

She couldn't.

But Serine could. "Five years ago my husband and I were searching for a baby to adopt. A social worker brought us this boy baby. She told us his mother was in jail, but she was sure that in time we would and could adopt."

"I never signed the papers."

"My husband thinks that you want some compensation, er, money." Serine laughed. "You're not going to get any." She glanced at her watch. "Oh, I must go." As she passed Bailey, she paused at the door. "We'll get Gary. The court will eventually rule you to be an incompetent and unfit parent." She nodded at Joseph. "You've seen how easily Bailey throws a fit."

Bailey's rage left her trembling. "I will never give up my son."

Petunia arose. "I'm leaving, but, Bailey, I'm telling Dave everything you've said."

"He already knows."

"Come now." Joseph stood between them. "We're family. Surely this can be resolved."

"Never!"

Bailey stood back as Serine and Petunia stormed past her. Then she wobbled into the hall and touched the eagle's head on the cane. The beady eyes had seen everything. She bowed her head. Stan would be so disappointed.

Joseph, the priest, waited.

She dropped the cane and turned to face the books and her half brother. His face was contorted with grief.

"You're the only family I have."

"Families don't always get along." She saw his lips tremble. "I'm sorry, but James is my son. She calls him Gary, but even that isn't right."

"Bailey, I'm sorry about this. I didn't know Gary, er, James belonged to you. Serine has always had him and brought him to services with her. He's a bright little fellow. He's well thought of in the parish."

She nodded. "Thanks."

"Bailey, will you visit me again?"

His hopeful face seemed honest, and yet she couldn't trust him. He had led her into a trap.

The walk to her car extended like miles. Her heels rang on the sidewalk and echoed against the building as if she were again in prison about to hear the gates and doors shut. She opened the door of her car and stood looking back at Joseph at the entrance. So much had happened in such a short time. She would never know or understand it all, but she didn't have to know. She didn't have to understand. She didn't have to return, but as Joseph waved, she thought maybe it would be nice to have a brother, even if he were only a half brother and also a priest. Slowly she drove away.

Chapter 24: Valentine's Day

As Bailey crafted a valentine for James on the computer, her door bell rang. "Just a minute."

"Dave!" She opened her arms and walked into his hug. "Oh, honey, it has been so long!"

His fingers traveled up her arms, across her back, and held her close. "Um, you smell so good!" The kiss was lengthy and sweet. "Bailey, come with me today." His nose stroked her cheek between short smacks that worked back to her mouth. "I have something important to show you."

His kisses dipped below her chin, and she didn't want them to stop. "Where?"

"It's a valentine surprise."

"Can James go with us?"

"James?" He pulled away. "Is he living with you?"

"Not yet, but today is my day with him." Her arms wound tightly around his neck to pull him back to her. "I was making a valentine for him on the computer. Do you want to come and see?"

She felt his resistance but pulled him toward the desk. The screen was full of little red hearts upon which she had notated little sayings and cartoon pictures. "I used the program called paint. It's so easy with paste and cut. These I enlarged."

Dave stepped an arm length away.

Bailey tasted his coolness, studied his sober face, and waited.

"I came to see you and spend the day entirely with you." A little boy pout pursed his lips. She turned on her brightest smile. "I'm so happy to see you, too, and I'm delighted to spend the whole day with you." She stepped toward him as he stood with arms stiffly at his sides. "I love you, Dave. You mean a lot to me." She touched his face with her middle finger tip and felt him tremble. Her lips brushed his cheek bone, and his arms encircled her waist.

"Oh, Bailey!" The groan vibrated all through him as he clutched her. His face came down to nuzzle her neck, and his arms tightened. "I've thought of you all the time. I'm miserable without you."

They stood there, and Bailey felt a warmth tingle from her breasts to her toes. He held her as if waltzing without music, and his hand moved up her backbone, to her neck, and became tangled in the hair that had grown past her shoulders. Once again the kiss became lengthy and sweet, luring her into a deeper relationship than she had ever known or thought existed.

"When do you get James?" His voice was husky with emotion.

She pulled back to see the clock. "In fifteen minutes. Oh, I didn't run off his card." She twisted out of his embrace and ran to the computer. Clicking and sliding the mouse, she heard the door close behind her. She whirled. Dave had left.

There was no time to mourn his disappearance. James rapped on the door and rang the bell three times wanting out of the Indiana cold. The wind had picked up, and light snow was expected, but the sun shown gloriously, making the crystallized world glimmer in thousands of colors. Where had Dave gone? She didn't see any tire tracks in his driveway.

"I brought you a valentine, mother." James shinnied out of his outdoor clothing and dug through the book bag that bore Serine's touch. "We made them in school today. I had to make two, one for you and one for my other mother. Which one do you want?"

She studied the two red-and-white pieces of construction paper, choosing the lesser so that Serine could have the better looking one.

"I told the teacher you would know which one I made, 'cause you're my real mother." His little face glowed. "She said you wouldn't want to see the paste, but I knew it wouldn't matter." He turned to the kitchen. "I'm hungry."

As he nibbled on the heart shaped cookies and drank his milk, she continued to glance through the picture window at the driveway across the street. Dave had evaporated.

"Mother?" James patted her hand. "What are we going to do next?"

"Do you have homework?"

"A math paper and some reading."

"Well, let's get at it."

He opened the back pack. "This folder is all my take home papers. Do you want to see them? My other mother is always too busy. Sometimes my father glances at them, but most the time I stuff 'em in my drawer. Then mother cleans it out and throws them away."

"That's probably when she looks at them."

"No, she just throws them away." His head bent over the colorful math page, and he pressed the thick pencil lead into the paper. Each stroke showed tremendous concentration as his tongue touched his lip.

Bailey remembered her mother scolding her once for holding her mouth open. She picked up the folder of finished work and pulled out the packet of loose and assorted pages. "These are very good grades, James. I'm so proud of you." She felt tears coming into her eyes. "You are so smart." She gave him a hug.

"You can put them up on your refrigerator."

"I'd like that." Bailey found her cellophane tape. James showed her how to make loops of tape to stick behind the valentine. Then they positioned his work around the valentine like petals on a flower.

"Mother, why are you crying?"

"Because it looks so pretty, and you're so precious." However, Bailey didn't really know why she was so emotional about a few homework papers, but she had lost one treasure in gaining another.

"Dave came to see me yesterday." Matron Macintyre closed Bailey's front door and allowed Bailey to take her coat. "He wanted to know if you were going to get James or if Serine was adopting him."

Bailey stared out the window at the house for sale. "Oh?" She could feel the tears collecting inside her eyes.

"Did he come to see you?"

"Yes." Bailey rolled her engagement ring around her finger. She turned and tried to smile. "He didn't stay very long. He wanted to go somewhere, but James was coming here, and I couldn't go with him."

"Stan has also talked to the priest."

"Yes, I went, but I didn't like it."

"What happened?"

"Petunia and Serine were also there. Joseph said they were both my sisters."

The matron sat down in the big chair and pulled papers out of her briefcase. "Bailey, we can't choose our family. I would think you of all people would know that. Serine is your half sister and is serious about adopting James. You are going to have to make a decision."

Bailey dropped to the sofa. "What kind of a decision?"

"Well, I can't make it for you, but I can make some suggestions."

"Like what?"

"You can continue battling for James. Serine will continue to hate you, and it won't be good for your relationship with Dave or James."

"He's my son."

"He's also in a fine family. Serine and her husband love him as theirs. They will continue to raise him if you would allow them that right. She is your half sister. That means James isn't really going to be lost to you. You can continue visitation rights, but that would have to be drawn up in the adoption papers."

"You want me to give him up?" Her surprise tightened her chest. "James is all that I've ever possessed. When I was in prison, I dreamed of having a home with him. It kept me going when everything around me went sour."

"I know." The matron reached over to touch Bailey's hand. "This isn't something that will be easy for you, but it probably will be the best for James. You and Dave can get married and have another family."

Dave didn't want James. The thought knifed through Bailey. Couldn't he understand a mother's love for her child? How could she give up her son?

"Bailey, I can't make this decision for you. I came only to try to help you. The judge and I have been talking. If you and Serine could just get along, it would be so much better for James and both of you. As it is now, the two of you are both headed for trouble. Serine and her husband are on rocky waters, just as you and Dave."

"She doesn't want to get along."

"I don't see it that way. She is afraid that you are going to take James away from her. If you would change your position, I think she would come around."

"And if she doesn't, I lose my son."

The Matron shrugged. "Bailey, you're not a child. Wake up! Adults have to make decisions that will be the best for everyone, not just what they want or think they want." She squeezed Bailey's hand. "Look, I love you very much. You've become as close as a daughter to me. I know I wasn't supposed to get so involved when my boss assigned you to my case, but it happened." Now Matron Macintyre had tears in her eyes.

"I'm sorry."

"It's not your fault. I just saw you so vulnerable that I couldn't help it. Then you proved you could handle the situation with your mother and her housekeeping. I've been on your side ever since."

Bailey handed over the tissues. "Thank you. I love you, too. You've done so much for me that I could never repay you. But this adoption? I just don't think I can do it." Sobs from deep inside erupted.

The Matron left, and Bailey stared out the window.

What did she want? She had always thought she wanted a home with James. Now she wanted Dave. Why couldn't she have both? *Oh, God, what should I do?* The cry came from her heart. How could she know the will of God? What was the best? Hadn't God made mothers to raise their children? But James had two. Which one was best for him?

Chapter 25: Tough Decisions

Bailey's mind couldn't follow all the legalese. Was this really the best for James? She had formed a friendly relationship with him in the last few months. This past week he had visited again.

"James, do you want to live with me or your other mother?"

He had looked up from the dinosaur he was turning a bright purple with a water marker. “I don’t know.” The green eyes looked so innocent. “If I live with you, will I see my other mother and father?”

“That could be arranged.” She bit her lip. He needed to know the other option and the consequences. “Would you rather live with your other mother and father?”

“Could I see you like now?”

She nodded. “But which would you rather do?” It was a terrible question for the child to answer, but she had to know in order to form her own decision. Beanie’s toenails clicked across the linoleum, and he sat beside her leg. She dropped her hand to pet his head, and he yawned.

James had seen it. “Will Beanie always be my dog?”

“Definitely.”

“Even if I live with my other mother and father?”

“Even if. He’ll always be here for you.”

“Will you always be here for me?”

That question made Bailey pause. If she married Dave, would they live in Lakeside? She didn’t know, and his e-mails had been mere sentences lately.

James dropped his marker, and she bent to the floor to pick it up.

“Well, will you always be here for me?”

The decision had to be made. “James, I want to marry Dave. If he would take me to Indianapolis, there would always be a place in our home for you."

"Would Beanie be there?"

"I don't know. Dave is allergic to dogs and cats."

"Oh."

"We would work that out. Beanie will always be yours."

Bailey e-mailed Dave. "I am thinking of allowing Serine to adopt James. What are your thoughts?" She hit the send button and waited—and waited. She checked her e-mail almost every hour.

The next morning she turned the computer on before she dressed or had her first cup of coffee. Dave had not replied, so she sent another e-mail. "Should I keep James?" Again she checked her e-mail every hour. By afternoon she was a nervous wreck.

"I e-mailed him twice," she told Matron Macintyre. "By this time he could have read it fifty times."

"Dave's a working man. This decision is yours—not someone else's."

My decision?

Bailey searched her Bible. Hannah gave her son to the priest in the temple when he was seven years old. She saw him once a year and took him a new coat. She prayed. Her decision teetered up and down. She had to talk to someone besides the Matron.

"Stella, do you have a minute to talk to me?"

"We're going away to a retreat, Bailey. Can you hold on

for a few days?"

"All right." Bailey hung up the phone, but her mind was so bothered that she found herself dialing Tonia Sue. "Do you have time to talk to me?"

"When?"

"Right now."

"It'll have to be short."

"I'll be right over." Driving down the street reminded Bailey of her mother. Would she ever know where Narla had placed her? Thoughts of her mother brought to mind how vehemently her grandparents and parent had been about adoption. Had they been right?

Tonia Sue had hot tea waiting. "This has been the coldest winter, I do believe. You been keeping warm?" She set out a package of cookies with the cellophane ripped off one end. "Help yourself."

"I came to ask if you thought I should give up my son James for adoption."

"What ever gave you that idea, child?" Tonia Sue set her cup down on the table so hard it splashed. She reached behind her for a towel hanging on the oven handle and sopped it dry. "You a mom just like I is. We both have a son. Do you see me giving up my Teddy for adoption even if he bad?"

For a short talk, Bailey didn't think she would ever be allowed to leave Tonia Sue's house. Tonia Sue followed her to the door chatting about Teddy. When Bailey slid through the door, Tonia Sue stood in the entry talking about the jail ministry and Stella. She came out of the house as Bailey walked to her car.

"James only have that one mom--you. Don't you forget it."

Bailey saw her in the rear view mirror until she turned the corner. James was her son. Even if she allowed him to be adopted, he would still be her blood, but she was so mixed up that she turned a wrong corner and found herself in front of the Catholic Church.

Joseph seemed surprised when he opened his office door and saw Bailey. "Come in. What brings you here?" His cheerfulness turned on like Christmas tree lights.

"I've come for advice."

His green eyes seemed to smile into hers and waited.

She twisted the tissue in her hands. "I've never had a brother or anyone except Matron Macintyre to confide in, but she thought you could help me."

His smile warmed his face. "Is this a confessional?"

"No."

"Well, I'll do the best I can, as a brother that is. I've never been consulted on those grounds."

"James is my son. Like you and me, he was conceived by rape. I raised him the best of my ability for two years before I went to prison. Serine has kept him for five."

"She tells everyone she wants to adopt him."

"I know." Bailey paused. This was so hard. She took a huge breath. "If I sign the papers for her to adopt him, can you tell me how to get on better terms with Serine so she will allow me to see him?"

The priest drummed his fingers on the desk. "I wish I could guarantee that, but none of us can control the actions of another person." He swiveled the chair around and stood. "James could be the answer to your prayers, mine, and Serine's. We are family. Families need to get together."

"What do you mean?"

"She would do anything for James. If he wants to see you, me, or whoever; she'll do it for him. Love grows slowly like a tree, but the roots go deep."

"I don't understand."

"Bailey, this is going to take time, but it is already progressing."

She bowed her head. "I don't know how much time I have."

"Are you ill?"

"No, that's not what I meant. The judge wants answers. I don't know what to do."

Joseph walked around the desk. He laid his hand on her shoulder, but she didn't flinch.

"Serine loves that little fellow, but she knows the only one who could take him away from her is you. You will always have access to him if he's adopted or if he isn't."

"Not if she continues the suit that I'm an unfit mother."

"How can she prove that? How have you neglected him?"

"I was in jail."

"Mothers with a jail sentence still have rights to their children. What would keep you from getting James?"

"Serine."

"Ah, but there you're wrong. The strongest ties in the world to a child are those to his blood related mother." He pointed to the picture of Mary the mother of Christ. "Catholics believe that all over the world."

"But the question is whether I should give James up for adoption."

"Bailey, even if you don't, Serine will want to see him often. He's like a son to her. James can become the bond we need to unite our family."

Bailey left the church office stepping high. Joseph wasn't a bad guy, and she needed a good friend, but she wasn't any closer to a decision than before.

Clark was not on her list to be consulted, but she stopped at the grocery to get a gallon of milk and some oranges. He found her bending over bananas.

"Well, well, well."

She recognized his voice and stood slowly, dodging the hand that fell on her arm. "Don't touch me."

He stepped back. The smile turned into a hard line to match the stare. "What's wrong with you? All I want to do is talk to you."

"Talk fast."

"Now, Bailey, talk takes time, time alone. I can never get you alone." His hand snaked out, but she jumped back, knocking the apple display to the floor.

She picked up one and lobbed it right at his face. Then she leaped across the mess and down the closest aisle. Cutting across the meat section, she doubled back through the baking aisle to the checkout counters and slid out to the front door.

"You pack a powerful punch." Clark stepped out of the shadow, rubbing the jaw on his leering face. "Come on, Bailey. Grow up. Quit playing these childish games." He grabbed her arm above the elbow. "Yell, and I'll break your neck."

"Let me go."

"After we've had a little talk."

"Where are you taking me?"

He laughed.

"Clark, let me go!"

"Shut up." He slapped her hard, snapping her head back like volley ball. Then he continued to pull her across the parking lot. He pushed her behind the wheel and over the bench seat of a pickup. "Don't try to get out. I'll run you down."

He whipped the vehicle across the intersection and into traffic. The motion threw her on the floor. She struggled to get up and hit her head against the glove box. She was about to crawl up on the seat when he hit the brakes so hard, her body slammed the floor again. The truck roared off, and she lay in a fetal position.

"Well, Babe, I finally got you." He laughed.

She stretched out, kicking his leg and foot off the accelerator. The motion of the truck jolted her into the door, but she had tensed her body for several more kicks.

He swore and twisted the steering wheel back and forth, making her body reel, but she continued to kick. Suddenly he braked. Her head hit the door, and she lost consciousness.

Minutes later she awoke. Cold air hit her body like ice water. Clark had opened his door to get out. She lay still waiting for an opportunity. He shut the door. She reached up and locked her door, scrambled over to lock the driver's door, and realized he had left the key in the ignition. She started the motor and put the automatic in reverse.

"Bailey, stop!" Clark grabbed the door handle and stood on the running board.

She backed out on the street while he continued to pound the window by her head with the palm of his hand.

"Woman!"

Bailey drove away from the salt box, the house she recognized from her visit with the Matron and the real estate agent. It didn't look like any improvements had been made, and she wasn't about to share it with Clark for any period of time. At the corner she had to brake for a stop sign and hit the pedal hard. His body flapped on the outside, but he held like super glue.

"Bailey, where you taking me?"

The question made her smile. He wouldn't answer when she asked, so she pursed her lips and pushed the accelerator. Again his body jerked.

She braked for Main Street. Wouldn't he just give up? She glanced to see his raging face and white knuckled grip on the door handle. They passed the school where children were out for recess in the winter sun, but she didn't look for James. Instead she headed for the jail and police station.

"Bailey, open this door!"

She couldn't find a parking place as she drove up to the front with the glass doors, so she braked and killed the engine right in the middle of the street. Then she pushed the horn in a multitude of continuous, short honks.

"Bailey, you're crazy!"

Officers poured out like ants in a stirred hill. Bailey continued to honk.

Clark jumped from the truck to confront the first officer. "Arrest her. She stole my truck."

As the cops surrounded the truck, Bailey unlocked the door and opened it. "I'm not armed. Arrest him. He tried to abduct me."

When Matron Macintyre arrived a few minutes later, Clark and Bailey were both being held for questioning.

"He caught me in the super market and took me out to that old house. Remember the trashy salt box? I locked him out of the truck and drove here."

"Bailey, this is serious. It could break your probation."

"No, don't put me back in jail." Her hands began to tremble. "I didn't do anything wrong. I was looking at the bananas, and he came up behind me."

"Liar!" Clark stood and stepped toward them. "She came out to my house to talk about James."

"I didn't! Please, believe me." She touched her face. "He slapped me. He yanked me over the parking lot. He threw me inside so I fell on the floor."

"Lying woman. She was stealing my truck."

"My car." Bailey searched the matron's stern face. "It's still at the grocery. That'll prove I'm telling the truth." She grasped the matron's hands. "If I'd gone out to his house, my car would be parked out there, but it's still in the parking lot at the super market."

Matron Macintyre faced her chief. "Book him for kidnapping and assault and battery."

Clark turned to the officer. "I want a lawyer."

Bailey met Serine's husband, a tall thin man with sandy hair and a lined face. His cold handshake was limp, but his lips worked with emotion. Bailey couldn't keep from staring at the pair as they settled in the theater seats of the court room across the aisle. Serine's happiness gave her proud face a glow of beauty. As always, her blue pantsuit with the wide collar and peach camisole was as impeccable as her coiffure. But the man's limp, cold hand remained on the woman's knee. The solidarity of their relationship spoke loudly in that silent touch.

"Will the court rise?"

The judge entered in her black robe from a side door. Bailey watched her cross to the high desk, sit, and tap the gavel. "You may be seated."

Soon Bailey was summoned and faced the judge. Serine and her husband came behind her.

“Ms. Berkley, do you fully understand the boundaries of this document?”

“Yes, your honor.”

“You are giving up your rights as a parent to your son James, right?” The judge’s eyes penetrated like those of a hawk.

“I am.” Bailey turned to Serine and her husband and smiled. “I feel this must be done for James. I want the very best for him. Serine has been very kind and loving to him.” She faced the couple. “I know you will provide James with the best of care. I only would like to see him frequently.”

“Ms. Berkley, face the bench.”

Bailey turned, but the sobs in her chest had reached her throat and eyes. She raised her hands to her face.

“Here.” Serine thrust a fancy handkerchief into Bailey’s hands.

“Thank you.” Surprise numbed the hurt.

“Sign here.”

Bailey accepted the pen from the judge. She paused to glance at Serine whose hand had slid into her husbands. Small beads of perspiration dotted the woman’s forehead. Bailey set her left finger on the line and held the paper steady. She signed her name.

“Date your signature, please.”

Once again the pen tip met the paper, and she scratched across the surface.

Then she dropped the pen and turned to Serine. “I believe that James will be happy.”

"He always has been." Serine's head nodded towards her husband. "Now he will have a father."

Chapter 26: Confessions

Bailey walked to her car thinking of the last statement. James had a father. Unlike her, he had always had one. He had a loving home. She had no one. Joseph's face came to mind. She would talk to him again. There were too many questions without an answer.

She passed the entrance to the jail, remembering Rosenbaum's confession. She and Stella continued to hold Bible studies. The inmate came with an eager interest and open mind. Then one afternoon before they left, she broke down in tears.

"We was 'dirt poor.' Other children had nice toys, nice parents, nice homes. We didn't have nuthin'." The tall woman's thin shoulders bowed inward, and her sobs came out like the earth shuddering during an earthquake. "Paw drunk up everything. We lived inside some rough tree posts covered with tin, cardboard, and odd pieces of wood that maw found to cover the cracks." Her eyes strayed out the window. "Yah might say our house looked like the ugliest patch quilt ever made. When the wind blew, it shook like a scared rabbit. When it rained, there wasn't a dry spot to be had."

The silent group around the prayer table waited.

"Yah, maw used a battered tin pot on top of the stove with a few granules of coffee to give the water color, but there weren't no taste." Her eyes traveled around the group. "I guess our sink had running water. Maw sent us running with the bucket off the back wall to the cistern fed by the stream." Her gaze rested on Bailey. "A rag on a nail was used to strain it into the pot. Maw boiled dandelion and turnip greens for us to eat. We didn't starve, but we didn't own a pinch of fat either."

“How did you stay warm?”

“There was a cook stove in the kitchen. Its crooked pipe went through the ceiling, and we cooked everything on it: fried squirrel, hog jowl bacon, and grits.” A glimmer of a smile crossed her face. “You’d bake facing the stove and freeze on the other side.”

“And I thought I had it rough.” Bailey stared in wonder.

“Oh, I don’t remember feelin’ too bad about it. We youngin’s ran wild like the deer in the forest. Nuthin’ bothered us much.” Then she stopped. “That was a lie. Everything bothered us. We fought like hell cats: kickin’, screamin’, and cussin’ the air blue. I hated it.” Spit collected in her mouth, but she quickly swallowed it.

Bailey handed her a tissue.

“Thanks.” Rosenbaum wiped her mouth and chin. “Where was I? Oh, yah. Early on I found a bunch of older boys. They had all tried me out and said I’d do.” Tears came to her eyes, and the tissue paper melted into a knot. “They introduced me to chew, the corn cob pipe, and some other herbs I never bothered to name. But it was the still on the hill that brewed more trouble than it was worth.”

Stella looked at her watch. “We don’t have much time.”

“I’m almost done. The guys drunk themselves silly. Petty offences didn’t bounce off the walls. They formed alliances against each other, drew lines in the dirt to dare the others to cross, and fought until their bodies dropped on the ground panting and heaving for air. I held them together.” She sniffed. “I towered over the lot like out here in the exercise yard, and they would cringe in fear. I ruled with a cruel tongue and a fast backhand. None dared cross me."

Her eyes roved around the table. "Yah, it's just like here. None dared disobey. All of them worshiped me like royalty, but it's funny. None of them really loved or cared for me. I held them together like a pack of wolves giving them a living. Not a one came to my rescue when I was shoved in the slammer."

Bailey rose from her chair. "God cared. He sent Jesus to save you."

"I know, oh how I know!" The woman beat her breast. "He's forgiven me for that first baby died. We buried the little fellow in a hollow log under the hickory tree. I declared I'd never change or wash them dirty diapers and dropped off my next two at maw's."

"What happened to your children?"

"I don't know. I didn't care, and I didn't go back to visit. Babies and children were unnecessary trouble. I had no time." She scanned the ladies at the table once more. Her proud face grew grim, repentant. "I'm a bad woman, aren't I? An awful, old woman."

Stella's tissue was soggy with tears. "Oh, Rosenbaum, ask Jesus to forgive you."

"How could He? I'm the worst of the worstest."

"He loves you anyway. All you have to do is tell Him what you've told us, and ask Him to forgive you."

The woman shivered. "There's more." Her eyes shifted to Bailey. "Stuff I cain't tell nobody. Cain't tell a living soul."

"You can pray silently." Stella had all the answers.

"Silently?"

"Yes. I say the words out loud. You think them in your mind like you're talking face-to-face with Him. He'll forgive you."

"How will I know if He forgives me?"

"You'll know." Stella turned to those around the table. "Please pray with us."

The air held a spiritual battle. Bailey could almost hear the swords of the fighting angels, but Stella prayed. Rosenbaum prayed. All the ladies prayed. Bailey couldn't say exactly the second the peaceful presence flowed over them like a bursting dam, but a joy rang in her heart. She lifted her tearful face to those around her. There wasn't a dry eye in the crowd.

Rosenbaum beamed. The lines in her face disappeared, and Bailey thought, she's beautiful. The brow lost the tortured frown. The lips curved naturally upward, and the cheeks blushed with God's love. The long, wet, curling lashes accented the light blue eyes whose iris had an indigo edge. Hers was the face of royalty.

"I feel clean." Rosenbaum laughed, but the jeering tones were gone. The sound came deep down, more than a throaty chuckle. The vibrant, womanly tone rang like chimes in the wind. "He did it—He did!" She stood and raised her hands heavenward. "Oh, wonderful, wonderful Lord!"

The warden stepped in the door. "Time's up."

Rosenbaum was first in line. "Marm, I'm sorry for causing trouble. Will you forgive me?"

The police woman's surprise made Bailey giggle, but she held her hand over her mouth as the inmates marched like kindergarteners back to their cells.

That evening as she watched the sunset through the picture window, the phone rang.

"Hi, Bailey."

Dave's voice sent shivers through her. Why had he disappeared on Valentine's Day? Why hadn't he answered her e-mails? Did he want to break their engagement? Did he want her to give back the ring?

"Hi." Her voice squeaked with the effort.

"Honey, I have only a few minutes. I joined the army. That's why I haven't been able to contact you the last few weeks."

"Joined the army?"

"Don't be too shocked. I didn't like my job at the library in Indianapolis. I missed you so much, but I wanted you to bond with James. Then I realized that my life needed to stand for more. I thought I could get it here."

Her mind raced. "Dave, I signed the adoption papers. James belongs to Serina."

"You did?"

"Yes, where are you?"

"In Fort Benning, Georgia. Oh, Bailey, I've made a terrible mistake."

"How long are you going to be there?"

"That's just it. I've got another eighteen weeks of basics."

"Half a year?"

"Not quite. Honey, I have to hang up. I'll send you a letter soon. I can't e-mail. Love you."

Before she could reply, the line went dead.

Chapter 27: The Job

Matron Macintyre faced Bailey. "I think you need a regular job."

"I am making enough to support myself."

"I know that, but you're too alone." She paced Bailey's front room. "You need to get out more in the public."

"Like a job." Bailey stared at the computer. "I'm doing the only thing I know."

"You know how to serve tables and fix food."

"I'm not working in a bar."

The Matron sighed. "You know you can be difficult at times. I am not referring to bars and saloons. There are some nice family restaurants in town. You could apply at one of them. I always see signs begging for help."

"Okay." But Bailey didn't like the suggestion.

"Look, Bailey. You need some structure. When did you go to bed last night?"

"I didn't. It was three in the morning."

"That's what I'm talking about. You have bags under your eyes from a lack of proper rest."

Bailey was inflamed. She waited until the Matron left before she faced the mirror. Her hair needed washed and combed. She'd take a shower. To cover the bags under her eyes, she applied some makeup. Then she called the beautician for a cut.

A help wanted posted on the front window intrigued her. “What kind of help do you need?”

The stylist grinned at her reflection in the wall high mirror. “I’m looking for sort of a jack of all trades—answer the phone, greet the ladies coming in, push a broom when it’s required.” Her smock wore a colorful name tag, Wanda. She winked a brown eye. “Are you interested?”

“You’d have to train me.”

“I don’t think that would be too much a problem.” Wanda leaned over the back of Bailey’s head. “Have you ever considered coloring? I think a light ash brown with a streak or two of red would make you gorgeous.”

“I had a permanent before Christmas.”

“It’s about time to do it again. Then we’ll discuss the coloring.”

When Bailey’s hair was finished, she reached for her purse.

“Hair cuts are free if you’re coming in this afternoon to answer the phone.” Wanda’s wishful smile and her hopeful face beamed encouragingly. “You could start right now.”

“All right.”

“Hang your coat over there and stick your purse under it.” Wanda answered the phone as the door opened, the bell rang, and two more customers walked into the little shop.

That evening when she got home, Bailey called Matron Macintyre. “I found a job. I’m working at Hair Cuts as a receptionist.”

“That’s wonderful. I’ll call tomorrow for an appointment.”

Bailey awoke the next morning excited and alert. She prepared her house for James’ visit after school and went to work. The phone kept her busy planning appointments. She enjoyed meeting the customers. About noon Wanda tapped her on the shoulder.

“Yah done great! Don’t yah think yah need a break?”

“A break?”

“Yah worked through yah break, but yah go to lunch.”

“Oh, okay.” Her hand automatically reached for the ringing phone.

“Got it. Take the hour if yah need it.”

Bailey slid into her coat and grabbed her coat. Outside on the street she looked both ways. She wasn’t really hungry, but Cindy’s Cup on the end of the block seemed appropriate. She entered remembering the Sunday she met James. She chose the booth at the back where she and the matron sat waiting for him.

“What would you like to drink?” The waitress set down a frosty glass of ice water.

“Oh, water is fine.”

“I’ll be back when you’re ready to order. Our lunch special is onion soup, chili mac, or fried cheese sandwiches.”

“The soup, please.” Her mind replayed the boy standing in the midst of the restaurant attracting the notice of all the customers. She loved him.

As Bailey ate, she watched the other diners come and go.

She recognized a couple of ladies, customers in Hair Cuts, but she slid out without talking. Work waited.

"I need to leave at a quarter till." Bailey told Wanda about James. Then she swept up the last hunks of hair and walked out the door. Clouds covered the sun. The wind blew through her coat and chilled her bones. Shivering, she opened the door of her car, but the Chevy wouldn't start. James was due in minutes. She panicked and began to run home.

She was crossing the highway, when Matron Macintyre pulled the squad car up beside her. "Bailey, I thought this was the afternoon James came."

"It is." Bailey slid into the seat. Her lungs burned. She coughed. "Hurry." She searched her purse for a tissue, blew her nose, and coughed again.

"Where is your car?"

"It wouldn't start." She glanced up to see the Matron pulling into her driveway. James was standing at the door, pushing the doorbell and pounding on the door. "I left it at Hair Cuts."

"Get a mechanic over there and get it fixed." The policewoman backed her car out of the drive as Bailey's door opened.

"Mother, where were you?" James watched the squad car until it disappeared down the street. "Did you have to go to jail again?"

"No, Matron Macintyre gave me a lift." She reached for another tissue to blow her nose again.

"Your clothes smell funny."

Bailey couldn't smell anything. "Would you like a cup of hot cocoa?"

They settled down with his homework, and she forgot the car.

The next morning Bailey awoke with a slight cold, but she took a hot shower, drank some green tea, and swallowed a couple of tablets. When she picked up her keys, she remembered that her car wasn't even close. She called a cab.

"I'm sorry I'm late. My car didn't run last night, and I had to call a cab."

Wanda nodded in her direction and returned to work on the latest customer filling her chair.

Before she could remove her coat, the phone rang. Bailey dropped in her chair and picked up the receiver. As she finished the call, the finished customer turned to stare at Bailey's reflection in the mirror that stretched across the wall. Bailey stared back at her sister Narla and shrugged out of her coat. She placed her purse and coat on the hook and turned to see Narla's eyes had followed her every move. Lifting her shoulders, Bailey walked back to the ringing phone. Narla was just another customer.

"Since you work here, my haircut is free." Narla's fake smile tried to hide the sneer in her tone.

"Absolutely not! Twenty dollars." Bailey waited for the money.

"Twenty dollars!" Narla snarled. "I never pay twenty. Since

I come in every week, I get a two dollar discount."

Bailey rose to talk to Wanda.

Her boss's thin and delicate eyebrows rose on her forehead. "Okay for this time, but twenty if she comes back next week."

Narla had already slipped out the door before Bailey returned.

Wanda grimaced. "Double next week."

Bailey nodded. Her chest burned, and her head throbbed. She looked at the clock, but the phone rang again. Two permanents that afternoon aggravated her breathing, but she suffered silently. As the shop closed for the evening, she struggled to sweep up the hair.

"How are yah getting home?" Wanda already dressed for the outside waited as she struggled into her coat.

"I was going to call a cab."

"I'll take yah home." Inside the car Wanda asked, "What happened with Narla? I watched her stare at yah the whole time I did her hair."

"She's my half sister."

"Oh, that explains it all. Bailey, don't let her dominate yah. Next week she doesn't sit in a chair until yah have the forty dollars." She pulled into Bailey's drive. "I'll pick yah up a quarter till tomorrow morning."

"I'll be ready. Thank you."

"No, thank yah, Bailey. Yah don't realize the pressure yah saved me by being in the shop. Yer a jewel."

"A jewel." Bailey repeated the words several times that evening. No one had ever given her such a nice compliment. She reveled in it.

"We're off tomorrow." Wanda announced on a Tuesday. "I mean, yer off unless yah want to come with me and carry my stuff. I go to the nursing home every week or so to do the ladies' hair and cut the men's."

"What nursing home?"

"Well, there are three in town. We hit all of them sooner or later."

So Wanda picked her up the next morning at the regular time. Inside the facility Bailey kept her eyes open. Maybe she would find her mother.

"I'm going to teach yah how to wash heads. I'll curl them, but come and watch."

She was doing the third lady when her mother wheeled into the room.

"Bailey! Where have you been? Why haven't you come to see me? Get me out of this horrible place. Nobody will get me any liquor, and it's just about to kill me."

Wanda's eye brows lifted, and her quirky grin crossed her face. "Yer mother? I didn't know."

Bailey continued to rinse the woman's head in her hands, but her mother was on the rampage.

"Don't you ever listen to me? I want out of here."

Wanda came up beside her. "I can do her by myself. Go get us some pop. My mouth is dry." Her head was beaded with perspiration, and she nodded toward the door. "Don't yah hurry none. Take yer time."

"Mother, I'll be back." Bailey left the room. She had known the possibility of finding her mother would arrive sooner or later if she continued to work for Wanda, but she had still been surprised. Her mother actually looked younger. Her voice was stronger, oh, so much stronger. She had to be healthier. But why was she in a wheel chair? Was this a protest?

Wanda took her to Cindy's Cup for lunch. "So that was yer mother. I would have never guessed." She took a sip of her sweetened iced tea. "The first time I did her hair, I almost had to shave her head to wash it. She grabbed the shampoo and threw it at me." She chuckled, and her eye brows twitched. "And I would never have thought yah and Narla sisters."

"We're only half sisters. Our fathers were different."

"Oh, that explains a lot." Her order of a hamburger and fries arrived. "How can yah survive on only a cup of soup? Here take some of my fries. I don't need them all." She patted her stomach and laughed.

"When is your baby due?"

"Sometime in May. I'm so glad I found yah. Now I know I won't have to shut the shop down."

Dave's letter lay in her box. She pulled it out and studied the handwriting. His presence floated around her.

Darling Bailey, I really messed up big time joining the

army. I admit I was angry that you have James, and he always seems to be in the way, but I really like the little kid. I didn't expect you to sign him over to Serine. Oh, Honey, how could you?

I thought I was in pretty good shape until I got here. Sarge marches us for miles, and puts us through all kinds of calisthenics for maybe a smile or raising an eye brow. He never seems happy with anything that any of us do. I don't know how my brother Jim survived all of this.

I beat the rest of the guys today in the mile, but ole Sarge made me do a hundred pushups. I had a coughing fit so he sent me to the infirmary. It's a blessing I've slept half a day in here, and have the chance to write this letter. You can't believe how Sarge keeps me going.

Love, Dave

She slept that night with the letter.

"Clark's hearing is tomorrow. The judge gave me a subpoena for you." Matron Macintyre handed the paper to Bailey neatly folded as if going in a legal envelope. She glanced around the room. "This is a nice place."

"Thank you." Bailey used her receptionist voice. "Please be seated. The stylist will be with you as soon as she finishes another customer."

The Matron's surprise appeared in her stepping back. Then she smiled. "You're doing fine, Bailey. I'm proud of you." She found a chair and faced Bailey. Between phone calls they gave each other a knowing nod.

The hearing became quite controversial. Clark brought up her past to discredit her testimony, but the Matron verified Bailey's words. The judge looked tired. Finally she tapped her gavel.

"The defendant is sentenced to five years and court costs. Court dismissed."

Bailey returned to Hair Cuts, bouncing like a rubber ball. Clark couldn't touch her.

"Bailey, we've missed you, and your friend Rosenbaum asked for you." Stella Brown stood in the vestibule of the church on Sunday morning.

"I'm working at Hair Cuts."

"Would you go with us if we scheduled our visits for the hour after you are off work?"

"Sure."

"I'll make arrangements with Tonia Sue and the jail."

Bailey walked to her Sunday school class. So much had happened in so short a time. When Dave moved away, she had taken over his class downstairs. The kids were always asking when he would return, but she couldn't answer that or some of their other questions. She wondered if she should be teaching kids when she knew so little herself.

"That's the way to learn," Pastor Brown assured her. "Let me know what their questions are, and we'll get them answered." With a wink and a pat on the back he had left her standing in the basement class room.

It must have been inspiration that gave her the idea to provide a pencil on a string, a pad of paper, and a shoe box with a slit in the lid. "When you have questions that I can't answer, write them down. Put them in the box, and I'll see the pastor answers them for you."

"Are you going to read them?"

"Only if you want me to."

"How are you going to know the difference?"

Bailey brought another box. The one marked PRIVATE always had more notes, but she didn't mind. She had solved a problem and could move to other matters.

Rosenbaum's hair, recently washed and curled, framed her thin face that glowed with an inner beauty. Bailey had never seen such a transformation. God's grace had not only cleaned up the inside, but He had shined up the outside as well. The woman brought back Bailey's old Bible and sat next to her.

"I missed you." The tone wasn't accusatory.

Bailey was surprised. "I have a job."

"Oh?"

For the inmate to show interest in anyone except herself was a miracle. "I am working at a beauty shop."

"Yah cut hair?"

"Not yet, but I'm learning."

Stella's lesson was on friendship and relationships with others.

She brought a paper cross that required Bailey's help in holding it up before the class. "This upright piece goes up to God and down to us. We couldn't save ourselves, and God knew it. So He sent the best He had in Heaven, His Son."

"That was Jesus."

"Yes, Rosenbaum, Jesus could save us because He was without sin. His blood paid for our sins."

Stella turned back to the cross. "This horizontal arm is like a person stretching out their arms for a hug." She dropped the paper to demonstrate by opening her arms.

Rosenbaum came out of her chair and stepped into Stella's arms. "I ain't had no friend, no real friend afore."

Bailey had to swallow. The truth hit hard. Rosenbaum had followers, a crowd, but nobody who really cared for her. Any of them would have paid her in full behind her back, but they were all deathly afraid of her fury.

At one time Bailey could have honestly said she had no friends, but now she had Stella and Tonia Sue. Those two loved her and would do anything they could to help her. She had Matron Macintyre who had risked her career, position, and job in overt friendship so many, many ways. Now she had Wanda. God had even given her Dave. She could feel an expressible joy arising to over flowing within her. Then she turned and saw Rosenbaum coming toward her with arms spread wide.

"I love you, Bailey." The thin, skinny arms wrapped around her body. The inmate's face burrowed into her shoulder, their cheeks met skin-to-skin. The woman's lips touched her neck.

Her love softened Bailey's heart. "I love you, too, Rosenbaum."

Chapter 28: Dave

The March weather brought out the robins that she could easily see in the bare branches of the trees. Almost hidden in the melted, dirty, and crusted snow left in the shadows, crocuses peeked out to catch the warming sun and show off their purple and yellow-orange outfits.

"Sorry, you're too early for Easter," Bailey told them as she walked around her house searching for each and every bloom. The crisp fresh air energized her so that she left the car in the garage and jogged to work. Bennie whined when she left the house, and she knew he wanted to run with her. "Sorry, fellow, you can't come today."

Wanda's baby was showing. "He kicked up something terrible last night." She waddled around the shop, unable to bend over. "I think he'll play a lot of soccer and football." Her laughter rang through the room, cheering the customers.

Bailey's fingers slid through hair so her trimming didn't resemble Wanda's but a chop-chop. However, she could set hair. Her boss would explain which direction to run the curlers and work on another customer. The clientele appreciated Bailey, except for one customer—Narla.

Her sister sauntered in like she owned the joint. Bailey learned to find something to do in the back room when Narla's face appeared in the doorway. Wanda knew exactly how to handle that gal.

When they went to the nursing home, Bailey's mother arrived to complain. Again Wanda stepped between them, and everything smoothed out like warm margarine on toast.

"What will I do when you're gone?"

"I'll only be gone a day or so. Yah can handle the customers that need a wash and set. Book the others for when I get back." Wanda's laugh filled the place. "Bailey, yer a worry wart. The baby isn't coming for another two months."

"But I need to know how."

"Go to the back room. I've set up some dummy heads for yer to practice on."

Bailey struggled.

"Yah wallow them dolls around until yer break their neck if they had one." Wanda's cheer brightened everybody's day. "But yer learning."

Yes, she was learning, but not fast enough. She also worried about Dave.

His next letter came within a week.

Dear Sweetheart, I've been spending more and more time in the infirmary. The pollens are out down here big time. My sinuses plug up when I'm doing all the physical activities outside, and this time I fainted right in front of Sarge. It was so embarrassing.

The doctors have been giving me different pills for allergies and asthma, but nothing seems to be working. I'm a failure, Honey. I can't do it. I don't understand how my brother Jim did it. I'm trying hard, but I'm not making the grade.

Then again, the computer courses I'm getting are really great. The army wants to use me for an air controller. I'd sit up there in the tower in front of a computer and guide the planes in and out. It's like a video game and really a lot of fun. I'm good at it. And the pollen doesn't affect me up here.

Well, I must post this.

I love you very much. See you in ten weeks.

Dave.

Bailey prayed, Oh, God, bless Dave. Heal his sinuses. Help him to make it. It seemed so unfair that he would have found a job he loved and yet be struggling.

The phone rang, and she answered it. “Hair Cuts. Can I help you?”

“Hello, Bailey.”

“Dave!” Her shout of joy made Wanda stop and smile at her.

“How are you?” His husky voice thrilled her.

“I’m fine. I’m working.”

“Take a break. I’ve been discharged from the army because of my asthma. When can I see you?”

“Where are you?”

“In front of your house, sitting in my car.”

She laid her hand over the receiver. “Wanda, can I take the afternoon off?”

“Sure. Just don’t run off and elope tonight. I need yah.” She patted her tummy. “We’re depending on yah.”

“Thanks!” She spoke into the phone. “I’ll be there in fifteen minutes.” Then she thought of the ten minute jog. “Make it twenty.

I'm jogging."

"Stay there. I'll pick you up in five minutes."

She stared at the hair on the floor. "I'm sorry."

"Don't yah worry none. I can do it." Wanda's face beamed. "I can't wait to meet this fantastic fellow." Her laugh sent Bailey scurrying out into the sunshine.

He leaned over the seat and pushed her door open. "Get in."

She slid in, replaced everything on the console between the seats, and sat on top.

"Hey, Bailey, you'd be more comfortable if I shared my seat." Dave scooted over to the door, wrapped his arm around her, and pulled her in beside him. "Now this is what I've been yearning to do for months!" He kissed her.

She had to come up for air. "Dave!" They were still in front of Hair Cuts. Wanda and her clients watched intently out the windows as if it were a TV sitcom. "Aren't we going somewhere?"

"Yeah." He started the car, and it leaped into the street. With difficulty he guided it into a back street alley. "Now the only watchers will be alley cats." He pulled her back into kissing position. His hands flowed up her backbone under her coat. After his lips pulled away, he cuddled her. "Honey, I have been lost without you, utterly lost. Nothing worked, but now here you are, and I couldn't be happier."

Bailey began to smell the stench from the garbage that had missed the cans. "Isn't there a more pleasant spot to spend the night?"

He looked around. "You know, the court house is closed. We can't get a license, but first thing tomorrow morning I'll be standing before the clerk."

"And?" She allowed the side of her finger to run down his jaw line.

He caught her hand and kissed each finger and the palm. Before he reached the elbow, she stopped him.

"We're still in the alley, and those aren't tomcats peering out the window."

Dave removed his arm from about her, and backed out onto the street. "We need to see Pastor Brown and set a wedding date."

She settled back under his arm, enjoying the warmth, smell, and touch of him. It had been so long that she had forgotten the headiness of being with him. His face had lost the roundness, and the chin squared under lean cheeks. His muscles and body were smooth and hard. He had a tan and the shortness of his haircut made him look so masculine and handsome. His hands gripped the steering wheel until the knuckles grew white.

The car careened around the corner and swung into the driveway. Dave braked so hard that her head swung forward, but he caught it. "I'm so sorry, honey. Are you all right? He began to kiss her cheeks, her forehead, and her lips. The car thumped.

"Dave, you backed off the curb."

"Oh, I didn't set the brake." This time he parked the car and pulled her out into his arms. "I just can't get enough of you."

"The neighbors."

"Let them get a full view." He whirled her around like a dance step, stopped her, and kissed her squarely on the mouth. "I'm just practicing for the wedding." Then he loosened his grip enough to lead her up the steps and ring the doorbell.

Dave had kissed her several more times. "No use wasting time."

She caught Stella standing in the doorway watching. "John, look who's come to visit."

"Hi, Dave and Bailey. Come in." Pastor Brown waved them inside. "What can we do for you?" His eyes twinkled, and the smug look on his face convinced Bailey he knew exactly what she and Dave wanted.

"We want to get married as soon as possible."

"Let's talk about that." As Pastor Brown led them into his living room, Stella disappeared into the kitchen area. She came out with a tray of lemonade and cookies. "Do you have a marriage license?"

"Not yet, but I'm getting one tomorrow morning."

"Indiana requires each of you to get blood tests. You can also go to the clinic tomorrow or run to the Emergency Room at the hospital tonight."

Dave smiled and pulled closer to his side.

Stella sat down beside Bailey on the divan. "Do you have a dress?"

"No."

"Do you want to try on mine?"

"Yes!"

"Come with me while the men talk." Stella led the way to a back bedroom and opened a large closet. "I've always kept it thinking I'd have a daughter of my own. Guess what! You qualify." She closed the door behind them, slipped off the plastic protection, and laid it on the bed.

"Oh, Stella, it's beautiful!"

"Try it on. Let's see if we need any alterations. You can get them done at the laundry tomorrow."

Bailey slipped off her clothes and ducked under the full length skirt as Stella held it over her head. It zipped up easily.

"Feels big."

"But it is going to work without any alterations. Thank the Lord!" She reached up to the top shelf and brought down a round hat box. "Here's the veil. Oh, it's a bit crumpled, but we can press it out." She lifted it onto Bailey's head. "You're beautiful. Come look in the mirror."

It was a smallish mirror, but Bailey could see enough to be thrilled.

"Oh, Stella, I never dreamed I would be a bride."

"Come now. Let's get you out of this for now. I want to know what the men are doing."

Bailey glanced back at the bedroom. Her heart pounded with excitement. Stella nodded to her husband. "We have a dress."

"Wonderful. The wedding will be after the morning service."

"John, let's make it an afternoon wedding. Give people time to go home first."

He smiled. "Stella, my bell, we can have a fellowship dinner after the wedding." He looked at Dave. "Do we have the money to cater it, or should Stella call all the ladies of the church to bring in something?"

"What do we need?" Bailey could already see a monstrous list.

"We'll use the prayer line-phone system. It will take only one call, but we need to have our meal planned so we can inform the ladies what to bring." Stella reached for a pad that she gave to Bailey with a pen. Then she got another for herself. "Let's go in the kitchen. I can think better there, and the table makes it easier to write."

"Who are you wanting to invite that do not come to church regularly?"

"Matron Macintyre and Stan." Bailey had a second thought. "I wonder if Stan would act in the place of my father and give me away?"

"There's the phone. Let's find out."

The next morning at Hair Cuts, Bailey made her announcement.

"Are yer inviting me?"

"Yes."

"Well, my present to yah will be to do yer hair." Wanda flipped the long strands. "I've been wanting to cut into this for a long time." Her laugh made Bailey laugh. "We'll do a facial, too, and yer nails."

"So when's the big day?"

"Sunday after the morning service. A pot luck follows."

"Have yah ordered a cake?"

"Cake?"

"Call Cindy's Cup. She'll do a bang up job." Wanda continued to help her plan the wedding between customers. "Yah'll need something borrowed."

"That's the wedding gown."

"Something blue."

Bailey just shook her head.

"What about yer flowers? Blue could be one of yer colors."

"I hadn't thought about flowers."

"Every bride needs a bouquet. Call the florist." Wanda took the comb out of her teeth. "Oh, don't forget boutonnières for the groom, the best man, and Stan. Yer need rose peddles for the flower girl."

"I don't know any girl."

"Just choose one from the church, and ask her mama to dress her prettily."

By noon Bailey's list had doubled. When Dave arrived, she learned that he wanted to take her to the jeweler to get rings.

"I never dreamed a wedding is so involved."

He laughed. "We could be already happily married if we'd done it in Florida."

"It wasn't the right time."

"No, it wasn't." He pulled her close. "Where do you want to go on your honeymoon?"

Chapter 29: Wedding Wishes

"We're striving for the natural look." Wanda's confidence increased Bailey's tenseness. "Now I can't be there to touch yah up for the wedding, but I'll be there for the ceremony."

"But what if I mess up?"

"Yer'll do fine, trust me."

Bailey stared into the mirror. "I can't believe the bride is me."

"That's yer face and none other." Wanda lifted off the veil and hung it carefully so the tulle would hang without wrinkling. "I'm so glad Stella allowed yah to bring this over so I could plan a hairstyle around it." She peered at Bailey through the mirror. "That new brand of eye shadow really brings out the beauty of yer eyes."

The phone rang, and Bailey hopped off the chair to answer it. But all morning she would glance at the mirror just to remind herself.

Dave had other worries. "We've got to make it to the clinic to get those blood test results or the wedding is off."

"I thought you were going to do that while I was at work."

"I got hung up at the cleaners with the tux rental." He sighed.

"We're going to make it with minutes to spare." He pulled into the parking lot and took a moment to kiss her. "Your lipstick tastes like strawberries."

"I remembered how you liked the smell of my shampoo."

He squeezed her. "Come on."

Inside the clerk fumbled through the files. "I can't find it. Are you sure the test would be in today? It takes forty-eight hours, you know."

Dave stopped pacing. "It should have been in yesterday, but it wasn't. We've got to have them before Sunday. The wedding's Sunday, and I'm not postponing it another day."

The clerk had raised the phone to her ear and was dialing. "Just a minute. I'll check with the lab." When she reset the receiver, she said, "I'm going down the hall to talk with them right now. Please be seated."

Bailey sat, but Dave strode halfway down the hall after the clerk.

"Please go back and sit down."

So he chose a seat beside Bailey and continued to fidget. "The jeweler wanted me to bring you in to fit the ring."

"I thought we already did that."

"He called me. He wants to make sure it's a perfect fit."

Bailey had her own list.

Stella mentioned the need to decide on what to throw on the bride and groom after the ceremony. "The traditional rice is out. Birdseed was popular last year, but I think you should get rose petals. They don't throw very far, and nobody gets hurt."

She put off telling her mother, and she didn't have a phone number or address for Narla. Her grandparents were another matter. If they were in Florida, they wouldn't be able to come. James was to be the ring bearer. Serine had been so excited about getting him a tux. And then she hadn't spoken to Joseph or Penelope. Should she even invite them?

"Bailey, I think we ought to park my car in your garage. We'll let Teddy and his pals decorate yours as the get-a-way car." Dave was peering down the hallway at the returning clerk. "Did you find them?"

"It's all here, but there isn't any doctor's signature. Let me call one over the intercom." She looked up at a fellow behind her. "Oh, doctor, would you please sign this paper?"

He glanced at it and added his hieroglyphics.

The clerk removed the back copies and gave Dave the original. "That will be $120, please."

"One hundred twenty dollars?" Dave looked at Bailey. "I don't have that much on me."

"I'll write a check."

"You have it?"

She smiled and pulled out her checkbook.

The next day Wanda needed her services all day at the nursing home. Bailey faced her mother. "I'm getting married Sunday."

"To that loser."

"Dave isn't a loser. He's a very nice person."

"Every man I've ever known is a loser." Her mother pushed past her to argue with Wanda about her hair.

Bailey was washing another lady's hair when she heard her name and commotion behind her. She turned to recognize her grandfather.

"Hello, Bailey." He stood an arm's length away, studying her. "Your mother said I'd find you here. I hear you're getting married."

"Yes." She rinsed her hands and stepped forward. "I wanted to send you an invitation, but I didn't have any address."

"We've moved."

"I know." His pale eyes glanced around the room. "There isn't any place here to talk."

Wanda intervened. "Bailey, I can handle things for a few minutes. Take him down to the lunch room and have a cuppa out of a vending machine."

"How you been?" He sat at the round table with his elbows on top, his arms cupped around the steaming coffee, just like she remembered. The shirt front that was hard to keep buttoned because of his potbelly was hidden beneath the table. His heavy jowls sipped the hot liquid.

"I'm fine."

"You got out of jail."

She nodded.

"I wanted to tell you that I found out you didn't steal that money from the cash register.

Some came up missing after you left. I set a trap and caught Narla. She wouldn't confess, but I knew then I'd done you wrong."

"I forgive you, grandpa. I'm a better person now. I found Jesus, and He's taken care of me."

"Good. Somebody has to. It seems we didn't do much of a job of it." His throat cleared. "And that wasn't all. It was your mother stealing all that liquor out of the cellar." He rose to leave.

She caught the cuff of his sleeve. "Grandpa, where's grandma?"

"Buried in Florida. I couldn't help it. I had to leave her down there." His lips pursed together. "She was the love of my life. I don't know how I'm going to get along without her."

"When?"

"About two weeks ago. I couldn't stand it down there without her. I stuck the mobile in the wind and came home."

"Would you come to my wedding?"

"I'd sure like to. And I want to see what kind of a fellow you picked. He'd better treat you right." His face pointed away, across the room. "God only knows that we didn't."

While Bailey and Wanda cleaned up the accumulated mess from the hours of beauty work at the nursing home, Narla stalked into the room.

"Yer'll have to phone in an appointment at Hair Cuts." Wanda picked up a plastic crate of curlers and made a wide pass around Bailey's sister. Narla waited until the stylist was out of sight.

"You're getting married. What's wrong with you? I as your sister should be matron of honor. My daughters must be the flower girls and attendants."

Bailey focused on the imitation silk that revealed her sister's deep cleavage and huge hips. The neon colors swirled like her thoughts. Narla had stolen the money and allowed her sister to take the blame and serve five years when she was innocent. She closed her eyes to blot out the thoughts.

"Going to sleep on me or ignoring me?"

"Neither." Bailey raised her chin. "I have not seen you since you were asked to leave my home."

"All those times in Hair Cuts don't count?"

"Did you leave your address?"

"It had to be on the checks."

"I don't handle the money."

"Wanda is one smart woman. She knows who she can and can't trust." Narla turned to see Wanda standing behind her. She forced a smile. "I will call Hair Cuts tomorrow."

"We're closed tomorrow." Wanda picked up another plastic crate and handed it to Bailey. Her head motioned for her to move it outside.

Bailey shook her head. "I have to handle this myself." She turned to Narla. "Grandpa just told me you were the thief. You didn't speak up. Your testimony sent me to prison for five years. You have never been kind to me, and I'm to make you matron of honor? Not on your life. That position is already filled. Wanda is my matron of honor."

Narla left.

"Very well said." Wanda laughed. "But I don't have a blue dress that fits." She patted her tummy and picked up the last box. "Let's get out of here before she comes back."

Bailey stopped at the library and didn't recognize the woman watching the desk.

"Can I help you?"

"I wanted to talk to Petunia."

"If she isn't in the computer lab, she's probably upstairs in the children's area."

As Bailey stepped up the padded stairs, memories of Dave reading *Horton Hatches an Egg*, and James jumping into the giant bean bag nest made her giggle. Petunia met her face-to-face with her grim lips.

"Dave isn't here."

"I know. We're getting married tomorrow, and I wanted to invite you to the wedding." She glanced around at the colorful paper flowers popping out of the bulletin board. "You have made this room very attractive."

"Thank you."

"Dave just came back from the army, and we wanted to get married quickly. Otherwise, I would have sent you a formal invitation."

Petunia stood there, but she wasn't frowning.

"James is the ring bearer, and Serine has ordered a tux his size. Joseph is coming, and we all wanted you to come, too."

"I don't know."

"Oh, Petunia, please come. I would have asked you to be one of my attendants, but there wasn't enough time to find you a dress."

"Is Serine your other attendant?"

"To tell the truth I'd asked my boss from Hair Cuts, but she doesn't want to stand up there showing eight months. I hadn't thought of Serine. The two of you would be perfect. You are my sisters."

"So Serine doesn't have a dress either?"

"Like I said, I didn't have time. Dave and I decided to do this three days ago."

"I'll call Serine, if you're serious about us being your attendants."

"I'm serious."

Petunia sent the first smile ever in Bailey's direction. "We'll come up with something. What color?"

"Blue."

"That shouldn't be difficult."

Bailey found Stella and Tonia Sue in the fellowship hall of the church stringing blue and white streamers across the room. Tables were covered with white. Blue and white carnation centerpieces and the white paper bells adorned them.

"It's beautiful." Bailey twirled in excitement. "I can't believe this."

Tonia Sue pointed at a roll of cellophane tape. "Grab that for me. My arms are screaming mercy."

Stella showed Bailey the nuts and mints waiting to be opened. The refrigerator held pop and juice for punch. "I brought over my punch bowl."

"Do we have enough cups and plates?"

"John went to the whole seller and bought more this morning, including plastic ware." Stella grinned. "He's treating you as if you were the daughter we never had."

Bailey's eyes opened. "Oh, thank you. I don't deserve this."

"Why not?" Tonia Sue stood in the doorway with her hands on her hips. "You one fine girl. Everybody love you."

"Come upstairs. John and Dave are practicing the ceremony."

The sanctuary had a palm plant on opposite sides of a huge bouquet of white gladiolas sticking up like the head gear of the Statue of Liberty. Blue and white carnations, baby breath, and ferns flowed in front of it. Behind the pulpit was a huge candle with two smaller ones beside it.

"Come, Bailey." Stella guided her through the ceremony. "Our pianist will be able to play the march. I thought she would be here."

"She had a problem this evening." Pastor John came up behind his wife. "Now that we're all together, let's ask God to bless this union."

That night Bailey lay in her bed, so excited that sleep wouldn't come. *O God, how great You are! How could You have brought me, a barmaid out of prison, to this absolute joy?*

Chapter 30: Abducted Joy?

Bailey awoke on her wedding day to let Bennie out of the house. With all the lists how could she have forgotten the little dog? She would be gone on her honeymoon for ten days. Maybe Teddy Sommers? No, she'd promised James that Bennie belonged to him. Would Serine accept the little dog for just a few days?

"Serine, I need to ask a favor."

"What is it this time?"

"Could James take care of the dog while I'm gone?"

The silence on the other end of the phone almost made her believe that Serine had hung up on her, yet the dial tone didn't buzz. Bailey waited. She watched the clock. She had to shower, fix her hair, and put on her makeup. Bennie whined at the door, and she rose to get him. Still Serine hadn't returned with an answer. Bailey didn't dare end the call. Ten minutes passed. Fifteen.

She had to get a shower. Bennie whined. She fed him. A whole half hour ruined. She couldn't wait any longer. She hung up the phone.

Sometime while she was showering, Serine called. The answering service didn't have a message, only the phone number.

Bailey dialed it and heard James's voice, "Sorry we can't come to the phone right now. We're all busy, but please leave a message." Serine must have coached him.

"I would like to know if James could take care of Bennie while I am gone on my honeymoon. Bye." She hung up and started to pin up her hair.

The phone rang.

"Hi, Honey. I tried to call earlier, but you must have been talking to someone." Dave's cheerful voice carried so much love and excitement.

"I forgot to ask Serine if James could take care of my dog while we're gone."

"I'm sure she would. Don't worry about it. When do you plan to get to the church?"

She finished putting in all the curlers and started on her facial, following Wanda's detailed notes. A steamed wash cloth. Don't scrub. Allow the pores to open. Another steamy wash cloth. Wipe gently. Now a cold cloth. Another cold cloth.

The phone rang.

"Serine."

"I'm sorry, Bailey. Blaine doesn't think James is old enough for that kind of responsibility, and he doesn't want me to add another pressure. This wedding is just about to do us in! Oh, Petunia did call. We have similar dresses and will stand up with you."

"Thanks." Bailey hung up thinking, *But no thanks!* Now she had to call Teddy Sommers.

Since she couldn't find her car keys in her purse, she checked the kitchen. Things had been so hectic lately that she might have left them in the bedroom, her coat pockets, or the car. She opened the garage to find Dave's car. He had her car, hiding his to prevent someone painting it with shoe polish, but how was she going to get to church? He hadn't mentioned getting her.

"Stella, Dave hid his car and has mine. I have no way to get to church."

"I'm sorry. Neither John nor I can get you."

Bailey dropped the receiver into its cradle and spoke aloud to Bennie. "Well, I'll have to drive his car." She slid her purse onto the passenger seat, and studied the gages and knobs on the front panel. With resignation she started the motor.

When she entered the parsonage driveway, the garage door was open. She drove in, parked Dave's car, and closed the door. No one was at home. She walked across the street to the church and down to her Sunday school class.

"Bailey, are you really going to get married today?" The kids collected around her like chirping birds. Their mouths twittered while their legs jumped, their bodies whirled, and their arms flapped.

"Yes, now let's calm down a bit." She searched for her place in the quarterly, laid it open on the podium, and passed out the lesson leaflets.

"Will you wear a white dress?"

"Will Dave kiss you?"

"Will we all get to see him?" The girls swooned. Groans and yucks proceeded from the boys as they punched one another and thumped the underside of the table with their toes.

"Yes, all of you will go to the wedding. Does anyone have prayer requests?" All the hands raised, and Bailey heard them one-by-one. She bowed her head and asked God to bless them. "Now let's look at the first page. Bobby, read the first verse, please." The structure of the lesson brought the youngsters' minds back to Sunday school. They memorized the verse, and she passed out stars for them to paste on the little squares of the poster. Each one colored a page, and she posted a few on the bulletin board. They decorated some Bible bookmarks with glitter and stickers. Bailey was cleaning up the mess, when Teddy stuck his head in the room.

"Bailey! Someone stole Dave's car from your house, and kidnapped you." He stopped. "Wait a minute. If you were kidnapped, how did you get here?"

"I didn't get kidnapped."

He slammed the door, and she could hear his feet thundering up the stairs. He was shouting. "I found Bailey!"

As she walked into the hall way, she noticed policemen interspersed among the crowd. She didn't have time to ask anyone. She dropped her attendance sheet on the counter of the church office and walked over to the parsonage to get dressed.

Stella and Tonia Sue were waiting for her. "We've been praying for you. How did you get away from the kidnapper?"

"What kidnapper?"

"The one who stole Dave's car."

Bailey blinked her eyes. "No one stole Dave's car."

“He drove over to get you. His car was gone and so were you.”

“I drove Dave’s car over here and parked it in Stella’s garage. Come and see. It’s right there.” They followed her and witnessed that the car was definitely in the parsonage garage.

“Then where were you all this time?” Stella tried to connect the dots.

“I was in the church basement teaching the primary kids.”

Tonia Sue began to laugh. “Oh, Bailey! No wonder we didn’t see you.”

“I’m calling John. Everybody needs to know the mystery has been solved.” Stella listened to his reply. Her eyebrows rose, and she began to chuckle. Then she closed her cell phone. “O girls, you haven’t heard the half. Teddy went downstairs and found Bailey. He rushed up to tell Dave. Dave came down and couldn’t find her. The police thought she had been abducted and are searching the entire town of Lakeside.”

Bailey in her gown led the parade to the church with the ladies holding up the trailing hemline and train. Then Serine, James, and Penelope arrived.

“Ah, there you are.” Matron Macintyre stood beside her nervous husband. “Oh, Stan, you’re not getting married. Bailey is.”

Bailey hugged her friend. “I’m glad you agreed to be mother of the bride. You are gorgeous in that silk suit. Oh, thank you so much!” She looked around. “Stella is taking the part as the groom’s mother. She’s already seated. I think it’s time for the ushers to seat you.”

Stan whispered. “If I weren’t already married, I’d give Dave a run for his money.”

She giggled.

James started down the aisle. His back was as straight as a soldier’s. A small girl that Bailey only knew as Ann followed him. She smiled and flirted all the way to the altar.

“She’s going to break a lot of hearts.” Stan crooked his arm for her.

Serine was followed by Penelope down the aisle. A mystic moment hung over the audience. Dave turned to stare at her. His smile broadened. The chords on the organ brought everyone to their feet. Stan hummed, “Here comes the bride,” and she was waltzing down to meet Dave, her train flowing behind her like the robe of a queen.

“Do you, Dave, take Bailey to be your wedded wife, to have and to hold from this day forth in sickness and in health till death do thee part?”

He smiled into her eyes. “I do.”

“And Bailey.” John turned to her.

She could never remember anything but the thickness of her tongue and the weakness of her voice. Somehow the vow was spoken. “I do.”

“I now pronounce you man and wife. You may kiss the bride.”

“She was right. He’s kissing her right in front of us.” The little girl’s voice held awe.

“Gross.”

A mother's voice hushed the lad, but Bailey felt Dave's arms surrounding her like a welcomed protection. His lips found hers, and she closed her eyes, leaned into his body, and absorbed his love.

The wedding march swelled. She stumbled over the folds of the dress in turning. Dave pulled her straight and strode down the aisle. She was laughing as she tried to keep up with him, and her joy overflowed like a foaming cup of cocoa. If only the entire world could be as happy as she!

Pastor John lined them against the wall of the stairs so the congregation could file past to congratulate the couple as they went to the fellowship hall for the meal.

"What happened to you?"

"Nothing. I was here all the time." The constant repetition made her mouth dry. Then she smiled and smiled as picture after picture was taken.

"What did you do with my car?"

"It's in the parsonage garage."

Dave looked perplexed. "I thought you knew I wouldn't forget you."

"I didn't remember your saying you would come after me. Isn't there an old myth that the groom shouldn't see the bride on her wedding day until she comes down the aisle?"

"It doesn't mean anything. I just hope none of these young fools are painting my car or tying cans to the bumper."

She fed him cake, and the crumbs fell down the front of his tux.

"Please, Bailey, be more careful with the punch." He sipped without a spot, but she nearly choked on hers. "Swallow."

Nonetheless the meal went fine. They opened their gifts. Bailey stepped up the basement stairs and tossed the bouquet. Her sister Penelope caught it.

"Now aren't you glad you came?" Bailey teased.

"It's been a lot of fun, even if you weren't kidnapped."

Chapter 31: Happy Endings

Wanda brought her baby to the shop. The soft little bundle passed from one lady to the next. A crib was set up in the back of the room where he slept, and Bailey learned to change diapers between phone calls.

"I don't know how I ever managed without yah." Wanda nibbled on a sandwich brought from Cindy's Cup. "Yah almost run this place, but I like it."

"That was before you had the baby." Bailey settled him down for a nap. "Wanda, do you think there's room for another crib?"

"Bailey, yer expecting?"

She nodded. "The doctor says around Valentine's Day."

"Wonderful! We'll have a shower and throw a party." Wanda pointed at the ceiling. "We'll hang pink and white streamers—oh, Bailey. What if it's a boy?"

The news spread even to the nursing home. Bailey's mother greeted the tidings with her frowning condemnations, but grandfather's back straightened and his chest puffed to the proper dimensions.

"I'm so glad you decided not to go back to Florida."

He nodded. "I've been thinking of selling the mobile home. There are some assisted living apartments a block away that are mighty nice. I'm getting a little old to be pushing a vacuum."

"Have you heard from Narla?"

"She separated from that man of hers. I don't like it, Bailey. Those poor little girls have to go through all that misery." His fist thumped the table where they were sharing some coffee and a few of Bailey's homemade cookies. "Why couldn't she settle down like you?"

"Grandpa, I couldn't do it alone."

"You did."

"No, first I gave my heart to Jesus. Then He supplied the people to help me." Bailey thought of Matron Macintyre, Dave, Tonia Sue and Teddy, Stella and John, and Wanda. All of them had encouraged her in her walk with the Lord. "Grandpa, do you ever feel lonely?"

"Almost all the time except when I'm with you."

"Wouldn't you like a closer friend?"

"Now, Bailey, don't start any match making. I'm too old for that." He started to get out of his chair, but she laid her hand on his arm.

"I wasn't thinking of a woman, Grandpa. I just wanted to share my friend Jesus. We have all sinned and fallen short of what we should be, but God loved us so much that He sent His Son to die in our place. Wouldn't you like to ask Him to forgive you?"

"Bailey, I don't rightly know how. You know what I think

about religion, what that priest did to your mama."

"I wouldn't be here otherwise. Don't you see? It wasn't God's fault, but God went ahead and worked it out for our good. I wish I could convince mother of that."

"Well, maybe some day you will." His hand covered hers. "I love you, Bailey. Next to your grandmother, you're the best thing that ever happened in my life."

"Grandpa, wouldn't you like Jesus to forgive you of your sins?"

He looked into her eyes with a yearning that almost broke her heart and nodded.

"Then let's pray."

The simple sinner's plea changed the old man's heart. Immediately Bailey saw the difference in his relationship with her mother. Then Grandpa and Joseph became buddies. It pleased her to see the two of them walking the streets of Lakeside and discussing the doctrines of the Bible.

Rosenbaum had changed, too. Her appearance blossomed into beauty that matched a growing love of the Lord in her heart. Bailey saw the ministry of the jail double in just a few weeks because of the inmate's witness.

"Do you know what made me decide to become a Christian?" Bailey reveled in the chance to talk to her friend on a one-to-one visit. "I was so afraid of you, that I sought the safety of Christians. Then I saw they had something good, and I wanted it, too."

"Yea, yer always got to watch yer back in here." Rosenbaum

turned pages in her well thumbed Bible. "I'm sorry, Bailey. I was a hateful witch."

"But I want to thank you for it."

"Thank me?"

"Yes, if I hadn't been so afraid, I might never have found Christ. While you were a sinner, in a way you brought me to Him. I owe you big time."

"Now yer know that ain't so." But Rosenbaum seemed pleased.

Later that summer Dave and Bailey invited Serine and Blaine to bring James camping out on the river. Dave brought his boat and life preservers.

"Look, mother." James caught the attention of both Serine and Bailey. "I can paddle." He sat in the middle splashing away while both fathers sat on both ends holding the craft steady. The boat circled like a dog trying to lie down.

Bailey laughed so hard she had to hold her rounding tummy. Serine stood beside doubled over as well. As the males came into shore, Bailey thanked God for His guidance. She had been so wise to give up what she couldn't keep so that she could have both her son and her sisters.

"Dave told James on New Year's that he would bring him out in the boat."

Serine nodded. "James talked of nothing else for weeks. It made me so mad because I thought I'd lose him forever."

"That's what I was afraid of, too. You were so determined to keep him, and I wanted him so badly." Bailey stepped closer to her sister. "Now I have both of you."

"And we have Penelope, too. You know, I went to the library yesterday to find a book on tape to listen to while I clean house. Penelope showed me her engagement ring. She's planning a fall wedding."

"Catching the bouquet must have some powers."

Serine laughed. "Maybe, but Penelope has chased Larry for years. He wasn't interested in marriage until he saw Dave's reactions at yours."

"And what was that?"

"Dave ogled you." Serine searched for words. "I think it was because Larry saw how happy Dave really was and wanted it, too."

"Oh."

Dave and Bailey shared one sleeping bag.

"You awake?"

"Um-hum." He pulled her closer to his body, and the warmth blessed both.

"I've been thinking of our little one." She felt his hands touch the rounding of her belly. "What are we going to name her?"

"You sure it's a she?"

"Well, he or she isn't an it, Dave. I have a little person living inside me."

"I know, but he could be a boy."

“So we need two names.”

He kissed her neck. “Name he or she whatever you wish, Honey. I’ve had a long day.” He fell asleep, and Bailey could hear the gentle flutter of his snore and feel his chest move with every breath. Dave worked hard at the computer lab in Lakeside. His demanding customers were always doing something crazy to their lap tops or PC’s and expecting him to know how to fix it.

She could feel herself getting drowsy, but the persistent question of names reminded her of how she had named James. After he was born and they brought the birth certificate to her bedside, she remembered glancing up at the attending physician’s tag and copying his name down on the paper. James’s name had become quite a controversy when that first foster mother, whoever she was, tried to change it to Gary. Bailey didn’t want anybody changing the identity of her next child, so she would be well prepared this time. This time--

About the Author:

Rose Goble has several other Christian romances on Amazon.com which you may enjoy. She has written for take home Sunday school papers and devotionals. Her interests are as diverse as her books. God bless you as you read.

Made in the USA
Middletown, DE
01 May 2025

75014107R00183